Praise for Trisha Sugarek

Song of the Yukon is a powerful historical novel that opens in the Yukon in 1923 and tells of one strong woman's long-held dream of homesteading and how the Homestead Act led her to build a new home, sweetened by her discovery of gold on her property.

The story begins with this dream and works outward as it follows LaVerne's efforts to hone and realize her desires upon discovering that the Alaskan frontier offers her a unique opportunity.

But Sugarek, in her eighth novel, covers more than music growth, more than homesteading in the wilderness, and even more than testing one's abilities against a foreign environment. Most of all, it's about one woman's determination to achieve her dream against any odds. It is a commanding saga. ~~ Diane Donovan, Midwest Book Review ~~

'It takes a tightrope artist of a writer to create chapters that successfully delve into a killer's thoughts (*Angel of Murder*) without revealing his identity in the process.' ~~ *Midwest Book Review*

Women Outside the Walls ~~ 'Step inside the sisterhood of the women with men behind bars. These women all come together in the waiting room and then visitor's room at the prison while waiting to visit their men. It will touch your heart in ways you wouldn't expect and is a book well worth spending the time to read. You'll come away with a new respect for women in this situation.' ~~ *Fresh Fiction*

D1524232

More praise….

'Love can see people through the roughest times. *Women Outside the Walls* is a novel from Trisha Sugarek as she explores the nature of women outside the prison walls who are trying to get by as their men are serving time. Finding an unusual friendship through their tough time, more plight comes their way and challenges what they have left as independent women as one of their daughters goes missing. "Women Outside the Walls" carries a positive message, and shouldn't be overlooked, very much recommended.'~~*Midwest Book Review*

Song of the Yukon

by

Trisha Sugarek

For my friend, Doug, fondly, Trish Sugarek

WITHDRAWN

39999000030825

Little Elm Public Library
Little Elm, TX 75068

Notice

Copyright (c) 2016 Trisha Sugarek. All rights reserved. No part of this book may be used or reproduced in any manner whatsoever without the written permission of the Author. Printed in the United States of America. For information contact author at www.writeratplay.com

The Library of Congress has catalogued the soft cover edition of this book as follows: Sugarek, Trisha, Song of the Yukon, Trisha Sugarek -

This is a work of fiction. Names, characters, places, and incidents either are the product of the author's imagination or are used fictitiously and any resemblance to actual persons, living or dead, business establishments, events or locales in entirely coincidental.

1. Female friendship-Fiction.   2. Alaska-Fiction.   3. Liberated women-Fiction.   4. Gold Rush-Fiction.   5. Romance-Fiction.   6. Historic women-Fiction.

ISBN 978-1489558206

FIRST PAPERBACK EDITION
10 9 8 7 6 5 4 3 2 1

Cover Design by David White, Illustrator

Song, 'Swiftly I Go' by Gary Swindell, Composer
Additional lyrics and poetry by Trisha Sugarek

To view all of the author's play scripts and fiction go to:

www.writeratplay.com

Quotes: The Best of Robert Service, Copyright 1940 by Robert Service. Publishers: Dodd, Mead & Company, Inc.

Also by
TRISHA SUGAREK

Fiction

Women Outside the Walls
Wild Violets

The World of Murder
Art of Murder
Dance of Murder
Act of Murder
Angel of Murder
Taste of Murder
Beneath the Bridge of Murder

Poetry
Butterflies and Bullets
The World of Haiku with Sumi-E Artwork
Haiku Journal -- a companion book

Available at all fine book stores.

Dedication

To a hundred years of Guyer girls....
still going strong.

Prologue

The Yukon
1922

"Heave! Heave!" Milo shouted as six brawny men guided the corners of the roof into place. LaVerne's neighbors, Milo and Stan straddled beams, ready to guide the roof joists as they settled into place. Three more men handled the pulley and wench as the roof slowly rose up the side of the log building.

Nearby the women were putting out a potluck meal for all the workers and their families. The rich aroma of Cariboo stew mingled with the fresh baked smell of sodbuster biscuits. Several children, with eyes round as saucers, stood off to one side and watched, speechless with excitement.

"Okay, lower 'er into place!" Milo called to the men manning the pulley and when it settled into position a cheer went up.

"Food's ready, boys!" Charlie, a strapping woman in her earlier thirties called out.

"Take a break now and come get it while it's still hot." Primeval forest ringed the clearing where the unfinished cabin stood, the trees dappled with light and shadow in the afternoon sun. A new garden space was set off to one side. Tiny bright green shoots were visible, bravely reaching for the sky.

Beyond the garden chickens clucked importantly behind a wire fence. Goats bleated their displeasure at the disruption of their life.

In front of the cabin and well away from the work, the men had set up a makeshift table by nailing a couple of boards down on top of two stumps. One of the women had spread a cloth over it and now dishes covered the table. Everyone had come not only to help with the roof raising but to also contribute a dish for the meal.

A bon-fire crackled and roared taking away any chill in the late afternoon, as the sun sank behind the trees. The forest was gilded as the sun began to slip away. The men put down their tools and gathered around. Taking tin plates heaped with food from the women, they congratulated each other on the work accomplished so far.

"We can close 'er up before night fall," Stan said. "Come back tomorrow and put the shingles on."

"Tight as a tick in a horse blanket, it'll be, Milo told LaVerne. "And none too soon…I smell snow."

"Ha! You and your nose, Milo! You can't *smell* snow." one of the other men grinned.

While everyone laughed good naturedly Milo scowled, "You just wait and see if we don't have a dusting over night. One final spring dump of the white stuff, or my name ain't Milo Robbins."

LaVerne walked to the table and picked up a battered, old tin mug. She hit a spoon against the side of it to get everyone's attention. She was the picture of what one would imagine a pioneer woman would look like. Hand sewn canvas trousers held up with no-nonsense suspenders with a cambric blue shirt tucked half way in. Heavy leather boots were laced half-way up her calves. A blue rag tied her long, black hair away from her face. Nothing, but nothing could detract from her beauty. Her face held the classic lines that spoke of her French heritage. Dark chocolate, slanted eyes sparkled with health and happiness. Her generous mouth was a rosy pink.

"I just wanted to thank you all for your hard work. I could'a never gotten the cabin buttoned up so quickly without you. So, thank you..." Her voice thickened with emotion as she beamed across the clearing at her best friend, Charlie.

In a few moments Charlie, who was originally Charlotte Donovan from Boston, strode across the space and slung her arm around LaVerne's shoulders and hugged her.

"Come on now, no point in getting girlish. We do for each other when there's a need. A woman, on her own up here needs her neighbors to help out."

"Here, here!" yelled a couple of the men.

"And besides, Miss LaVerne, you do for us when we need you. Besides, you play some awful pretty music," Milo's face reddened as he paid her the compliment. Everyone applauded and the men hooted and poked Milo in the ribs. It was an ill kept secret Milo had feelings for LaVerne. The only one who seemed unaware was LaVerne.

As the group of neighbors and friends ate they shared the latest news of finding gold, the anticipated fishing harvest out of the Yukon River this year, and who had received mail from family in the lower forty-eight.

LaVerne stood off to the side, alone for a few minutes, and admired her new, much anticipated home. She would be able to move in by mid-week and it couldn't be soon enough. She'd camped in an eleven by nine foot shack while she laid the timber for the walls of her cabin. It had taken her, with help from her new friends, three months to lay and chink the logs. When she'd moved out here permanently she'd found that her neighbors had cut down, debarked and stacked enough logs to begin building. It had saved her months of cutting down trees and hauling logs to her homestead.

She'd worked in town for the first year after arriving in Alaska, saving every penny for this day. But, at heart, she was no city girl and the moment she had arrived in Fairbanks, she dreamed of homesteading. She had explored the Tanana Valley and then staked her claim to this eighty acres under the Homestead Act. She had planned to work in Fairbanks for at least two years to save enough for her stake. But everything changed the day she discovered gold nuggets in the creek that ran through her property.

A voice called out, breaking her reverie. "Hey, Vernie, how 'bout some music?"

Part One

The Journey

Little Elm Public Library
Little Elm, TX 75068

One

Tumwater, Washington
1921

The three middle girls in the family shared a bedroom in the over-crowded Guyer farm house. There were thirteen kids in total but rarely was everyone home at once. The boys, now in their late teens were always somewhere in the state, in the deep forest, logging with their father. Lillas was working in Seattle. But when all the siblings were home every inch of the two storied, rambling house was used. In mild weather the screened porch slept two and the boys would bunk in the barn.

On this night, LaVerne, the youngest girl and baby of the family, knelt on her bed and gazed out the window at a half moon. Across the room, soft snores could be heard out of her two older sisters. Quietly LaVerne recited a poem by her hero, Robert Service.

'Were you ever out in the Great Alone, when the moon was awful clear...and the icy mountains hemmed you in with a silence you most could hear;

With only the howl of a timber wolf, and you camped there in the cold,
A half-dead thing in the stark, dead world, clean mad for the muck called gold;
While high overhead, green, yellow, and red, the North Lights swept in bars?-

Then you've a hunch what the music meant...hunger and night and the stars...

In the bed against the other wall, Violet rose up on an elbow and spoke in a harsh whisper.

"LaVerne! Wake up! You're talking in your sleep, *again.* Shut up and go back to sleep." She punched her pillow and flounced back down under the pile of quilts.

Watching the moon glide across the night sky, LaVerne dreamed a dream of Alaska. She longed to follow in the poet's footsteps, doing without, experience being 'hemmed in by silence'.

She whispered to the moon, "'*Can you remember your huskies all going, barking with joy and their brushes in air; you in your parka, glad-eyed and glowing, Monarch, your subjects the wolf and the bear. Monarch, your kingdom unravished and gleaming;*

Mountains your throne, and a river your car; Crash of a bull moose to rouse you from dreaming; Forest your couch, and your candle a star.

You who this faint day the High North is luring unto her vastness, taintlessly sweet; you who are steel-braced, straight-lipped, enduring,

Dreadless in danger and dire in defeat; Honor the High North ever and ever, Whether she crown you, or whether she slay; Suffer her fury, cherish and love her-- He who would rule he must learn to obey.'

"That's what I want, to rule and obey," she told the moon.

LaVerne stood and stripped off her voluminous nightgown. Under it she was dressed in a pair of her brother's work pants, a plaid flannel shirt and heavy boots, all borrowed from the men in her family. She wound her long braid of hair around the top of her head and pulled one of her brother's caps down over the whole mess.

She picked up her wool coat, duffle bag, and guitar case where she had stored them at the end of her bed. She crossed to her sisters' bed and poked Ivah's shoulder.

"Ivah!" She whispered. "Ivah, wake up!"

Her sister moaned and turned away from LaVerne. "Go away...it can't be morning yet." She groaned as she cracked open one eye. "It's still dark out. Are you crazy, La Verne? Go back to bed this instant!"

"Please, Ivy, wake up for just a minute. This is really important. Really, *really* important."

Ivah sat up. She was a pretty girl, not a beauty like Violet but pleasant looking with a rapier sharp sense of humor.

"What is it? And stop calling me Ivy, I am not a plant," she growled at her baby sister. "This had better be important or you are dead. What is it?"

Violet pushed away towards the wall and buried herself deeper in the covers. "Shut up, Ivah! Or *you* are dead!"

"Oh yeah? And whose gonna make me? Not you."

"Shh...Will you two be quiet? You're going to have the whole house in here."

Violet snorted. "Gladly. Get back to bed you two."

Ivah, now completely awake, sat up in bed and plumped the pillows behind her. "Okay, squirt, what's so earth shattering it can't wait 'till the morning?

"I'm leaving--I couldn't go without telling someone--I don't want Mama to worry..."

"Leaving? What'd ya mean, leaving?"

It took a moment for Ivah to take in the fact that LaVerne was dressed and carrying a bag and her beloved guitar.

"What the h-e-double toothpicks is going on? You've got a coat on--what's in the duffle? What are you talking about?"

"I'm leaving--for the Yukon. Tonight."

"Yukon? You mean in *Alaska!?* Are you nuts? Go back to bed. You're sleep walking...or I am."

Suddenly LaVerne pinched Ivah's arm.

"Oww! What'd you do that for?"

"To prove to you that you're awake. I'm not sleep walking and neither are you. I just wanted to say goodbye."

"Goodb...?" Ivah turned to her other sister and shook her shoulder. "Vi, wake up this instant! LaVerne thinks she's running away. Wake up!"

Violet rolled over and glared up at her two very noisy sisters.

"What the devil is going on? LaVerne, why do you have your coat on?"

"She's leaving, you slug. Wake up, I need your help."

"Vernie, take your coat off and go back to bed. You're not going anywhere. You're the baby, re-member?"

"Shut up, Vi, and listen." Ivah ordered.

"Who are you telling to shut up? You're not the boss of me."

"Please..." LaVerne whispered. "You're going to wake up Mama. Maybe I better just go."

"No, no!" Ivah yelled in a sotto whisper. She poked Violet with her elbow again.

"Oww--stop poking me!"

"Vi, it's obvious LaVerne has a problem,. Let's be good sisters and hear her out. What's going on squirt?" Ivah patted the bed next to her. "Sit down, honey, and tell us all about it."

"Yeah, spill it so we can go back to sleep." Violet sighed. "It can't be that bad, Vernie."

"I've been thinking about this for a long time. I've read gobs on Alaska and that's the place for me. You can chase your dreams there, be whoever you want to be--no one telling you what to do and what not to do..."

"But, Vernie, you're way too young..." Ivah said.

"No, I'm not--I'm seventeen!"

"You are? Already?" Ivah asked, truly surprised.

"Let's get practical for a moment." Violet offered. "How are you going to get to Alaska? Do you have any idea how far away it is?"

"Oh, yes, I've done the research. I'm going to hitch a ride up to Seattle. Then I am going to sign on a freighter, and work my way north to Alaska." LaVerne sighed at the romance of it all. "That's how Robert Service got there."

"Just one little problem, Vernie. Robert Service was a guy. Who's going to hire a girl to work on a ship?"

"I'm not going as a *girl*, Ivah. I'm going to hide my hair under a cap and wear Eddie's old clothes. This way I can sign on as a kitchen helper or a steward...I think that's what they call them. By the time they find out I'm a girl, either they won't care or it will be too late to turn back. They can't very well throw me overboard."

"Wanna bet?" Vi scoffed.

All three girls were silent for a moment. Her sisters could not dissuade her from her plans. *They would work...they had to work. This is my chance.* LaVerne vowed.

"Of all the hair brained ideas, Vernie, this takes the prize." Violet flopped back down in bed and turned her back on them. "Go back to bed."

"Hold on there, Vi. Let's hear Vernie out." Ivah turned to her sister and took her hand in both of hers. "What's wrong, squirt? Why are you leaving us?"

Violet mumbled from under the bedding. "I would love to be rid of a pesky little sister and finally have a bed of my own."

Ignoring her sister, she tried to explain, "Everybody's leaving. Lillas got married and is working in Seattle. You just got engaged and when you get married you'll be gone. And Vi's on her way to San Francisco to play basketball. Everybody's having an adventure except me. I don't want to be left here all alone." LaVerne's chin trembled.

"You'll still have Pa and Mama--and the boys. And all of us will be home for holidays to visit."

"That's different. I won't have any sisters here. I'll be the only girl. Besides, I feel like...well..."

"What? You feel like what?" Vi asked.

"Different from you. You all see yourselves married with children. I want different things."

Violet sat up, "I don't! Want kids, that is. I see myself playing basketball for a few years and then opening my own business." Violet boasted.

"See, Ivy? Everybody else gets to have their dreams. How come I don't?"

"Oh, everyone feels like this at your age. I thought I was adopted for a whole year when I was fourteen. It was the worst year of my life," Violet told her sister.

"You're just growing up, Vernie." Ivah added.

"No it's more than that," LaVerne struggled to put her feelings into words. "My feelings, they're different..."

"How?" Ivah squeezed her hand.

"I'm afraid you'll laugh at me."

"No, I promise we won't. Don't we promise, Vi?"

"I'll promise anything to get you two to shut up and let me sleep."

"Vi will laugh. She always laughs at me."

"Vi promises not to laugh." Ivah poked Violet again. "Promise her, Vi!"

"Okay. I promise not to laugh, Vernie. Now what *is* it for gosh sakes?"

LaVerne straightened her spine and jutted out her chin. "I want to go to Alaska and write songs."

Violet sputtered, trying to keep her promise not to laugh. LaVerne gasped at her insensitivity and tears filled her eyes.

"See? She's laughing. I knew she would!"

"No, no...I'm not..." Violet quickly fake-coughed. "It was just a cough."

"Oh, Vernie, just ignore Vi. You know how she is. *Everything's* funny except when it comes to *her* life."

"That's not true..." Violet said loudly.

"Shhh...!" Both sisters shushed Violet.

"Vernie, I know you love your music and writing and all. I love the songs you've played for me. But, can't you write them here? Mama loves your music. We all do."

"No. To be a great writer, you have to suffer. When Mr. Service went to Alaska, after years of suffering, he got very sick and had to come home. It took him a long time to recover."

LaVerne spoke with relish about the gore and romance of it all. "He got dysentery, lice, and he almost died from pneumonia."

"Holy Christopher! You're going to Alaska to suffer? Stay at home and I promise to make your life miserable every day. Now! Can we, please, just go back to sleep?" Violet sighed. "Good grief."

"You're mean, Vi, you know that? I knew you wouldn't understand. I'm sorry I even woke you up to say goodbye."

"So am I. Believe me, so am I."

"I...vah!" LaVerne wailed.

"Never mind her. We all know how selfish Vi can be. Just ignore her." Ivah paused with a new thought on how to dissuade her baby sister from leaving. "Vernie, have you thought about Mama? She is going to be so worried and hurt."

"That's why I woke you up, Ivy. I thought maybe you could talk to her after I'm gone. Make her understand. Tell her not to worry."

"Telling her not to worry is like telling the sun not to set. She'll never understand. You're her baby, Vernie."

"See? That's just it--I'm the *baby*. I've been the baby my whole life. I don't get to do anything. Well now, I'm going all the way to Fairbanks. Just like Robert, I want to see the Aurora Boreattics, the..."

"Borealis..."

"Huh?"

"It's Aurora Borealis."

"Yeah, that. The wolves and the glaciers. The polar bears, and the streams filled with gold. Did you know that Robert Service rode with the mail carriers on their dog sleds? He traveled over a hundred miles with them delivering the mail and writing his poetry. He…"

Violet rolled back over and sat up, exasperated. "He's a man! Men do stupid and dangerous stuff like that."

"Robert isn't just some man! He's the Bard of the Yukon, not that *you* would even know what that means."

"Not that I even *care* what that means. What a bunch of nonsense."

"I don't care what you think, Violet Marie Guyer! I'm going to ride with the mail and write my songs."

"Good grief. You don't know anything!" Vi said as she turned over and pulled her pillow over her head. "There's no talking to her."

"Do something for me, Vernie?"

"I'm leaving--you can't talk me out of it."

"No...I'm not going to try and talk you out of anything. I just want you to wait one day--okay? Let me think about all of this. I didn't know that what our sisters and I were doing was upsetting you so much. We've all been so wrapped up in our own lives and plans we haven't given much thought to how you must be feeling."

"Oh, Ivy, please don't blame yourself. This is something I have been dreaming about ever since I was a little kid--I want an adventure--a big one!"

"Holy Christopher." Vi grumbled under her pillow.

"You're not supposed to swear, Vi. I'm telling!"

"It's not swearing. Besides, how can you tell on me? You won't be here."

"Oh, yeah. Well, Ivy will tell."

"You're ridiculous! Shut up and go back to bed, this instant!"

"Okay for you, Vi. Everything is just perfect for you!" LaVerne cried, forgetting that it was the middle of the night. "You get to go to a big city, play your stupid ball game, and show off in front of a bunch of men. Probably fall in love like everyone else around here and get married..."

Violet sat up, shocked by LaVerne's outburst. "Whoa! I didn't mean anything by what I said. I just meant..."

"Oh, shut up, will you, Violet? You're just making everything worse." Ivah said.

"Oh, like you know everything. Just because you're marrying a big shot lawyer doesn't make you the Queen of the World. You're still a small town girl from the sticks..."

"Well, she sure knows more than you do Vi."

"Well, thanks very much. See if I bring you anything when I come back from Frisco..."

"Anyway, Vernie. Will you promise? Wait one more day, okay? Just one day."

LaVerne thought for a moment, sliding her hands behind her back and crossing her fingers against the lie she was about to tell. "Well, okay, Ivy. I promise."

"Good girl! Now let's all get back to bed. I'll see you in the morning, squirt."

"*Finally.*" Violet muttered.

"I have to go to the 'necessary'. I'll be right back."

Already snuggled under the quilts, Ivah sat up, "Do you want me to go with you?"

"No thank you. I'll be fine. Go to sleep."

"Hurry back. Watch out for bears." Ivah laughed and lay back down.

LaVerne crossed to the door and was gone.

Ivah whispered in the dark. "Vi? Vi! You awake?"

"Um-huh."

"Can you believe it? Vernie thinking she can get clear up to Alaska? Of all the crazy ideas, that beats all."

"Um-huh."

"You're going to have to help me talk her out of it."

Violet made no response. Ivah poked her in the back. "Vi? Violet Marie! Answer me."

"Um-huh?"

"Are you going to help me or not?"

"Yess!" Violet hissed. "Now leave me alone and go to sleep."

A few minutes later LaVerne crept back into the bedroom. She stood in the dark listening to the regular breathing of her two sisters.

"Ivah? Vi? I've been thinking about what you said. I think you're right. I couldn't possibly get to Alaska by myself. Ivy? Are you awake? Vi?" She waited in silence for a response. "Okay then."

LaVerne picked up her coat, her guitar, and duffle bag where she had dropped them by the bed. She quietly walked to the door and opening it, she turned back to her sisters.

"I'm sorry to break my promise to you, Ivy," she whispered. "But I *must* go."

She paused, wanting to say more. Then she quoted a few favorite lines from Robert Service, almost as a benediction, for herself or for her sisters, she knew not.

'Why join the reckless, roving crew of trail and tent?
Why grimly take the roads of rue, to doom hell-bent?'

'Columbus, Cook and Cabot knew, and yet they went.'

"Goodbye. I love you both. Kiss Mama for me." With tears in her eyes, she walked into the hall and closed the door quietly behind her.

❧❧❧

An hour later, LaVerne walked through the silent town of Tumwater and then crossed the road to the north-bound side. Trucks of all sizes and descriptions lumbered by. Thumb stuck out, LaVerne began to walk north and marveled to herself. *These are my first footsteps on my adventure. Soon I'll be walking in snow, mountains surrounding my travels; a lone wolf's cry greeting me.*

LaVerne was startled out of her reverie when a large truck hit his breaks and slowed beside her. The passenger door swung open.

"Where'ya headed, son?" the driver yelled.

"Seattle, sir." LaVerne was astonished that her disguised worked so well.

"Hop in, time's awastin'. I'm drivin' straight through."

Two

LaVerne's luck was holding. The trucker who had given her a ride was delivering his load to the docks in Seattle. It was easy from there to walk from ship to ship looking for work. The fourth freighter she inquired at was not only headed for Anchorage but was named the 'North Star'. She found that providential. And they needed what they called a 'kitchen boy', to help the cook. It offered a bunk and three squares and paid a little something besides.

She told the first mate that her name was 'Verne' and that she was experienced in a kitchen. That wasn't exactly a lie; Mama made certain that all the girls knew their way around a stove. Without much discussion the job was offered to her and she accepted immediately. Early the next morning, on the outgoing tide, LaVerne stood at the railing and watched the town of Seattle slip by.

Grinning, she descended a long ladder and after a couple of wrong turns arrived in the galley. The cook, nicknamed Grub, was a man who was as wide as he was tall. His face was covered in a white beard and his gray hair was pulled back into a pony tail that reached the middle of his back.

"Peel those spuds, lad." He ordered.

"Yes, sir," LaVerne sat on a stool and began. She would show Grub that she could peel a potato with the best of them.

As the days went by and innumerable meals were prepared and served to the crew Grub told LaVerne stories of his life in Alaska. He had worked at E. T. Barnette's trading post in Fairbanks, had run a trap line for furs in the winter, and worked on a fishing boat in the summer.

Did Verne know where he was headed when they reached Anchorage? Grub recommended Fairbanks to LaVerne because of the Tanana Valley. It was rich in furs, wild-life and had good soil for growing vegetables.

"I want some land, Grub." LaVerne told him.

Grub laughed, "Well, we got plenty of that in Alaska. Just be sure to file your homestead when you find the right spot."

"What's a homestead? How much will land cost me? Are there jobs in Fairbanks?"

"There's always jobs waitin'. People work a little bit and then they get the gold fever and off they go to the creeks and streams. Land don't cost nothing but a lot 'a sweat and blood. A homestead is free land the government gives ya to settle there permanent like. Eighty acres, all yours for the takin'."

"Really? Free?" LaVerne was amazed.

"Aye. I think you have to build your cabin within two years, or somethin' like that, before the land is yours for keeps--but they'll explain all that to ya when you file. That what ya gonna do, file for some land, laddie?"

"The minute I arrive!"

"Well, get a job first, take your time--scout around for a good parcel. Make sure you got good water and timber. You'll be wantin' to build your cabin with your own trees nearby. And make sure there's lot'sa game. 'Course that ain't never a problem up there. Like I said, take your time. Everybody's in such a damn rush these days."

"I'll have plenty of time. I figure I'll have to work a job for at least two years before I have my stake."

LaVerne absorbed every word her boss uttered. She would travel cross country to Fairbanks, get a job and explore the area for the perfect spot to homestead. *Homestead!* That one simple word held all her dreams in it. *Homestead. A place all my own.*

"All right then, laddie. Let's get these spuds in the oven and start breaking eggs into that bowl there. The boys love steak and eggs."

Suddenly the galley tilted and bowls and pans started to slide across the counters. A railing around the entire top stopped the cooking utensils from falling to the floor.

"Whoa!" LaVerne cried as she grabbed for her bowl full of eggs.

"Ahh--we just left the Pacific and sailed into the Gulf of Alaska. It's always this way--choppy." Grub stood with his legs slightly apart and steady as a rock. "It'll smooth out a'fore ya know it."

And after a few minutes the ship righted itself as if Grub had ordered the seas to behave.

"How can I get to Fairbanks, Grub?"

"Train's the best way, during the summer. And it's cheap if ya don't mind sleepin' sitting up."

"And in the winter?"

"Dog sled's about the only way. But, it's a harsh trip. Best to ride with a mail carrier. They are the only ones that get through--but 'tis a harrowing trip."

"Lucky for me, then, that it's summer."

"'Tis, laddie. Find a place to stay through next winter, have a look at the area and have your homestead filed by spring. That would give you the whole of the summer to build your place."

"What will you do next when we dock in Anchorage, Grub?"

"Och, it's the fishin' boats for me this summer, then back to cookin' on this tub," he laughed affectionately as he referred to the grand North Star as a 'tub'.

LaVerne noticed Grub's expression turn serious. "Was ya ever gonna tell me who you really are, *Verne*?"

LaVerne ducked her head and made busy work for her hands. "Don't know what you mean, Grub."

"Not many men walkin' around can pull the wool over these ole' eyes—much less a little slip of a girl," he scoffed.

LaVerne sagged down on a stool, shoulders bent, chin resting on her chest. "How long have you suspected?"

"Girl, I got me four granddaughters—from ages twelve to twenty-three. I know the difference between a man and a girl." He stared at her. "I will tell you this. You did a good job of binding your chest and making sure your clothes were baggy. But oncet I saw you in silhouette, I knew you was no boy."

"I'm sorry I lied to you, Grub."

"Well, no harm done. You're a good worker. Better'n a few kitchen boys I've hired. But, your travels are going to be more dangerous, being female an'all. Best keep up your disguise until you get settled somewhere, make some friends."

LaVerne looked at him with tears of gratitude. "Thanks, Grub. I really appreciate all you've taught me and told me about life in Alaska."

The grizzled older man blushed. "Ain't no skin off'n me. You just be careful, ya hear?"

Three

Fairbanks, Alaska
Three months later

Dear Mama and family,
I am writing you from Alaska. I'm sorry I haven't written before now; even though it was an exciting trip to get here, it did have its challenges. I worked on a freighter as a galley boy; yes, I pretended I was a boy and no one was the wiser. Well, except for Grub, the cook. But he kept my secret and we became friends. It took three weeks to sail from Seattle to Anchorage. Then with my money from working on the ship I was able to pay for a third class ticket on the Alaskan Railway to this outpost. The very first place, I asked for work, hired me and now I work as a clerk at the E. T. Barnette's Trading Post.
Mr. Barnette opened the post in 1901. When they discovered gold near here he turned the one room temporary stop into a four room permanent post. It's a store with hardware, supplies for the trail, panning items (for gold) and a post office. Oh yes, there's also a barber shop. Mr. Barnette is now Fairbanks' first mayor. There's a rooming house at the end of the main street and I was able to find a room there.

Don't worry, Mama, it's respectable. You would absolutely love Ma Powers who owns it. She clucks around me like a mother hen. I am the only girl in the house so she scolds any of the other boarders that even look my way!

When I get time off from work, which isn't very often, I rent a horse, (thank goodness Pa insisted we girls learn how to ride) and I explore the countryside west of Fairbanks. I am slowly working my way up the Tanana Valley but my free time doesn't allow me to go as far as I would like to. If I can get some extra time off, the locals tell me I can ride cross-country to the Woods River and get passage on a flat boat up to the Yukon River which is where I want to look for my homestead. I despair of this happening any time soon as Mr. Barnette is very strict about being on time and at work every day.

Enough about me. How are my pesky sisters? Still up to pranks? I cannot wait to have a letter from you, Mama. You can address it to Barnette's Trading Post, Fairbanks, Alaska and it will find me.

Just know that I am safe and so happy to be here. I feel the same emotions that Mr. Service felt when he wrote his poetry. Only I want to write music about the purity of this untouched, beautiful place. It's exactly like Mr. Service described,

'There's a land where the mountains are nameless, and the rivers all run God knows where; there are hardships that nobody reckons, there are valleys unpeopled and still; there's a land…oh, it beckons and beckons, and I want to go…'

Give Pa and the brats my love. Tell Pa to hug you for me, will you?

Your loving daughter, LaVerne

Two months later, the long awaited letter arrived from home. LaVerne frequently helped to empty and sort the mail bag and when she saw her mother's familiar script she left the pile of mail on the counter and dashed out the back door of the trading post. Sitting on the step she ripped open the envelope. As she opened the letter a twenty and a five dollar bill fell to the ground.

"Oh, Mama, it is so like you to worry about my being able to support myself," she whispered as she scooped up the money.

'My darling girl. At last! You gave me the fright of my life disappearing like that. At least your sisters were pretty certain where you were headed from your conversation with them the night you left. And now, finally, a letter from you. I am so relieved that you are alive and have not been eaten by a polar bear! How is life in the wilderness? I try not to worry about you but I do. Your letter put some of my worries to rest but then I imagine you traipsing all over the wilderness by yourself and I have new worries. I miss you and often remember all the evenings we sat while you read aloud to us. I pray Alaska is not as ferociously wild as Mr. Service's poetry describes it.

Those were good days with my children all around me. Even if your brothers and sisters complained about your incessant reading of poetry, I still miss it and you. Things here at the home place are as usual. Ivah and Arthur have set a date for a summer wedding. Lillas and Bill and little Maxine are doing well in London but Lillas complains about, of all things, tea! She says every time she turns around someone is offering her 'a cuppa' when what she really wants is a good old fashion,

American cup of coffee. She says they can't even do that right. Ha ha.

She tells us the weather is so similar to home that sometimes she forgets she's in a different country. With the exception of London's fog (which we've all heard about) it's rainy and cool most of the time.

Little Maxine is growing like a weed. Lillas enclosed a photograph of her in her last letter. She's grown from a baby into a little girl. I enclose it here for you so you will have a little piece of home.

LaVerne gazed at the small snapshot of her niece. A lump of home sickness formed in her throat as she turned back to her mother's letter.

Violet continues to lead her hellion life in San Francisco. Something is just not right there, but I can't put my finger on it. Violet's letters are full of excitement and success with her basketball career but no other news, at least none that she wants to share with me.

Your father and the boys are working up on the Snoqualmie Pass and will be gone at least three weeks. It's so quiet here with everyone gone. I just can't imagine you homesteading a parcel of land in Alaska, like any man would do. It sounds like beautiful country from your descriptions, but won't you be lonely? There, all by yourself?

Well, daughter, the bread's about ready to come out of the oven so I'll close for now.

Your loving Mama

PS. Rochester, that devil of a rooster, died.

Four

Fairbanks, Alaska
1922

LaVerne lounged on the porch of the boarding house. It was early evening and she groaned as she stretched muscles that, nine months ago, she hadn't known she owned. Her tall, lanky, boyish figure was in peak condition due to the physical work at the trading post. Loading and unloading supplies, stocking shelves, cleaning and a myriad of other chores included in her job description.

The sun wouldn't set for several more hours. *It sure took some getting used to,* she thought, *a few hours of darkness every night.* Sleeping with light pouring through the curtains of her room was nigh on impossible.

LaVerne picked up her guitar and strummed some chords to limber up her fingers. She then picked out a simple melody of her own making and hummed the melody. Stopping, she picked up a pencil and some paper lying by her side, and wrote down ideas for the lyrics.

Gold! The word echoed from mountain to strait,
soon to be heard in the lower forty-eight,
    city slickers bought a pack --came to meet their fate
  illness of gilt...easy to kilt...gold fever...
    dying alone in the great beyond

gold fever leaving behind a family of grievers..

She chewed on the end of her pencil and studied the words. *Not bad for a start.*

The screen door creaked open and then slammed shut. From around the corner of the wrap-around porch Ma Powers appeared.

"Lordy, child, you make the prettiest music these old ears have heard in a coon's age."

She plopped her considerable girth down in a rocking chair. "Mind if I sit and listen a spell? These old dogs of mine are barkin' by the end of the day." Pulling aside her ankle length dress and apron, she raised one foot, clad in a rubber boot with stockings sagging around the top.

"Not at all, Ma. I'm just noodling' around with a new idea I had for a song."

"Will you play me one, girl?"

"Certainly. How about I Swiftly Go?"

Ma Powers laughed. "You know that be one of my favorites. It's so--I don't know…true."

LaVerne struck two chords as an introduction and then launched into it.

Whirling winds & whipping ice
beating hard -against- my- skin
As I swiftly go
Beasts of burden straining hard against their ropes
To pull me ever closer to my destiny
before the night falls
Before I'm swallowed by the winds
I swiftly go, through time and snow. I swiftly go
I swiftly go -
towards reflection of the sky and frozen mountains
and have to wonder which is sky and which is ice.
Frozen water, ground, & sky
beneath me/ all around me/ inside me

As I swiftly go through time and snow I swiftly go

For-ward-still-I-go
ever blinded by the white of swirling snow
For-ward-still-I-fly
Even blinded by blue illusions, that turn the ice to
sky
I swiftly go. I swiftly go. I swiftly go.

By the time LaVerne had reached the second chorus other boarders had wandered out and sat or stood listening to her play. Stewart, another boarder, slipped his mouth-organ out of his pocket and quietly accompanied her. Cecil went back in the house and soon returned with his fiddle. The song ended amidst much hooting and applause.

"My word, child, you do have a way with words," Ma exclaimed. "Swallowed by the wind--just lovely, that."

"Hey, LaVerne, do ya know, 'Stardust'?"

LaVerne played the intro to the song and the boarder who requested it grinned at her. The violin and harmonica joined in a few bars later and a few boarders who knew the words began to sing along.

'Sometimes I wonder why I spend
The lonely nights dreaming of a song
The melody haunts my reverie
And I am once again with you
When our love was new
And each kiss an inspiration
but that was long ago

Now my consolation is in the stardust of a song
Beside the garden wall when stars are bright
You are in my arms

The nightingale tells his fairy tale
Of paradise where roses grew
Though I dream in vain
In my heart it will remain

LaVerne looked up and saw more than one rough n' tumble man wiping his eyes, thinking of home and a loved one he had left behind. She ended the song and leaned back, staring at the far horizon where the snow capped mountains rose silently into the perpetual dusk.

Suddenly, heavy steps were heard mounting the porch. Around the corner lumbered Mr. Barnette, himself. Topping out at six foot, four and weighing close to three hundred pounds, he was an impressive figure. His handle-bar mustache was waxed to perfection and swept half way across his cheeks. He wore heavy corduroy pants, a home-spun shirt and steel toed boots. His brightly colored, embroidered waistcoat was his one weakness and he was known throughout the territory, for his collection. A dead but very large cigar stub stuck out of his mouth.

"What's all the caterwaulerin' about?" he asked no one in particular.

"Evenin' Mr. Mayor." A couple of boarders tipped their hats.

"It ain't caterwaulerin' from where I'm sittin', you old goat," Ma Powers scolded him. "This here gal's got real talent."

"Well, now, Ms. Powers, I didn't say I didn't like it," Mr. Barnette told her.

"Humph," was Ma's only response.

"Good evening, Mr. Barnette," LaVerne said.

"LaVerne! I had no ide're you was musical."

"Yes, sir, it's a hobby of mine."

"Humph, it ain't just a hobby. This girl was meant to write her music and give it to the world," Ma Powers exclaimed. "Whad'ya want, Edward?"

"I just wanted to stop by and tell LaVerne that she can have her three days off next week." He turned to LaVerne. "With your regular day you'll have four days all tol'."

LaVerne jumped up. "Oh! Thank you, Mr. Barnette!"

"Now, don't gush, girl. You been workin' real hard for the store," he blustered. "Just be sure you get back on time. I don't abide tardiness."

"No, sir. I'll be back to work on time."

Mr. Barnette started to leave and then turned back. "Come see me tomorrow, Vernie, I think you should start a musical night over at the post."

"Really?" LaVerne was stunned.

"I said it, didn't I?"

And with that Mr. Barnette lumbered away.

LaVerne turned and grinned at Ma Powers and the other boarders.

"Now, that's a fine idea, if I ever heard'a one," Ma said.

"Do you think anybody would come?" LaVerne asked.

"We got very little entertainment in this here part of the world," Cecil, the violin player, told her. "The whole town will be there, Vernie."

"Will you play with me?" LaVerne asked them.

"Of course we will," the harmonica player assured her.

"Doesn't the post have a pie-an-a? Seems like I saw one," one of the men asked.

"But we don't have a piano player," LaVerne said.

"Oh yes, we do." And all the boarders looked at Ma Powers.

"Now you all cut that out. I'm so rusty...my fingers won't know what to do if they ain't holdin' a pan or a spoon. I haven't touched the keys in years."

"So practice a little, Ma." LaVerne pleaded. "Please, it will be so much more fun if we have a piano."

"It's probably way out of tune, child, even if I could play."

Cecil laughed, "Fortunately, I can tune it right up for you, Ma."

Everyone cheered and Ma Powers blushed.

"Please, Ma?"

"We'll see, child, when the times comes." Ma rose. "Gotta get back to my kitchen. I got a mess of dirty pans needs my attention. Play loud so's I can hear ya from there."

Five

The moment LaVerne ended her shift at the store, on the night before her four days off was to begin, she rode a rented horse three hours over land to the Woods River. She was deeply grateful for the endless dusk of summer nights. The stable owner in town had assured her that her horse was trained to stand quietly on board the flat boat that would transport them up the Tanana Valley to the Yukon River fork.

She arrived at the river landing late. Sleeping in the rough with no fire and no hot food, she caught a few hours of sleep in the hollowed out trunk of an ancient tree. Up river on the Yukon, the boat would land on the west side and she would then be able to make her way to the village of Tanana and explore the area around the village. She was certain that she would soon find the site of her future homestead.

At dawn she awoke to the clanging of a ship's bell and she scrambled out of her bedroll. She pulled on her coat and boots. Tying her bedroll on the back of the saddle she quickly removed the hobbles from her horse and cinched up the saddle. She slung the reins over the horn and led the horse down the path and onto the boat.

"That'll be fifty cents for you and a quarter for your horse, Miss." The captain informed her.

LaVerne dug into her trousers and produced a dollar bill. "Thank you." she said as the captain gave her back the change.

The boat had an in-board engine and it grumbled and spit as they cast off and slowly moved down the river. A moose cow and her calf were grazing in the shallows and raised their heads to stare impassively at the boat. Then, with a sudden burst of energy, mother and calf bolted onto the shore and disappeared into the trees.

LaVerne stayed close to her horse and soothed it with unintelligible mutterings to keep it calm. The horse seemed impervious to the trip on the river but LaVerne was taking no chances. The river remained calm until they reached the fork where the Woods River and the Yukon met. The water churned and boiled for several yards as the rivers fought each other for dominance on their way to the sea. Once the boat entered the Yukon it became calm and peaceful once again.

As they chugged up the Yukon against a strong current, the native Alaskans aboard the boat had been quietly speaking to each other in their own language, Athabascan. Their tone became slightly more animated as they neared the landing. *I guess whoever you are or wherever you go a person gets excited when they're near home,* LaVerne mused.

The boat nudged into a crude dock and the deck hands secured lines front and back. LaVerne gathered her pack and tied it to the back of her saddle. Leading the horse by its bridle, she moved carefully toward the stern of the boat. A ramp lowered and lay in the shallows. She stopped to ask the captain about the return trip.

"Excuse me, Captain, what time should I be here in two days time to catch the boat back down to Fairbanks?"

"I'll be here this same time, every day, young lady," he replied. "But don't be late, I don't wait for man nor' beast."

"Yes, sir. Thank you."

LaVerne led her horse to the apron that had been lowered to the shallow water along the shore. Her horse balked briefly at stepping off and then docilely walked onto shore and up the bank of the river. Off to her right she could see smoke rising in the air. Since most of the passengers were walking that way, she could only assume that the trail led to the village of Tanana.

In no time she was walking down a muddy main street. There were perhaps six buildings, mostly cabins and shacks made up of whatever material the owner could find. Racks of drying fish and chained sled dogs announced that people lived in these shanties. The best constructed building was larger than the other structures and LaVerne guessed it might be the tribal lodge. The next largest building declared itself a trading post with a homemade sign over the door: *Village Store.*

Tying her horse to the railing, she entered the building, hoping to obtain a map of the area. A tall middle-aged man stood behind the counter. He had the reddest hair LaVerne had ever seen. His little round eye glasses perched upon a bulbous nose.

"Good day to ya, Miss. Just off the boat, are ye?

"Yes. How do you do? I'm Miss Guyer."

"Nice to mee'cha I'm sure. I'm George, George McGregor. What can I do ya for?"

"I'm thinking of settling in the area and wondered if there might be a map or information about land available to homestead."

The man laughed. "No such thing as a map, lady. But, if ya got a bottle of whiskey as payment, there's Black Eyed Joe who'll guide ya. But, I recommend that you don't pay 'im 'till the job's done and he's guided ya back here. These In'juns love their fire water." He laughed.

LaVerne didn't care for nor understand the slur about the native Alaskans but she kept her opinion to herself. "Excellent! Where might I find this guide?"

"Well, now, you're in luck there; he's in the back of the store, snoozin' it off by the stove." George slapped his knee as he laughed again.

LaVerne thanked him and, navigating her way around barrels of flour, sugar, and sorghum, she walked toward the rear of the store. Sitting in chairs around a pot-bellied stove were three men. Two natives and one very old white man.

"I'm looking for a guide by the name of Joe." LaVerne asked.

One of the Alaskans poked the other to wake him up. The sleeping man sat up abruptly and looked around wildly.

"Huh? Wha? Wha's wrong?"

"Mr. Joe?" LaVerne repeated.

Black Eyed Joe stood and wiped his mouth with the back of his hand. "Yes, I am known as Black Eyed Joe." In spite of his accent he had an odd dignity about him. His face had the leathered look of a man who spent all of his life outside in the elements. His round face and eyes spoke of his Mongolian heritage and his black hair was neatly braided and tied at the back of his head.

"I'm Miss Guyer. I am spending the next two days looking for my homestead and I need a guide."

Brushing off his none too clean shirt, Joe stood and tucked it into his pants. He finger combed strands of his raven black hair that had escaped from the braid.

"I am the best guide around. Everyone will tell you this."

"Excellent. I will pay you one dollar per day. Sun up to sun down. Is that agreeable?"

"Yes, Miss. When would you like to leave?"

"Immediately. There's still five hours of daylight and I'd like to be up the trail and ready to begin in earnest tomorrow morning."

"Let me find my horse, Miss."

At this statement the other two men laughed and poked each other.

"I shall meet you back here in one half hour. Will that give you enough time?"

"Yes, Miss."

LaVerne turned and walked back to the front of the store. She smiled to herself. This was an excellent start. She hadn't thought about a guide until the post's clerk had uttered the words. A much better idea than striking off on her own into territory that she would have found completely foreign.

♪♪♪

Six hours later Black Eyed Joe and LaVerne sat around a small camp fire. Joe was mopping up the last of his dinner with a chunk of bread.

"Good beans and pork fat, Miss. Thank you."

"You're very welcome. Do you mind if I ask you a question, Joe?"

Joe nodded and mumbled around a mouth full of bread and gravy. "Umm-uh…"

"Your English is very good. Did you go to school?"

"Yes, when I was a boy there was a missionary school in Kayukuk, my village. If we did not speak proper English the priests would beat us. We learned very swiftly."

LaVerne smiled and offered him a tin cup of steaming coffee. "How will I know what land has not been claimed?"

"When a homestead has been filed on, the man stacks a cairn of rocks on four sides of the land. Then he must build a dwelling soon. Then after five white man years, it is his, or so they think."

"What? Does the government not honor the Homestead Act?"

"No. The white man's government has no say. The land belongs to no one and to everyone."

"Whatever do you mean?"

"A long time ago my people traveled to this land from far, far away, from a land that had snow and ice every day. The Mother Spirit greeted us with fresh running rivers, many animals to hunt and days of sunshine. She instructed us to respect the land and pray to any animal that gave up its life so that we might have its meat and fur. She gave us the land to care for on her behalf." Joe shrugged his shoulders. "No man owns what Mother Spirit does not freely give."

"I see." *What a charming folk tale,* LaVerne thought. *And Joe seems to believe it. I could use the story as a basis for one of my songs.*

Joe lay down and pulled a blanket over his body. "We should sleep now. Tomorrow comes very soon."

LaVerne lay down in her bedroll and stared up at a star packed sky. Soon waves of green, gold and red color danced across the star studded night sky. *What an amazing place this is. Soon, with some luck, I shall lie on my own land and watch those spirals of color ghost across the piece of sky that blankets my homestead.*

As she dreamed of her future homestead, her eyes drifted closed.

Six

LaVerne woke to the smell of rich, dark coffee. She snuggled deeper into her bedding, resisting the idea of leaving her warm nest. Through half closed eyes she watched Joe as he cut thick slabs of bacon and threw them into a sizzling fry pan on the open fire. Soon a full bladder had her up and walking toward the thicket of trees nearby.

When she returned she detoured to the hobbled horses and gave them each a handful of oats from a satchel hanging from her saddle. Joe's horse snuffled her hand and the oats for a minute before greedily inhaling the treat. LaVerne laughed and rubbed his forelock. Crossing to the camp fire, LaVerne saw that Joe had made a rich gravy from the bacon drippings. Joe handed her a tin plate where bacon and gravy covered the camp biscuits Joe had made using a Dutch oven she had brought along.

"This looks wonderful, Joe. Thank you."

"It is part of my job as guide--to share camp work." He shrugged and dug into his own breakfast.

After the meal the two of them made short work of the cleanup. They walked the horses down to the creek that ran by their camp site. The horses drank as LaVerne and Joe washed the dishes, using creek bottom sand and fresh water to scrub them clean. An hour after daybreak they were saddled up and on their way.

As they topped a slight rise, Joe stopped and waited for LaVerne to ride up next to him. Half a mile away and below them the Yukon River ran swiftly by. It was over two miles wide and had several small islands in the middle.

"This is good land, Miss. Many creeks run into the Yukon and there are enough trees for three life times. Good trapping too. Plenty of meat."

LaVerne sighed in complete contentment. "I see smoke, Joe. Are there settlers about?"

"We see the smoke from Charlie's cabin, Miss. We shall be at that place in about one hour. If you choose the land I am thinking of, Charlie would be your nearest neighbor. If you like, we shall stop and say hello."

"Yes! I would like that very much."

Leading the way, Joe descended into a beautiful valley where their horses picked their way along the banks of the Yukon. Joe turned inland onto a well worn trail and a cabin came into view. There was a sudden chorus of excited barking. Some distance and to the side of the house were fifteen beautiful sled dogs yapping in welcome. Some stood on top of their small dog houses, watching the arrival of the two riders.

"Hallo! The house!" Joe yelled.

No one in their right mind would ride or walk right up to someone's front door without announcing themselves. If they did, they might be met with a double-barreled shotgun. After a moment or two the front door swung open and a handsome, raw-boned woman walked out on the porch. At her side stood a white and gray Husky that must have weighed at least ninety pounds. The dog's eyes were icy blue.

"Joe, you old rascal! What brings you up this way?" she asked.

"Showing the little Miss here the lay of the land, Charlie." Joe told her as he got down from his horse, stepped up onto the porch and shook hands with her.

LaVerne was somewhat taken aback to see that 'Charlie' was female. Tall for a woman, Charlie had thick auburn hair and whiskey-colored eyes. Her cambric shirt was tucked into corduroy work pants and a belt cinched the smallest waist LaVerne had ever seen. She wondered if she had a family and kids and if they would end up being neighbors?

"Well, step on down and come on in!" Charlie told both of them.

LaVerne dismounted and tied her horse's reins to the railing. Charlie came down the steps with her hand out.

"Charlie Donovan, nice to meet you, she said.

"LaVerne Guyer, Charlie, it's a pleasure," LaVerne replied.

Charlie was staring so intently at LaVerne that they both blushed. "Sorry, LaVerne, don't see many women up this way," Charlie stuttered.

LaVerne was dwarfed by Charlie's lean, big boned frame but instead of feeling intimidated, she felt somehow safe. She laughed easily. "I was guilty of staring too. I have to confess that I was shocked that the Charlie Joe spoke of turned out to be a woman."

"It's actually Charlotte but everybody calls me Charlie." She turned and retraced her steps up onto the porch. "Won't you come in and set a spell?"

"Your dogs are beautiful, but this one," LaVerne indicated the huge dog, "she is lovely. What's her name?"

"Moon," the dog thumped her tail against the floor when she heard her name. "Do you like dogs?" Charlie continued.

"Oh, yes. I miss the ones back on the farm so much."

"You got any of that fine coffee, Charlie?" Joe asked.

"Yes, I just made a pot." Charlie held the screen door open for the two travelers and followed them into the cabin.

LaVerne was amazed at how cozy and homey Charlie's cabin was. The first floor was open and had no walls. In the kitchen was a large wood stove with a water reservoir on one side for heating water. The sink had a bright red pump for water. A large raw, planed wood table served two purposes; a working counter and somewhere to serve meals.

There were six mismatched wooden chairs around the table. Against one wall was a beautiful china and kitchen hutch that displayed a few of Charlie's fine china pieces. It also had fold-out bins that held flour and sugar and other staples, LaVerne was certain.

In the parlor area there was a stone fireplace that took up one entire wall. A well-worn, comfy sofa and two deep-seated chairs separated the kitchen from the sitting room. Homemade quilts added splashes of color. Off to one side a ladder rose up to a sleeping loft.

"Your cabin is wonderful, Charlie."

Charlie turned from the stove, carrying two tin mugs filled with steaming coffee. "Thank you." As she set them down on the table she said, "Sit, sit. There's raw sugar there in the bowl. Do you use cream, LaVerne?"

"Only if you have it."

Joe and LaVerne joined Charlie at the table. "How long have you lived here?" LaVerne asked.

"Oh, gosh, what's it been, Joe? Ten years?"

"There a'bouts." Joe muttered as he slurped his coffee.

"Do you have children?" LaVerne asked and then gasped. "I'm so sorry, my Mama always said I shouldn't ask personal questions but I always forget and do it anyway."

"That's all right. No, I don't have children and no man, thank God." Charlie laughed. "What is it I always say, Joe?"

"Man too much work…" Joe chuckled.

LaVerne laughed and her eyes lit up like black onyx in the sunlight when she did.

"What brings you up this way?" Charlie asked.

"I'm looking to homestead and Joe is showing me around. But I only have three days before I have to get back to my job in Fairbanks. I doubt I'll be able to find the right place in so short a time, but it's worth a try."

"You work in Fairbanks? Not for that old fart, Barnette?" Charlie chuckled.

"Yes, 'fraid so. You know him?"

"Oh sure. The old pirate." She grinned. "He's the only supply post in the area so he gets top dollar for everything."

"Yes, that would be him. But he's always been fair with me. Gave me four days off to look for my place even though he knows it will eventually mean that I'll be leaving his employ."

"Oh, I like him well enough. In his shoes I'd probably charge the same prices. It just stings when a person is short on cash and we homesteaders always are," she smiled.

Charlie looked at Joe and he shrugged. "Joe should show you the parcel right next to mine. It's not been claimed and it's as pretty a piece of land as you'll ever find."

"Really?" LaVerne exclaimed.

"Wolf Creek runs through both properties on its way down to the Yukon. I've never seen it dry up in all these years. And it runs strong enough that you can pipe it, using gravity, right to your cabin."

"Well, if it's half as pretty as your place, Charlie, I won't have to look any further." LaVerne's eyes glowed with anticipation.

Joe stood. "If we want to use your time wisely, Miss, we should be on our way." He turned to Charlie. "I will show her the land you spoke of and then I think I will take her up Kanuti Canyon to see that parcel up there."

Charlie turned to LaVerne who had risen from the table. "That's a good piece of land too, but the winters are harsher on the slopes and the Canyon can be tricky during the snowy months."

Charlie spoke to Joe. "There's that parcel on the backside of the canyon, that you might show her. Good water, good timber. I'd hate to see my new neighbor so far away but it's a good homestead."

"Yes, I will show Miss many homesteads." Joe replied.

"If you're back in the neighborhood at nightfall you and Joe are welcome to bunk down here."

"Thank you so much for your hospitality." LaVerne offered her hand and when Charlie took it an electric shock shot up her arm. *What in the world?* She blushed like a school girl, that a simple handshake gave her the shivers. What was going on?

"Hopefully we will get back by this way before I have to return to Fairbanks."

Charlie looked deep into the mysterious black depths of LaVerne's eyes. "I hope so," she whispered.

Once outside Joe and LaVerne untied and mounted their horses. Joe led the way out of the yard and crossed to the trees. LaVerne turned in the saddle to wave to Charlie and found her still standing on the porch, staring after her. She lifted her hand to wave good bye but Charlie remained motionless as she watched them depart.

LaVerne caught up with Joe at the edge of the forest and they entered a virgin stand of old growth trees. Joe turned north, following animal trails, and soon they came upon a dancing creek.

"This is Wolf Creek, the one Charlie spoke of. Good water year round. Very important."

"How far are we from the river, Joe?"

"No more than one half of the white man's miles. No worries about the flood season reaching your land. The parcel's east boundary ends at the river so you have good fish netting in summer and ice fishing in the winter."

They forded the creek and rode further into the forest. LaVerne breathed deeply and inhaled the loamy, pine scent. She sighed happily and knew that she would follow Joe anywhere. This is what she had come to Alaska for. There suddenly appeared before them a natural clearing. Sun dappled the floor of the forest and a warm sweet grass smell rose to intoxicate the senses. LaVerne was drawn to this place in a deep visceral way as the damp, sun-filled, earthy aromas wove their magic around her.

They continued to ride for another two hours when finally Joe stopped and dismounted.

"This is the northern border of this parcel which joins up with Charlie's." He pointed up a canyon ahead and to the right of where they stood. "There is another fine parcel up that canyon. Would you like to see it?"

"Yes, of course. Lead on, McDuff!" She laughed.

"Excuse me, Miss, but my name is Joe. I know no one named McDuff."

Mounting again, LaVerne laughed merrily as their horses continued up the trail.

Seven

LaVerne and her guide entered the mouth of a steep canyon but the trail, with many switch-backs, was a fairly easy ascent. The walls were strewn with huge boulders and the trees seemed to climb straight up. LaVerne was so pleased with her day she began to recite a ditty of Robert Service's as she followed behind Joe.

'A bunch of the boys were whooping it up in the Malamute saloon; The kid that handles the music-box was hitting a jag-time tune;
Back of the bar, in a solo game, sat Dangerous Dan McGrew,
And watching his luck was his light-o'-love, the lady that's known as Lou.
When out of the night, which was fifty below, and into the din and the glare,
There stumbled a miner fresh from the creeks, dog-dirty, and loaded for bear.
He looked like a man with a foot in the grave and scarcely the strength of a louse,
Yet he tilted a poke of dust on the bar, and he called for drinks for the house.
There was none could place the stranger's face, though we search ourselves for a clue;
But we drank his health, and the last to drink was Dangerous Dan McGrew.'...

Joe turned in his saddle with a puzzled look on his face. "You have been to the post in Galena?"

"No, why do you ask?"

"Your song tells of the nights there."

LaVerne chuckled. "It's not a song, Joe, its poetry."

"I hear music when you speak it."

"Then I shall skip to a favorite part of mine."

As she began again, Joe turned and urged his horse into a lazy walk. LaVerne could tell by the set of Joe's shoulders that he was listening intently.

"'Were you ever out in the Great Alone, when the moon was awful clear,

And the icy mountains hemmed you in with a silence you most could hear;

With only the howl of a timber wolf, and you camped there in the cold,

A half-dead thing in a stark, dead world, clean mad for the muck called gold;

While high overhead, green yellow and red, the North Lights swept in bars?

Then you've a hunch what the music meant...hunger and night and the stars.'"

They rode on in silence, each to their own thoughts and dreams. At the top of the canyon, Joe veered off to the left and the horses scrabbled up a steep embankment. The top of the canyon was a plateau of sorts, free of trees and exposed to the weather. Joe dismounted and let his horse wander away. LaVerne stepped down and, with reins trailing in the grass, her horse began to graze.

"Yoyekoyh." Joe said.

"What?"

"Yoyekoyh. Our word for the north lights that your song talks about."

"Yo-ye-koh..." LaVerne struggled to pronounce it. "What language is that?"

"Athabascan. My people. The white man calls it 'Lower Tanana'. Would you like to hear the story of the Yoyckoyh?"

"Yes...yes, please." LaVerne sat in the grass and looked out over the vista. This high up the Yukon River was a narrow, shiny ribbon snaking through the valley floor far below.

"We believe that as a soul departs Mother Earth, their way is lighted by other souls, already gone, carrying flaming torches--or, as the white man says, the 'northern lights'. This is done so that the new soul crossing over is not left frightened in the eternal dark."

LaVerne sighed contentedly. "That is truly beautiful, Joe, and in future I shall always think of those souls when I see the northern lights."

Joe grunted. "That would be a good thing, Miss. The ancestors who have made their final journey should never be forgotten." He was silent for a moment then changed the subject. "This parcel is larger because of the canyon and mountains at your back. But you must think on this. You will have to haul your timber *uphill*." Joe pointed off to the right. "Also the creek is down there and you will have to haul your water too."

"This view is spectacular. But my mind was made up when we rode into that lovely glen not far from Charlie's property." LaVerne rubbed her forehead. "I don't know--it was strange--it somehow called to me. Spoke to me and told me that I was home."

"You are a chosen child of Mother if the land speaks to you so clearly, Miss." Joe stared at her. "I was going to take you down the other side of this canyon and then we could ride around the hill to a lake. Good marshes for the moose. Charlie fills her cache with moose meat every year."

"Oh yes. I would like that very much. Will we see moose?"

"If we are blessed by the Mother you will see moose with their young."

LaVerne jumped up and walked to her horse. Joe mounted and, crossing the plateau, followed a trail down the backside of the hill. Gathering her reins, LaVerne mounted and followed behind him. A short time later they came to several small lakes glittering in the sunlight.

Woven around and between the lakes was deep marsh land. Joe dismounted and indicated that LaVerne should do the same and motioned her to be very quiet. Following Joe's direction, she walked quietly leading her horse. Joe led her through the tall grass and squatted down. LaVerne looked to where he pointed and saw big splayed-toed prints in the mud. Off to the side he showed her scat that still steamed in the late afternoon.

He whispered, "Very fresh. They are close. Do not speak. We will tie the horses here and go on foot."

LaVerne nodded and led her mount to a tree. After securing it, she loosened the cinch on the saddle, ensuring that the horse would be comfortable while they explored the area. Joe did the same and motioned for her to follow him. Carefully following in Joe's wake, LaVerne thrummed with excitement. With luck she would see her first moose up close. Fairbanks was enough of a settlement that the elusive moose were never seen around town. She had yet to see one on her day explorations around the area.

Joe suddenly froze in his tracks. He crouched down and put a finger up to his lips. LaVerne followed his example and looked up ahead. She couldn't see anything that would have alerted Joe.

Taking her arm so she would stand beside him, Joe rose slowly and pointed, and there they were! A moose cow and her off spring feeding on the succulent growth under the water. Joe pointed again off to the right. A huge bull moose's head came up out of the water, its massive antlers dripping with plant life.

Silently, LaVerne grabbed Joe's arm in delight. Since the human beings stood upwind of them, the family was unaware of being observed and continued to eat. They grazed along parallel with where LaVerne stood with Joe. Suddenly the wind changed carrying the human scent to the beautiful animals. The bull raised his head and huffed and snorted. The cow and her baby immediately trotted ashore and into the safety of the trees. The bull charged a few feet through the water directly toward the threat. Joe immediately squatted down pulling LaVerne down with him.

Waiting a few tense moments, Joe slowly rose just enough to see where the moose were. Then he stood, saying, "They are gone. It is safe now."

"Oh, My God! Joe, that was wonderful! How beautiful they were. Thank you."

"Mother Earth found you worthy, Miss, or she would not have brought the moose to you."

Joe turned back to the horses. LaVerne lingered a moment and gazed over the marsh where the moose had been. Grinning from ear to ear, she turned and followed Joe.

The riders spent the remainder of the afternoon leisurely traversing around the base of the hills toward the parcel that LaVerne had decided upon. At the head of one lake they saw beaver repairing their lodge and at the edge of the trees deer stood quietly in the underbrush and watched them ride by. Getting LaVerne's attention, Joe silently pointed across to a hill where a Grizzly sow lumbered along. Her fuzzy, twin cubs scurried along behind their mother.

"Oh! They're so adorable, I want to cuddle them!" LaVerne whispered.

"Don't let their Mama hear you say that, Miss. She will tear you to shreds."

As if the bear had heard his words, she rose up on her back haunches, to an impressive height of over seven feet, and stared at them.

"We should keep moving; slow and steady but away from Mama bear. We do not want to give her any reason to consider us a threat to her babies." Joe instructed.

When they were well away from the brown bear family, LaVerne spoke in a reverent tone, "Joe, I would like to mark my parcel when we return there."

"Yes, Miss, if you are certain in your selection."

"I am very sure."

'We shall mark the north boundary as we ride. The boundary between you and Charlie we can mark also. The far west boundary will have to wait until tomorrow."

They rode an hour more until Joe pulled up. Dismounting, he let the reins fall to the ground. His horse was well trained and as long as he felt this slight resistance he was as good as tied up. LaVerne repeated Joe's actions and joined him.

"Now we look for rocks to build your cairn."

"Really? This is the north border of my land?" LaVerne grinned. "How do you know?"

"I know."

Joe walked around lifting rocks as large as he could manage and began piling them into a pyramid of stones. LaVerne brought rocks and contributed to the pile. When they had built a cairn about three feet wide at the base and knee high, Joe stood back and inspected the marker.

"Yes. That will speak clearly that someone has claimed this land." He turned to his horse and mounted. "We ride now."

LaVerne walked to her horse that was grazing a short distance away and mounting, she followed Joe. It wasn't long before they arrived back at the beautiful natural clearing that they had found earlier in the day. LaVerne stopped her horse and sensing the change, Joe's horse halted too. Joe turned back, a questioning look in his eyes.

"Joe, I would like to spend a little time here. Think about my cabin and garden and just absorb it all. Once I return to Fairbanks, I don't know when I can get back. Can I meet you back at Charlie's cabin in a little bit?"

"Of course." He pointed to the far side of the glen. "That trail leads directly to her place."

"Thank you. I'll see you in an hour or so."

Joe rode up close and pulled his rifle out of its scabbard. "You must not remain here, alone, unarmed. Can you shoot?"

LaVerne took the gun. "Yes. Thank you."

Handing the weapon to her, Joe wheeled his horse around and trotted down the trail, the trees swallowing him.

LaVerne dismounted and led her horse over to the sparkling creek. The mare drank deeply and LaVerne washed her face and hands. Then cupping her hands, she drank the ice cold water. Something winked at her from the creek bottom. Thinking it was an agate or other shiny rock, she dipped her hand back into the water and scooped up a handful of black sand and pebbles. Letting the sand filter out between her fingers, LaVerne inspected the remaining rocks. A burnished yellow colored pebble about the size of her little fingernail glowed in the sun.

Interesting. What kind of mineral would be this color? Placing it in her shirt pocket, she dipped again. Repeating the process, she let the sand fall, and then let the water wash her closed fist of rocks.

Opening her hand carefully, she inspected the remaining rocks. Four more yellowish pebbles of different sizes lay in her palm. A black one marbled in white was almost a perfect oval, made smooth to the touch by years of tumbling water and sand.

LaVerne moved up the creek a foot or so and dipped her hand in again. When she inspected the rocks and sand and silt she discovered flakes of the yellow material and two more ochre pebbles, this time larger. She removed her neckerchief from around her neck and laid it out on the bank of the creek. Carefully she washed each flake and rock and placed them on the cloth. When she was finished she wrapped them carefully.

She laughed at herself. *What did the miners call it? Ah, yes,* fool's gold. *Pyrite. Oh well,* they'll *look pretty on my windowsill in my room and remind me of what I am working towards.* Perhaps Joe and Charlie would know what the other rocks were.

Leaving her horse to wander nearby, she walked the perimeter of the clearing. *I think I'll build my cabin at the far end here with the trees at my back. It will break the north winds. Then my garden will be there, to the side where the sun is the brightest.* She planned it all in her head. Eventually she could pipe water to the house using gravity and water pressure, just like Joe had explained to her.

LaVerne walked over to where her porch would someday be and sat in the grass. The lowering sun beat warmth into her tired shoulders and back.

Ah, Mama, if you could see me now. I am home. I have found my homeplace as surely as you and Pa did when you migrated out west. She sighed. *I miss you so much. Apparently I miss my bratty sisters too; that's the only explanation I can find to explain my instant attraction to Charlie. I miss a female's companionship like your girls have always had, Mama.*

Aside from Mrs. Barnette at the store, there weren't any single women living and working in Fairbanks. And she was the only woman living at the boarding house with the exception of Ma Powers. As nice as the other married women were, they were older and she found they didn't have much in common. *They all think I'm cracked when I talk about homesteading on my own without a man. I wonder--am I, Mama?* She whispered to the trees.

The sun had made her sleepy and she lay back in the sweet grass and stared up at the sky. Pure cobalt blue bracketed deep green branches as if in a patchwork quilt nature had sewn. An hour later LaVerne awoke to the warm breath of her horse on her cheek. The mare smelled of the pungent grass she'd been eating as she snuffled LaVerne's hair. She stretched and sat up. The sun had dipped behind the trees by now and there was a chill in the air.

"Okay, girl, time to head toward Charlie's, huh?" She said as she stood up. "A bag of oats must sound pretty good about now."

The horse shoved LaVerne in the back with her head, as if to say, 'yes, I've done enough work for you today'.

Gathering the reins, LaVerne led the horse to the edge of the clearing. Turning back for a moment, she gazed around at her new homestead. She mounted and started down the trail. She knew she was getting closer to Charlie's cabin because even though she couldn't see it, she smelled the smoke from the cabin's chimney. *Funny how everything is so much sharper out in the wild.* The air smelled sweet and pure, the earth gave up its own perfume of loam, moss, grasses, and rotting wood. And the smell of man, like chimney smoke, traveled far.

She rode on a bit and then observed that Joe had stopped long enough to build another marker on the side of the trail, clearly marking her boundary. *What a thoughtful thing to do.* She pulled up her horse and stared at the cairn. *My land, my place. Now all I have to do is figure out how soon I can return.*

Eight

Charlie stepped out of the barn after putting the animals up for the night, and watched LaVerne ride into the yard. LaVerne did not see her standing in the shadow of the huge door.

She looks tired but completely content. Charlie thought to herself. *Joe said he thought she had found her homestead.* She knew that clearing and it was a pretty place for a cabin. She didn't want to be too hopeful but she would have been disappointed if LaVerne picked another parcel farther away. *Okay, Charlotte! There's no point in hoping for more. The girl's hardly grown and certainly does not share your feelings so snap out of it.*

Charlie walked out into the late sun. "Hello!"

LaVerne had dismounted and was taking the tack off her tired horse. Surprised at Charlie's voice, she turned, holding the saddle in front of her and grinned. "Hello there. Can I take you up on your offer of shelter tonight?"

"Absolutely. Why don't you bring your horse into the barn and we'll get her settled?"

Gathering the reins, LaVerne led her toward the barn door. Taking LaVerne's tack, Charlie turned and walked back into the gloom.

"You can put her in here," she indicated an empty stall and going to a wall, took down a curry brush. "There's a feed bag hanging on the wall and oats in that bin over there."

"Thank you." LaVerne said as she led her mare into the stall, its floor covered with fresh hay.

Joe's horse nickered from an adjoining stall. LaVerne scratched his ears. "Hello, boy. All cozy now? Did you like your dinner?"

As LaVerne left the stall, Charlie was entering with the curry brush in one hand and a pail of fresh water in the other. Their bodies brushed each other innocently and, as one, the two women stopped and stared into each other's eyes. LaVerne was the first to break eye contact and blushing furiously she stepped out of the stall. The women worked for the next half hour in silence. Charlie groomed the mare while LaVerne got her oats and attached the feed bag to her head. Shaking out the damp saddle blanket she laid it on the wall of the stall to dry.

"I've got moose stew simmering on the stove for dinner."

"I've never eaten moose meat. I look forward to it."

The women kept up a casual conversation until the chores were done.

"We saw a moose and her baby today," LaVerne said. "And a bull."

"Did you?"

"And a Grizzly with her cubs."

"You had a busy day."

"Yes, the country is as beautiful as I had imagined."

"What brought you to Alaska, if you don't mind my asking?"

"I began to read Robert Service at a very young age. I know it probably sounds stupid but I could feel the love he had for this country. *'Wild and wide are my borders, stern as death is my sway; from my ruthless...'*"

Charlie seamlessly finished the quote, "*'...throne I have ruled alone for a million years and a day...'*"

"You know Robert Service!" LaVerne exclaimed.

"Yes. I love his poetry. Another favorite part of mine is, 'Searching my uttermost valleys, fighting each step as they go, shooting the wrath of my rapids, scaling my ramparts of snow; ripping the guts of my mountains, looting the beds of my creeks, Them will I take to my bosom, and speak as a mother speaks...'"

"Oh, yes." LaVerne sighed and looked at Charlie, "I had to come."

Awkwardness gone, the two women smiled at each other in total accord. Finished with their chores, they walked side by side out of the barn and up to the cabin. Joe sat on the porch in one of Charlie's homemade chairs.

"You found your way from the clearing, little Miss." He stated.

"Yes. And thank you so much for marking that boundary for me." She smiled at Charlie. "It's my place. I know it."

"Quyana ailuci...you are welcome. Tomorrow we shall ride to the west and mark the final boundary. We can mark the river boundary on our way to Tanana."

"Can I file my claim in Tanana, Joe?"

"No you must file it in Fairbanks. We shall mark a map to show them."

Charlie pushed away from the porch post on which she had been leaning during this exchange. "LaVerne, I have a map of the area showing my homestead and the property you want to file on. You may borrow it, if you like."

"Oh, thank you so much. I don't know when I can return it to you, Charlie. It took a lot of persuasion to get just three days off from my work to come here this time."

"Don't worry, there is no rush to return it. Now! Who's hungry? That stew should be ready now."

Joe rose immediately and held the screen door open for the two women.

"Can I wash up, Charlie? Then tell me what I can do to help."

"Of course." Charlie moved to the sink and laid out a bar of homemade lye soap and two towels. "You can set the table, if you would."

LaVerne washed up and then Joe took his turn at the sink.

"I brought some more wood in while you were at the barn, Charlie."

"Thank you, Joe. Sit. Would you like coffee with your meal?"

"That would be good, tsin'aen. "

"You're welcome."

As they talked, LaVerne set the table with bowls, tin mugs, and spoons. At Charlie's direction she cut large slabs of homemade bread and placed it on the table.

"No butter, I'm afraid. Just bear fat to spread on the bread." Charlie explained as she ladled steaming stew into the bowls.

LaVerne poured coffee for everyone and then sat down. She tried to discretely inspect the stew. The meat, potatoes, carrots, onions, and other chunks of something she couldn't identify swam in fragrant brown gravy. It smelled divine. She eagerly lifted the first spoonful to her mouth and immediately drifted into heaven.

"Oh, my God, Charlie, this is wonderful!"

"I'm glad you like it. If you don't care for bear fat, dunking your bread in the gravy is permitted," she laughed.

"I can't believe this is moose meat. It's like the best steak I've ever had."

"The moose gave up his life to feed the people. It is the way."

LaVerne turned to stare at Joe.

"LaVerne, we homesteaders have adopted the native Alaskan's belief that every animal we kill for meat willingly gave up its life." Charlie explained. "We never forget to thank the animal by sending up a prayer at the time of the kill."

"I see." LaVerne thought about what Joe and Charlie were saying. "I think that's a lovely tradition."

After everyone had eaten their fill, they sat around the table with a second mug of coffee.

"When do you think you will be able to return to start building?" Charlie asked.

"I don't know. Probably not until next spring. I should have enough saved by that time. At least I hope I will."

"There are several homesteads already established around your parcel. You can count on all of us to help you in any way we can."

"Oh! I almost forgot to show you what I found."

LaVerne pulled the neckerchief from her pocket and opened it on the table. "Look, I found them in the creek bed."

Charlie and Joe leaned over to inspect what the cloth held.

"Pretty, aren't they?" LaVerne asked.

"*The muck called gold...*" quoted Charlie.

"Humph. The rock that drives the white man mad." Joe said.

"What?" LaVerne asked.

"They are gold nuggets, my dear. You have gold in your creek."

Charlie laughed at LaVerne's astounded expression.

"Really? But I thought it was pyrite--worthless."

"Indeed." Charlie thought for a moment. "I find one or two in my section of the creek but never like this--how long did it take you to collect this many?"

"I don't know--about ten minutes, maybe. I was just washing up after our long ride and saw something sparkly in the bottom of the creek bed."

"Well, this complicates things." Charlie observed.

"Whatever do you mean?" LaVerne asked.

"You'll want to keep these hidden away until after you file and get your homestead certificate. Best not to let anyone know what you've found."

"Are you certain its gold, Charlie?"

"I am. What do you think, Joe?"

"Yes. It is gold. See?" Joe picked up a good sized, long flake and tried to break it. But it just bent under his fingers. "If it were fool's gold this would break. Gold bends, like this." He held the glowing flake up.

"Did these nuggets remain at the bottom? While others floated?" Joe asked.

"I didn't use a pan. Just my hands. I was picking up pretty rocks to take back to my room."

Joe and Charlie smiled at each other. "Pretty rocks, she says," he scoffed.

"You've picked up about two hundred dollars in ten minutes, LaVerne." Charlie told her.

"No--you're joking me. That can't be possible."

"I wouldn't joke about this kind of find."

"But, that's wonderful, don't you see? I can accelerate my plans to move up here. With this money I can buy everything I need. A stove, traps, snow shoes, a gun." She laughed with delight.

"There's no end to my list! Joe! Can we ride through my clearing on our way back tomorrow? I want to see if I can find anymore gold."

"Yes, Miss. But be careful you don't catch the 'gold fever'."

"Do you have somewhere in your room where you can hide your treasure, LaVerne? Charlie asked, "You shouldn't even trust the bank in town. People talk. Word will get out before your claim is approved."

"Yes, there is a loose floorboard that I put my wages in. No one knows about it."

"Good."

Joe rose and stretched. "I will say goodnight. I will bunk in the barn with the horses."

"You know you are welcomed to sleep here by the fire, Joe."

"Tsin'aen, my friend. But I am more comfortable with the animals."

Charlie rose and walked to the door with Joe. "Goodnight then, old friend. We'll see you in the morning."

After saying goodnight to Joe, LaVerne began to clear the dinner dishes. She dipped hot water from the water reservoir in the wood stove and filled a large tin wash bowl. As she washed, Charlie dried the dishes and soon they had made short work of it. Charlie folded the drying cloth over a bar and poured hot coffee into their mugs. She walked to the fireplace where a cozy blaze crackled.

"Come…let's talk." She told LaVerne.

The two women sat across from each other, sipped coffee, and enjoyed the end of the day. Wanting to regain the camaraderie of their earlier talk Charlie quoted something from Service.

"*'Have ever you heard of the Land of Beyond, that dreams at the gates of the day? Alluring it lies at the skirts of the skies and ever so far away; Alluring it calls: O ye the yoke galls, and ye of the trail overfond, with saddle and pack, by paddle and track, let's go to the land of Beyond.'*"

"That's beautiful, Charlie. How does the rest of it go?"

Charlie rose and crossed to a single bookshelf that held a dozen or so books. "I can't remember much more. Let me see…" she took down a well worn, leather book. Flipping a few pages she found what she was looking for. "Here it is…" She sat back in her chair.

"*'Have ever you stood where the silences brood, and vast the horizons begin, at the dawn of the day to behold far away the goal you would strive for and win? Yet ah! In the night when you gain to the height, with the vast pool of heaven star-spawned, afar and agleam, like a valley of dream, still mocks you a Land of Beyond.'*"

Charlie lowered the book to her lap and stared into the fire.

"I love his poetry. He expresses how I feel when I can't." LaVerne explained.

"This next stanza reminds me of you and your dreams, '*Thank God! There is always a Land of Beyond for us who are true to the trail; a vision to seek, a beckoning peak, a fairness that never will fail…*'"

LaVerne sighed and watched the dancing flames.

"Would you like to borrow this?"

LaVerne looked up. "Oh, I couldn't. It's a treasure."

Charlie smiled, "If it means you have to come back to return it, I would love for you to take it."

Charlie watched as LaVerne blushed at the compliment. She leaned in and handed her the book. Their hands brushed and that strange electricity passed between them again.

"If you're sure you won't miss it, I would love to borrow it. And Charlie?"

"Yes?"

"My sisters and my close friends call me 'Vernie'. Would you?"

Charlie stared into her beautiful onyx eyes. "Yes, I would love that, *Vernie*."

"Good."

"Tell me about your sisters."

"Well, for starters, there are five of us."

"*Five!* My goodness."

"Ivah, Violet and I are all closest in age and when I think back, we must have given our Mama many a gray hair. We were always up to something."

"Do you have brothers?"

"Six."

"My word, what a family!"

"But in recent years the boys were gone quite a bit with our Pa. Cutting lumber all over western Washington."

"Are your sisters as adventurous as you?"

"I don't know. I guess Violet would be considered very brave and adventurous. She has gone to San Francisco to play on a women's professional basketball team. Our Pa about had a heart attack when she first brought it up."

Charlie laughed. "And the others?"

"Mostly homebodies. The wife and mother thing. My sister Ivah, who was a worse tomboy than I was when we were growing up, fell in love and can't wait to get married and settle down."

"You sound like you are all very close."

"Yes, in a way. But then I've always felt different. I can't imagine marrying a man and doing the 'honor and obeying' thing." She laughed. "I have a confession."

"What's that?"

"I ran away from home to come to Alaska. I was the baby in the family; I knew my folks would never let me go."

"My gracious, Vernie, how old are you?"

"I'll be nineteen next month."

"A child."

"*I'm not!*" LaVerne was indignant. "I worked my way to Anchorage on a ship and when I got to Fairbanks I got a job. I'm saving money and writing my music."

"Writing music? You continue to amaze me. You're a musician."

"Yes. And I wanted--no, *needed* to come to Alaska to write. And so here I am."

The two women talked long into the night. Finally LaVerne spread her bedroll before the fire and went outside for a final call to nature. When she came back in Charlie had extinguished all the lanterns and the room was lit only by firelight. She walked up to LaVerne and, loosely embracing her, kissed her cheek.

"Good night, Vernie. I hope you come back soon."

LaVerne returned the sisterly hug and leaned in to kiss Charlie's cheek. Charlie turned her head at the last minute and LaVerne's kiss landed on the corner of her mouth.

"Opps! Missed." Vernie chuckled, stepping away.

"Good night, Charlie. Thank you for everything --the book and everything..."

Charlie walked to the bottom of the loft ladder and then turned back, "You will always be welcomed here, Vernie. Sweet dreams."

Nine

The next morning, after a breakfast of eggs, bacon, biscuits and gravy, LaVerne and Joe saddled up to continue their journey. LaVerne wrapped the book that Charlie had given her in soft toweling and placed in the bottom of a saddle bag. As they mounted, Charlie stepped off the porch and rested her hand on LaVerne's stiruped boot.

"Hurry back. I will watch over your claim until you return. Farewell, Vernie."

"If I can find more gold, I will be able to come back much sooner. Thank you for your warm hospitality, Charlie."

Stepping away from the horses, Charlie turned to Joe. "Have a good journey home, my friend."

"We will meet again, Miss Charlie." Joe responded and turned his horse to the trail that led out of the yard.

For some reason LaVerne found it hard to ride away. *What is wrong with me?* She wondered as she looked at Charlie. *It must be the land that I hate to leave, and of course my first real friend since coming to Alaska.*

"Well, see ya." LaVerne gazed into Charlie's soft bourbon-colored eyes.

"Yes," Charlie said. "Come back soon."

LaVerne turned her mare and followed Joe.

Soon they were riding along the gurgling creek that led to LaVerne cabin site.

"You should first look for black sand, Miss. Then look for quiet, deep pools. As it is washed downstream, the gold settles there beneath the current of the water."

"How do you know so much about so many things, Joe?"

"I am a guide. Many men have needed me to guide them to the gold. But after I saw how the white men disrespected Mother I stopped guiding them. They would have to find their own way."

LaVerne stopped and then dismounted. "Here, Joe! Here's a pool." She knelt down and rolled up the sleeve of her shirt. "And look! Black sand."

Careful not to stir up silt and cloud the water she dipped her hand to the bottom of the creek bed and came up with a fist full of rocks. With her other hand she picked through the pebbles and sand.

"Ooo...look Joe." She held up a nugget the size of a dime.

LaVerne washed the nugget, and then taking the kerchief that she had been using from her pocket, she added the wet rock to the others so that it could dry.

She then repeated the process of dipping and pulling a handful of rocks, twigs and sand out of the creek. This time there were four more nuggets of varying sizes. She carefully washed them and added them to the small pile.

A third handful of debris and pebbles produced three more nuggets and several flakes of gold. LaVerne grinned up at Joe.

"I mustn't be greedy but surely this will buy my stake and I will be able to homestead much sooner."

"Mother Earth thanks you for taking only what you need. You learn quickly, little one." Joe said approvingly.

LaVerne began rolling the cloth back up.

"Here, Miss, use this." Joe handed her a small leather pouch made of the softest, almost white, deerskin with a drawstring made of rawhide. A beaded sun symbol had been embroidered on the side.

"Oh! This is beautiful, Joe. Did you make it?"

"No, my mother makes them. She sells them at the post in Tanana."

"Thank you. I shall treasure it."

Picking up her nuggets and flakes of gold she careful stored them in the deerskin pouch and then hid the pouch in her shirt.

"We should ride, Miss, if we want to get your two other boundaries marked and return to Tanana by dark. You must catch the boat tomorrow morning."

"Yes, I know." LaVerne looked around. "I find it very hard to leave, Joe."

"You shall return--soon."

Ten

At dusk the two weary travelers rode into the village of Tanana. Dismounting in front of the trading post LaVerne turned to Joe.

"Here is the sum we agreed upon, Joe," she told him as she handed him money. "There's a little something extra as a sincere thank you for all you did for me."

"Many thanks, Miss."

"I hope we can continue our friendship when I return." LaVerne continued.

"Where will you sleep tonight?" Joe asked.

"Ah--I hadn't thought that far. The stable with my horse, probably."

"That is not a safe choice for a woman alone. Much better you spread your bedroll in front of my mother's fire. Come." He told her and turned away to lead his horse down the street.

LaVerne untied the reins she had just tied to the hitching post and hurried to follow Joe.

"But, Joe. Your mother doesn't know me. I would be intruding."

"My mother would beat me if I left you alone this night. Always remember, little Miss, you are in the wilderness. There are no laws except the ones you make for yourself. Come."

LaVerne couldn't think of another argument to offer as to why she shouldn't be an uninvited guest in Joe's mother's home. There was nothing left to do but follow Joe. Very quickly they walked up a path branching off the one street in the village. Amongst the trees LaVerne could see firelight with silhouetted figures passing back and forth. When she got closer she saw that there were several tipis grouped haphazardly around a small lodge house. Joe walked to one of the lodgings where he greeted a woman sitting by the fire.

"Tr'axa, Mother. I hope this night finds you well and happy," Joe spoke very formally and in English for LaVerne's benefit.

The woman smiled up into Joe's face, "My son. You have returned from your travels."

"Yes, and I have brought a friend to pass the night with us."

The woman rose and turned to LaVerne. She was perhaps in her sixties, it was hard for LaVerne to guess, as she was very lovely. Her jet black hair was pulled back and neatly braided to fall to her waist. She had a strange tattoo, three lines that ran vertically from the bottom of her lower lip almost to her chin. LaVerne thought it very exotic. Her almond shaped eyes glowed in the firelight.

"You are most welcome in my home," she told LaVerne.

"Thank you so much, Mrs.--er--um..."

"Na'aay-tuu' is my birth name. Edna is my English name. Come, there are Cariboo fritters for dinner. One of my son's favorites."

Joe's mother led her inside the spacious shelter.

"I'll be in after I care for the horses, mother."

LaVerne, Joe and Edna lounged around the fire after a feast of Cariboo, fresh river greens, and dump bread.

"That was a wonderful meal, Edna. Thank you. Is the bread hard to make?"

"No, child. I will teach you over the morning fire. You only need your cast-iron skillet, some flour, water, soda, and herbs. Very good bread when you are on the trail or building a camp."

LaVerne turned to Joe who had been very quiet.

"Your son told me wonderful legends from your people while we rode the back country. Would you tell me another, Joe?"

"My mother is the story-teller in our family. Tr'axa, I was explaining to Miss that we take only what we need from the land and water. Tell her the muskrat story."

"You always loved that legend as a little boy. I have not told it in many years. Let me see if I remember...During the spring, the People used to gather nihts'iil, which are little roots that muskrats find and hide in their caches. One day a little Athabascan girl found one of these caches on a lake and took out all the nihts'iil to take home to her family. She was very excited and very proud of herself when she got home with the tasty food. "Mother!" she said, "I found a muskrat cache! Here's some nihts'iil."

"You must pay for the nihts'iil," her mother scolded when she saw the pile of roots. "Don't forget to leave something in the cache for the muskrat."

"But, Mother," her daughter answered, "who would ever know! The muskrat wouldn't know that I was the one that took the nihts'iil. What does it matter?"

"Yes," her mother answered. "The muskrat will know. You've got to pay for what you take. The muskrat worked hard to fill his cache, and you shouldn't empty it without paying for it."

The daughter still wasn't convinced. "What happens if I don't pay for it?" she asked.

The mother answered, "If you don't pay, the muskrat will go into our cache, and take out all our meat." She paused. "The next day the little girl took back half of the roots as payment to the muskrat."

LaVerne clapped her hands, "That's a wonderful story!"

"Little Miss, please tell my mother one of your song poetries. I know she will enjoy it."

"They aren't mine, but here is a great favorite--

And when I come to the dim trail-end,
  I who have been Life's rover,
This is all I would ask, my friend,
  Over and over and over

A little space on a stony hill
  With never another near me,
Sky o' the North that's vast and still,
  With a single star to cheer me;

Star that gleams on a moss-gray stone
  Graven by those who love me –
There would I lie alone, alone,
  With a single pine above me;

Pine that the north wind whinnies through –
  Oh, I have been Life's rover!
But there I'd lie and listen to
  Eternity passing over.

A log on the fire fell with a snap in the silence. Edna had gone far away to her memories and Joe stared into the embers.

Finally Edna spoke, "This man, he knows our land, our ways. Who is he?"

"A great poet--storyteller--from England. Robert Service. He lived in this land for many years."

"Ah, that would explain it. He allowed Mother Earth to teach him the way."

LaVerne suddenly gave a jaw-breaker yawn, "Oh! Excuse me. I am getting so sleepy."

"Forgive us, we have kept you from your bedroll," Edna turned to Joe, "Son, you will sleep outside by the fire. This child will sleep here."

"Yes, mother," Joe and LaVerne spoke simultaneously. "Oh, no, I'm happy to sleep outside."

"You are our guest. It is decided." Edna's tone didn't entertain any more discussion.

Eleven

Fairbanks
1 week later

"Hey LaVerne, how about some music Friday night?" Mr. Barnette yelled down the store aisle to where LaVerne was stocking shelves.

LaVerne straightened up and placed the last five pound bag of dry beans on the shelf. She walked toward the front of the store. "Do you think people will come?"

"Of course. The customers have been asking when we were going to start."

"Friday's good for me. I'll tell Ma Powers and the folks at the boarding house."

"Can you get the fiddle player and the mouth harp guy here too?"

"Yes."

Mr. Barnette tore off a piece of clean brown wrapping paper. "All right then. I'll just make up a nice sign and put it in the wind'er. What time should we say, Vernie?"

"I think seven o'clock? That will give us plenty of time to clear a space around the stove and set up chairs after store hours."

"Seven it is. What ya gonna call yourselves? You should have a name."

"Oh, I don't know, Mr. Barnette--it's not like we are professional musicians or a real band..."

"Ya gotta have a name." he motioned to the sign he was making, "if just for the advertising."

"Well, let me see." LaVerne stared out the front window for a moment. "I know! How about 'The Trading Post Players'?"

Mr. Barnette slapped LaVerne on the shoulder, almost knocking her over. "Ha! I like that! Advertisement for me too."

He repeated the name, savoring every syllable, "*The Trading Post Players*. Yes, that will do very nicely." He began to write it on the paper, using big block letters.

♪♪♪

At six thirty that Friday evening people were already arriving and staking out their seats in the back of the store. Mr. Barnette, the stock-boy and LaVerne had moved barrels, boxes and merchandise back against the walls. The piano had been rolled into a corner nearby. Chairs were placed in a semi-circle around a cleared area for the band.

By the time the musicians had set up there were at least three dozen folks gathered and the bell on the front door was still tinkling merrily as more people arrived. The Trading Post Players began the evening with current songs, *Ain't Misbehavin', Makin' Whoopee, and My Blue Heaven.* Many knew the lyrics and joined in the singing. A couple of the men had fine baritone voices and the harmony that they created surprised LaVerne.

Some of the women had brought Johnny cake and Mr. Barnette had supplied a barrel of hard cider. It was almost like they were throwing a party. After a short break and refreshments, the musicians picked up their instruments again.

"Hey! Vernie!" Mr. Barnette called out. "How 'bout one of your songs?"

"Yeah, LaVerne, let's do one of yours," Cecil said.

Pink stained LaVerne's cheeks. "Are you sure?"

The audience clapped and hooted and Stewart whispered to the others, "How 'bout Barefoot Dream?"

"Oh, I don't know. I wrote that when I was just a kid."

"Let's leave it up to the crowd. Hey, everybody! Wanna hear a little ditty that Vernie wrote as a kid?" Cecil asked, winking at the friends gathered around.

Alaska inspired LaVerne's music and most of it was about the wild, unforgiving nature of the territory. But this song was about a girl in the bloom of her life, free and wild. The harmonica wept with the sound of the sea, the fiddle moaned with the pending doom. The words spoke of an innocent girl stepping unknowingly into danger.

A pair of slippers skip
along the surf, clammy chill
seeped into supple leather
she dreamed a barefoot dream,

laughter and joy stream out
across the endless waves
superb freedom from society
she dreamed a barefoot dream,
a barefoot dream

stripped of sock and slip'r toes clinch
and let loose the sandy floor as it
trembled, as in the dance,
vanishing under foot fall

a barefoot dream

danced on the heads of ancient warriors,
lost sailors, drown'd lovers
foamy wet tickled the ankles

sandy grains rasp and scrape hardened heel,
tiny secreted bones ache with numbing cold,
purified in nature's bath

She dreamed a barefoot dream,
a barefoot dream
She dreamed a barefoot dream,

Silence met the end of her song and LaVerne dipped her head in embarrassment. Her songs weren't good enough even for this entertainment-starved crowd. Tears filled her eyes in disappointment when applause erupted from the audience. They clapped, whistled and stomped their feet.

"More! More!" they yelled.

"Vernie, what happened to the girl?" Someone yelled from the back of the room.

"She drowned. Went too far into the waves and her wet skirts dragged her down."

"Oh no," a woman in the front row sighed.

By eleven o'clock some of the Trading Post Players had been replaced by other musically inclined town folk, giving LaVerne and her friends a much welcomed break. As midnight approached the party began to disperse; most had jobs or chores to get to in the morning.

LaVerne helped Mr. Barnette clean up and put the store back to normal for opening the next morning. She waited on the quiet boardwalk as he locked up for the night.

Mr. Barnette turned to LaVerne, "You all right walkin' home? Maybe I should walk with you."

"Thanks, but I'm fine. I walk home every night after work, Mr. Barnette. But thank you for the offer."

"It was a fine evening, Vernie. Your songs are wonderful and I know everyone enjoyed it as much as I did. See you tomorrow." He turned and walked away.

LaVerne turned and walked in the opposite direction. She was elated about how her music had been received. Some had even caught onto her lyrics and sang the second chorus with her. She would always remember tonight.

She walked down the silent street, lit only the glow of a second story window or by an occasional night light left on in a store. She was so caught up in her triumphant evening that the two drunken miners were almost on her before she realized they were even there. Startled, she veered off to her right to walk on the other side of the street.

The two men stumbled to a stop and peered at her. "Well now, lookie here, Ben, a purty lady all by herself. Bet she'd like some company."

"It's wearin' buckskins, Sam. Are ya shlure it's female?" Ben was decidedly drunker than his friend.

"Oh yeah, it's a she and young too. Howdy, Miss, I bet you'd like to have a drink with us, huh?"

LaVerne kept walking, hoping that they would have their joke and continue on their way.

"Cat got your tongue, little puss?" The man called Sam changed directions pulling his friend along with him, they followed after LaVerne. She knew it would be a mistake to quicken her walk or run so she just kept walking, every nerve and hair on the back of her neck on alert.

When they caught up with her, Sam grabbed her arm and wheeled her around. "I asked ya if ya wanted a drink--or maybe it's a kiss you'd like'ta have instead."

LaVerne yanked her arm free, "No thank you. I don't desire a drink or a kiss. Now be good boys and go home."

"Ha! She's a spitfire, Sham." Ben slapped his knee and laughed at his friend.

Sam forcefully gathered LaVerne into his arms. "Come on, baby, gimme a little kiss."

LaVerne relaxed into his mauling embrace even though, with all of her heart, she wanted to kick, scratch and bite.

"That's more like it. Look, Ben, she likes me."

With her hands free, LaVerne caressed Sam's chest and moved her hand down to his groin.

"Wow! Yeah, let's get the party goin'," Sam said before he let out a high pitched scream.

LaVerne had grabbed a hand full of testicles and squeezed with all her strength, just like her brothers had taught her. Sam dropped like a stone.

Ben stood mouth agape. In a liquor soaked haze, he couldn't understand why his friend was laying on the ground crying and moaning. Understanding came quickly as LaVerne kicked him between his legs as hard as she could. Ben screamed high enough to break windows, grabbed his crotch and fell to the ground beside his friend.

LaVerne had never truly appreciated having five brothers until this moment. She wiped her hands on her coat. "Good night, gentlemen," she told them as she walked away

Twelve

Tanana Valley
One month later

'*Dear Charlie,*
Great news! I received my homestead certificate the other day. On your advice, I hid away my little nest egg of gold nuggets until my claim was recorded.

Yesterday, I made a trip to the bank here in Fairbanks to find out how much gold I have. I could scarcely believe it! Five hundred dollars! That means I can come back to my homestead next spring once the rivers thaw. I will spend this winter collecting what I will need to begin my life in the Tanana Valley.

My plan is to build a little shack, just big enough to live and sleep in while I construct my cabin.

Life plods along here in the big city. Ha ha. Mr. Barnette, my boss at the trading post, has hired me to have musical nights at the store so that will add to my savings. They are well attended. We have a little band consisting of a piano, a fiddle, a mouth harp and me with my guitar.

Are you ready for the dark months? Did you get a moose already?

I hope you will write back and please send me your list of things I might not know I will need.

Fondly, Vernie

PS. I am enjoying the book of poetry that you loaned me and hope you don't miss it too much.

Charlie sat back and stared into the fire. Vernie was coming back--much sooner than expected what with the windfall of gold out of her creek. Charlie wondered how she could help her new friend get a good start on settling her homestead. A splendid idea came to her as she watched the dancing flames. Before first snow fall Charlie would ask Stan and Milo and Joe to help her harvest the poles for Vernie's cabin. Stacked properly over the winter they would season and remain true with little warping. Then when Vernie arrived the logs would be ready to begin laying in the walls for her new home. The harvested lumber would be a house warming present from her to Vernie.

If need be she would pay the men in barter. All her neighbors admired her vegetables and they were in great demand. And the rest in much needed cash. Few people knew that back in Boston Charlie had come from a very wealthy family and need never want for anything.

Charlie went to her small desk in the corner and took out paper and pen and returned to her chair by the fire.

'Dear Vernie, I got your letter today and was so happy for you. Your plans are progressing well and you'll be back in the Tanana valley before we know it. I have been busy harvesting the garden and canning the last of the salmon. The moose are still feeding at the lake where Joe took you. I would like to get one closer to home because packing the meat and fur back is a big job! The Caribou will not be moving through here until we get some snow. But you can almost set your watch by their migration.

Here is a list of things you might not have thought of.

1. One rooster and a few hens. There is nothing like fresh eggs!

2. A half-dozen bales of hay; you'll need hay right away to mix with the water and mud, for chinking your cabin walls. However some folks swear by chinking with moss. More labor collecting it from the forest floor but it does work well and lasts for years.

3. Snow shoes.

4. In addition to your rifle, you should buy a sidearm. The trading post can help you with the caliber, etc.

5. Seeds for your first garden.

6. A water pump.

7. Lanterns and candles.

8. Kerosene.

9. Post-hole digger in addition to a shovel.

I was so happy to hear from you and hope you will write again soon. I am looking forward to your moving your 'musical evenings' to your homestead.

Your friend, Charlie

PS. Moon is pregnant. I'll save you a puppy, shall I?

Charlie sat back and thought about her first year here. There had been so much to accomplish before her first winter. Being the first female homesteaders in the area, she had had only herself to rely on. Vernie would have an easier road because in Alaska everyone helped everyone else. That's just the way it was.

Charlie rose and, finding an envelope in her desk drawer, she addressed it to LaVerne Guyer in care of Barnette's Trading Post. There was no telling when someone might come by, from Tanana, with her mail or to pick up her letter. If too many days passed, she'd saddle up and ride to the village to mail it.

Tomorrow she would walk over to Vernie's place and start marking the trees to be cut.

♪♪♪

The dark months of winter had come to the Tanana Valley early. The Yukon River was frozen three feet deep. The village was buried under five feet of snow and the temperatures plummeted to forty below on some nights. Ice fishing was plentiful. Eel was an excellent food for sled dogs in the winter when food was scarce. If a person who kept sled dogs was lucky, and timed it just right, he could net eel as they migrated up the river.

When someone traveled during the winter it was by dog sled. Checking their trap lines every other day, traveling to other villages, hunting, and running the mail, all was accomplished by six to eight dogs and a sled. Sled dogs were bred for size and endurance and a good one could run all day.

It had been over a month since Charlie had heard from LaVerne. It had been at least that since she had seen another human being. But Charlie didn't mind the loneliness, she didn't need people around her, chattering, complaining and making a general nuisance of themselves. What she *did* mind was not hearing from LaVerne.

Before the first snow flew, she and the men had harvested good timber for LaVerne's cabin and now it was stacked and seasoning under a blanket of snow. As she went about her daily chores she thought about how much she enjoyed Vernie's letters. Today she was chopping more firewood. As she replenished the wood pile by the back door, which led into the kitchen, she wondered how Vernie was surviving the winter.

Had she changed her mind about the homestead? Life in Fairbanks would certainly be easier than this life in the back of beyond. Maybe she had just given up and gone back home to the lower forty-eight. *If she went home, would she even think to write me a letter of 'goodbye'?*

Just then she heard dogs barking down on the trail and that set her dogs off. Someone hollered from the edge of the clearing that led to her cabin. It was Black-Eyed Joe. From her porch she watched, as in a flurry of snow and shouts, Joe's dogs and sled bounded into view and pulled into her yard. Like a well behaved team should do, they stopped on Joe's command. Tongues lolling, they were greeted by Charlie's dogs with yips and barks of joy. Joe's dogs dropped in their tracks, taking a much deserved rest.

"Joe! Welcome, old friend!" Charlie cried.

"Hello, slatsiin, how are you?" Joe called.

"Cold." She laughed. "What brings you here?"

"My trap line ends not far from here and there was mail for you at the village store. Yapping Dog is down sick with a cold and so the mail will not move until he is better. I thought I would bring you your letters," he said as he dug inside his shirt and parka and pulled out three envelopes.

Charlie's eyes lit greedily on the letters. She could hardly keep from grabbing them out of Joe's hand. He handed them over and Charlie stuffed them into her coat pocket. She could see LaVerne's handwriting on one of them.

"Thank you, slatsiin--friend. That was very kind of you. Come, we will get pails of water for your dogs and I have some dried fish to give them."

"They would like that very much," Joe grinned. "And do you have a cup of hot coffee for me?"

"Yes, of course. Let's see to the dogs and then go inside."

As they worked, getting Joe's dogs comfortable, they chatted about village matters and how the trap lines were producing this year. As they walked to the cabin Joe asked about LaVerne.

"Have you heard from the young Miss?"

"Not for over a month now, Joe. The last time she wrote she said the gold she found would mean she would come in the spring."

"That is good news," Charlie replied as she poured steaming coffee into two mugs.

Charlie pulled the letters out and placing them on the table, smoothed out the wrinkles.

"Oh! Here's two letters from Vernie. Both postmarked Fairbanks. I feared she had gotten discouraged and gone home."

"No, not Miss. She is determined to live here and share the land with Mother Earth. I see it."

Charlie rose and went to the larder. "Are you hungry, Joe? I have cold chicken and I made fresh bread this morning. How about a sandwich?"

"Yes, breakfast was many hours ago, I would appreciate your food."

Within minutes Charlie placed a thick sandwich in front of Joe. She topped off their coffee and sat again.

"So you were saying that you think a wolverine is robbing your traps of the bait?"

"Yes and the fur caught in them. It is the 'courageous one' for certain. Much sign. I will run the line, on my way back to the village, and see if I have trapped him."

"Be careful, Joe. The wolverine are vicious. He could hurt you."

"No, my friend, the wolverine, as you call him, is not vicious. He is merely being a wolverine. He keeps the forest clean. He is to be honored should he give his life to me."

"Yes, I suppose you're right."

Joe finished his food and drank down the last of his coffee. He rose and began to put his outer garments back on. A parka with a fur trimmed hood protected his face from the deepest cold. He picked up his mittens lined with fox fur, especially made for driving the dogs and sled.

"I must leave now if I want to return to the village by nightfall. Thank you for the food for me and my dogs, Charlie."

They walked to the door and Charlie stood on the porch and watched as Joe removed the anchor line that held the sled in place. The dogs bounded up and jumped over each other in their excitement to resume their trip. Over their joyous barks, Joe raised his hand and yelled, "Goodbye, slatsiin, stay well."

"Goodbye, friend, safe journey." Charlie called.

In a flash of dogs and sled and cries of 'Gee', Joe disappeared down the trail and Charlie turned back into the cabin.

She picked up her mail and crossed to her chair by the roaring fire. She could now see that all three envelopes were from Vernie and she eagerly tore open the first one.

'Dearest Charlie, I don't think this winter will ever end. I'm certain I am more impatient this year because it means I will be able to settle on my homestead as soon as the rivers thaw.

Life here in town is pretty routine. I work six days a week at the trading post. I am slowly collecting the things I must bring with me (thank you for your list) and Mr. Barnette has given me a corner of the storeroom to store them in. I had remembered lanterns on my list but had not thought of Kerosene to fuel them. Thank goodness for you! On the recommendation of several customers I have purchased a Colt .45 in addition to my Winchester rifle.

Our Friday musicals have become a regular event and people pack themselves into the store to enjoy our playing.

I think I told you in one of my other letters that Mr. Barnette dubbed us The Trading Post Players and it has stuck. We don't dare miss a Friday or there would be a riot in the store. Ha ha.

I have received your letters pretty regularly but wonder if you are getting mine? You have not responded to some things that I have written in mine so I wondered.

With these long, winter days (and nights) I find I am writing more music than ever before. Our audiences at the store insist that I play whatever I have written, for them. They are most generous with their praise.

I would adore one of Moon's puppies. I do want to start building a team of dogs and eventually learn how to drive a sled. You must send me a list of anything you might need from town so that I can bring it to you when I come.

Well, my dear friend, I shall close for now. I hope this finds you in good health and happy.

Fondly, Vernie

The letters lying in her lap, Charlie gazed into the flames. She decided that she would save the other two letters for later and spread them out over time to lengthen the enjoyment. She rose and put the three envelopes into a wooden box on the mantle. Donning her parka and gloves she left the cabin to finish the wood cutting and stacking.

Thirteen

Fairbanks
Four months later

The ice began to crack and break up as the Wood River began to rise with the spring melt. Huge chunks of ice pushed and shoved down river. The old timers predicted that the Wood and Yukon rivers would not flood this year as the snow high in the mountains was not heavy. But they loved to tell tales of other years when the melt rushed down the mountains and the six foot thick ice, the size of buses, broke up and pushed up onto the river banks. As it traveled downstream, at thirty miles an hour, it took anything that stood in its path with it.

During the day the temperature was a scorching twenty above. Spring was officially here. While snow and ice still covered much of the ground there were bare spots where the sun had burned away the winter and tender green shoots could be seen pushing up toward the watery sun.

LaVerne walked to the Trading Post and since she was early for her shift she went directly to the store room to inspect her growing pile of supplies. Just seeing it made her dreams more real than anything else could.

That and Charlie's letters that arrived regularly twice a month. For some strange reason, mail delivery was better outbound than into the village.

In Charlie's last message she had said she hadn't gotten any mail from Vernie for over a month and then got three in a bunch. LaVerne sighed as she ran her hand across the gear that she had collected. The chickens, milk goats and the hay bales she would buy at the last moment. Staples like flour, sugar, and beans would also be purchased from the store when she was ready to leave. She had already spoken to the stable in town and had arranged for a wagon and team to carry her supplies up river to her new home when the time came.

She had put a deposit down on the mild tempered mare she had been renting all this time. They had become friends and LaVerne couldn't bear to leave her behind so decided to buy her. She had negotiated a good price on the tack and a used saddle. She had named the horse Junie in remembrance of a half mule, half horse that Pa had had.

She would leave the moment the boats were back on the river. Build her shack so she'd have somewhere to sleep, cut the timber for her cabin, dig an outhouse, prepare the garden, build a shed and fenced-in yard for the goats and chickens--the list had no end. And it couldn't happen soon enough to suit her! LaVerne grinned in anticipation.

The bell over the front door chimed faintly, announcing the arrival of Mr. Barnette and time to open for business.

"Vernie! You back there?" Mr. Barnette yelled.

"Coming!" LaVerne hurried out of the storeroom and up to the front of the store.

"Vernie, I had the most wonderful i'dear."

Donning a clean bib apron, LaVerne moved behind the front counter. "What's that, Mr. Barnette?"

"Come this spring I'm gonna punch out that there wall," he pointed to the back corner of the store.

"and make a big area for our musicals. That way people can dance if they've a mind to, and we can get more folks in."

"That's wonderful. But you haven't forgotten that I'm leaving in the spring?"

"Ah, shoot, girl! You're still dreamin' of homesteadin' up yonder? Do you have any i'dear how hard that will be and how much work?"

"Yes, sir."

"And you're still gonna do it, huh?"

"Yes, sir. I hate leaving the store and the musical nights, Mr. Barnette, but the homestead is where I have to be."

"All right. I understand, Vernie. When I first come up here--what's it been now? Twenty some years ago--all I could think of was openin' my own store. And look at us now. A bon-o-fide trading post with music every Friday night."

"The music doesn't have to stop when I'm gone, sir. You've got some very good musicians right here in town and visitors sometimes pick up a guitar or sit down and play the piano."

"We'll sure miss your songs, Vernie."

"I'll be back once in awhile and I'll be sure to stop by and bring some of my music with me."

"When ya leavin'?"

"As soon as the rivers open up."

"Should be less than a month, then. Time for a couple more musical nights 'fore ya leave." He frowned. "You don't get on that river until we say it's safe, ya hear?"

"Yes, sir."

The bell tinkled over the door and the post's first customers of the day arrived.

"Good morning, Ma," LaVerne greeted her landlady.

"'Mornin', Vernie," she sniffed as she greeted Mr. Barnette. "Edward."

"Mornin' Mrs. Powers, ma'am. What can we do you for?"

"My usual weekly order, of course. Why else would I be in here?"

"All ready for you, Ma." LaVerne said as she began to place various sacks and large cans on the counter.

"And add five pounds of salt to that, will you Vernie? I'm makin' up a brine for some fish a generous boarder brought me."

"Yes, Ma'am."

"Help ya carry that Mrs. Powers?"

"Don't you go worrying yourself about carrying nothing for me, Edward Barnette. The day I can't carry for myself is the day they bury me six feet under."

In spite of her protests, LaVerne carried some of the larger burlap sacks out to Ma Powers' wagon.

"Thank you, child," she told LaVerne when they had finished. "See you tonight."

"What's for dinner, Ma?"

"Ham hocks and beans like every Thursday night."

"Yum! I do love your cooking, Ma."

"You young ones are always hungry. Nine o'clock in the morning and you're already thinkin' about supper."

The both laughed as Ma drove away. LaVerne turned back into the store and returned to behind the counter.

"Can I ask you something, Mr. Barnette?" she said.

"What?"

"Why is Ma Powers so prickly around you? Are you not friends?"

Mr. Barnette turned beet red and looked everywhere but at LaVerne. "Er--well--I'll tell ya..." He stuttered.

"I'm sorry. I shouldn't have asked."

"No, no it's alright.   It's timeworn history, happened years ago. Catherine Powers and the current Mrs. Barnette were both sweethearts of mine--back in ninety-nine--and I asked Mrs. Barnette to marry me. Catherine never forgave me. Been sour towards me ever since."

LaVerne was shocked. She never expected to hear a story of unrequited love--and never imagined Ma Powers once being young and in love. She was just Ma Powers who ran her boarding house with a motherly, but iron fist.

♪♪♪

The next night produced one of their best turnouts to hear the Trading Post Players. LaVerne and the fiddle player were tuning up with the help of Ma at the piano.

Mr. Barnette's booming voice could be heard in the front of the store.

"Well, I declare, if it ain't Johnny Horton, as I live and breathe! What brings ya' to the Yukon, son?"

LaVerne heard a man's voice reply and thought nothing more of it. A few minutes later Mr. Barnette appeared with two men, strangers to the city of Fairbanks. They wore city clothes, new, shiny cowboy boots and string ties. One man had striking, wavy black hair, slicked down with pomade. He had a baby face and his black eyebrows were thick, almost meeting in the center. He carried a guitar case.

"Vernie, you're never gonna guess who this is--not in a million years," Mr. Barnette gushed.

The man stepped forward and extended his hand. "Miss Guyer, I'm Johnny Horton. I've heard some good things about your song writing. May I present my friend, Mike Phillips."

LaVerne almost swallowed her tongue. Johnny Horton! *That* Johnny Horton? "Uh…how do you do?" she stammered as she shook hands with them.

Johnny grinned. "Mind if we sit in?"

Mr. Barnette scraped an extra chair next to LaVerne's. "We'd be honored, Mr. Horton, real honored."

LaVerne watched as the singer sat down and opened his case. From the velvet lining he removed the most beautiful guitar she'd ever seen. A Gibson. LaVerne had never set eyes one but had heard of the company and their craftsmanship. The other man opened a case and produced a mandolin.

The other musicians tuned their instruments off of Ma at the piano. Johnny acted like he sat down with folks like these all the time, quickly putting everyone at ease. He didn't make a fuss, just tuned his guitar and strummed random chords.

"We'll get started in about fifteen minutes, Mr. Horton. Can I get you somethin' to drink? We got a fine cider or hot coffee." Mr. Barnette asked.

"Why a glass of cider would be much appreciated." He turned to LaVerne. "Will you play a couple of your own songs tonight, Miss Guyer?"

"Yeah, Vernie, you promised to let us hear your new one." The fiddle player exclaimed.

"It's still rough, I'm not finished with it." LaVerne objected, blushing.

"That's how my songs start out too. I'd love to hear it--maybe before your audience arrives?" Horton told her.

"Yeah, Vernie, play it for Mr. Horton," Ma Powers piped up. "I heard it from the porch at my boarding house, Mr. Horton, and it's a fine song."

LaVerne frowned at Ma. They were really putting her on the spot.

Johnny grinned at her. "Please?"

LaVerne blushed, partly from having to play and sing in front of this famous singer, but also she had developed a slight crush on this handsome celebrity. *Get a grip, Vernie. Your sisters would never let you live it down if they caught you simpering over some singer!*

"It's just an idea--I'm not finished with the lyrics, but all right, if you understand that I'm still working on it…"

"I promise not to judge." Johnny assured her.

LaVerne strummed a few chords and began.

Big Sam left Seattle in the year of '93
With George Brant, his partner, and brother Billy too
They crossed the Yukon River and found the muck called gold
Below that old White Mountain
Just a little southeast of Nome
Sam crossed the majestic mountains to the valley far below
He called to his team of huskies as they mushed on through the snow
With the Northern Lights a runnin' wild in the land of the Midnight Sun
Yes Sam McCord was a mighty man in the year of 1901 Way up north
Way up north
North to Alaska
We're goin' north, the rush is on
North to Alaska

We're goin' north, the rush is on

Once the musicians caught the tune, they all, including Johnny accompanied LaVerne. People had begun to drift in and they quietly took their seats, somehow aware that they were witnessing a great song being born.

Where the river is a'windin', big nuggets they're a'findin'
North to Alaska, go north, the rush is on
Way up north, north to Alaska, way up north, north to Alaska

LaVerne abruptly broke off. "That's all I've got so far."

"How 'bout this for the next verse?" Horton strummed a couple of chords and stared into the rafters of the store.

George turned to his friend with his gold in his hand. Said, "Sam, you're lookin' at a lonely, lonely man. I'd trade all the gold that's buried here

For one small band of gold to place on sweet little Jenny's hand. 'Cause a man needs a woman to love him all the time

The musicians picked up the tune and played the chorus.

Way up north
Way up north
North to Alaska
We're goin' north, the rush is on
North to Alaska
We're goin' north, the rush is on

The audience cheered and clapped and stomped their feet. At the first break Horton waited until

LaVerne was alone and then approached her.

"Miss Guyer, if you'd like me to help you with your songs, I could take North to Alaska with me when I return home. I'm certain my record label would love to hear it."

LaVerne's eyes got round with shock. Had the great Johnny Horton just offered to help get her song published?

"Why, I don't know what to say. It's not even finished. But if you think its good enough, then yes, take it."

Fourteen

"*Dear Mama, the day has finally arrived! Tomorrow I leave for my homestead. The wagon I hired is all packed so early in the morning we hitch up the team, and head for the Woods River. I'm writing to you tonight because this is the last reliable mail for the immediate future. When you write back to me send it in care of the Tanana Post Office, Tanana, Alaska and I'm certain it will find me eventually.*

Did I tell you that I bought the mare that I have been renting for all my explorations? I couldn't bear to leave her. And tell Pa I named her after his Junie. I'm starting with one rooster, (pray he isn't a devil like old Rochester) and five hens. I decided on milk goats because they are so much hardier than a milk cow.

My dear friend, Charlotte, has given me one of her Husky's puppies and I can't wait to meet him. Hopefully I can start to build my dog team soon.

I shall live in a thrown together shack while building my cabin. You're not to worry, Mama. The shack will only be for sleeping as I will be busy from dawn to dusk. If you and Pa could do it, I can! Hopefully most of the bad weather is over and spring is truly here. It will only get better, God willing and the creek don't rise. Ha! I find myself quoting you in my head all the time.

I have so much to accomplish, Mama, in a very short season before the snow flies again. A garden, collecting meat and fish for the winter months, the cabin, of course, and dig a five year outhouse. I never thought the things that Pa tried to pound into our heads would ever come in handy. Can you believe that the daughter who would gripe about setting the table or collecting the eggs has this long list of chores that she can't wait to begin?

Finding gold in my creek has certainly been a life saver. I am able to buy what I will need for the first year and a couple of luxuries like a very good quality wood stove with a hot water reservoir just like Charlotte has in her cabin.

Shall sign off for now. As soon as I get settled I shall write again with all my news. Tell the family I love and miss them. Kiss Pa for me.

Your daughter always, LaVerne

Finding an envelope and stamp, LaVerne sealed up the letter and tomorrow she would put it on the front hall table. Someone would take it to the post office while doing their own errands. The last thing she did before going to bed was to pry up the loose floor board and retrieve her cache of money and gold.

She looked around the room that had been her home for over a year. Her duffle bag was packed except for the clothes she would wear tomorrow. Her guitar was care-fully wrapped in doeskin and locked in its case.

♪.♪.♪

Dawn, in the palest pink and gold, was just breaking over the snow capped mountains. The peaks reminded LaVerne of the strawberry ice cream cones her mother made when she and her siblings were young. She walked into the stable, and saw that her wagon sat exactly where she had left it, after packing it carefully with the supplies from the storeroom. A heavy tarp was draped over everything and was tied off with rope. Her mare whickered from her stall, begging for some morning oats or not to be left behind, LaVerne wasn't certain which. Picking up a small pan she filled it from the oat barrel and crossed to the horse.

"Don't worry, Junie. We're in this together for the long haul." She held the pan as the mare greedily lipped up the treat. "As if I could ever leave you behind."

LaVerne got the saddle, blanket and bridle down and began saddling up the mare. Just then Mr. Browning, the owner of the stable walked in.

"You're early, Miss LaVerne. You eager to get on the trail, huh?"

"Yes, sir, I am. Want to be certain I don't miss the boat."

"Well, then, I'll just get these nags hitched up to the wagon and we'll be on our way."

On the very back of the wagon LaVerne helped the stable owner lift and secure the crates containing her goats and chickens.

There was a loud symphony of 'naaa's' and clucking as the creatures made their displeasure clear. Twenty minutes later the wagon rumbled down the main street of Fairbanks and headed northwest to the boat landing on the Woods River. LaVerne, riding her mare, followed behind the freight wagon.

In the next few days I'll be on my land, staking out the footprint of my cabin, the thoughts gnawing at her. *Can I get a cabin built before first snow? Will my livestock survive next winter? Will we all have enough to eat?* A smile replaced her worried frown. *I'll see Charlie again.* The town was quickly left behind and the tall evergreens, the spruce, hemlock and birch trees enveloped the wagon and horses. LaVerne never tired of breathing in the peppery, warm air as the sun filtered through the foliage and warmed the forest floor. A majestic bald eagle watched their progress from a bare branch at the top of a tree. His handsome head turned, a yellow eye followed them, quickly disinterested as he decided they were not a food source. With a disgusted cry, he flew away to a better hunting ground. LaVerne laughed from the sheer joy of being alive and starting the first steps toward her dream.

They pushed hard up the trail, seldom stopping, to try and meet the flatboat today and not have to dry camp that night. Several hours later, LaVerne rode up ahead of the wagon as they neared the river. The boat was moored and people and supplies were being loaded.

"Hallooo, Captain," she yelled from the shore. "Can you wait a few more minutes for my wagon and driver to arrive? We were hoping you'd have room for us today."

The captain of the flatboat walked to the stern and scowled at LaVerne.

"Ain't ya the young lady I carried up to Tanana last summer? Back for more, I see."

"Yes, sir, that was me. I'm going to my homestead and my wagon of supplies is just behind me. Can you wait for us?"

"If yur quick-like. I've got a schedule to keep to, ya know."

LaVerne wheeled her horse around and galloped back down the trail. She rode up to the wagon, and turning, fell into step with the dray horses.

"The boat captain is waiting for us, Mr. Browning, but he said we must hurry."

"These nags have one speed, Miss. And that there captain always threatens to leave folks behind. He'll be there or he won't when we get there."

He snapped his whip over the backs of the horses, being careful not to actually touch them with it. "Hi-yup! Bess, Tom, move along now! We got us a boat to catch."

The two horses flicked their ears back at the driver as if to say, 'yes, we hear you and we'll get there when we get there.'

It seemed like it took forever before they reached the river bank. LaVerne sighed with relief to see that the boat had not left without them. Mr. Browning got down from the wagon and walked over the ramp that he expected his horses to walk over in order to board. He shook hands with the captain and announced that everything looked safe enough for his team. He went to the head of the gelding, Tom, and whispered sweet nothings into his nose. Bess nudged his shoulder insisting on equal attention.

LaVerne had learned from this experienced horseman that horses could 'read' your breath and thus be more likely to trust you. She had tried it when getting to know her mare, Junie, and the result was a strong bond between woman and horse.

Mr. Browning took Tom by the halter and gently led the team and wagon onto the boat without incident. The captain helped LaVerne and the stable owner to tie down the wagon after Mr. Browning had unhitched the wagon from his team.

"If this here contraption sank my horses wouldn't have a fighting chance still hitched up. I'll not have some gol'durn wagon drag 'em down."

"No boat of mine has ever sank and we ain't gonna start today." The captain huffed and turned away to untie the mooring lines.

The swift current quickly caught them and they were on their way.

When they reached the fork where the Woods River joined the Yukon LaVerne saw smaller chunks of ice floating by but, for the most part, the river was clear. Fighting the strong current, they traveled the last five miles up the Yukon to the boat landing. After docking, the horses were backed into their traces and the wagon was untied.

"G'up, g'up!   Get along now, Tom, Bess." Mr. Browning called, standing at the front of the wagon so he had a clear view of the beach.

LaVerne stood by her horse, waiting, in the event that Mr. Browning needed her help. But, the team who had made this river trip before just snorted and pulled and the wagon was safely delivered to the beach.

LaVerne waved to the captain and rode up beside the wagon.

"We'll travel the river's edge for a bit," Mr. Browning explained. "There's a shallower bank up ahead, nearer the village. No sense in making these nags work harder than they have to."

Part Two

Coming Home

Fifteen

As the wagon and riders lurched up the gentle slope from the beach they turned left at the fork and headed up a trail that would lead to LaVerne's homestead.

"Mr. Browning, I'd like to stop off at Charlie's place just to let her know we've arrived."

"Not a problem, Vernie, I plan on stayin' the night in Tanana. Gonna get their order, for next month, to fill back at the trading post. Be headin' back in the mornin'."

Suddenly they heard hoof beats pounding behind them. LaVerne turned in the saddle to see who was headed down the trail after them. Mr. Browning continued on without a backward glance.

Hair flying out behind her like a banner, Charlie rode at a gallop. Her hat flopped loosely against her back.

"Hey! Vernie!" she yelled, her smile so wide it was fit to crack her face in two.

LaVerne turned her mare and galloped back to meet Charlie in the middle of the trail. It had been a long winter and LaVerne couldn't believe how good it was to see her friend again. When their horses met, side by side, Charlie slapped LaVerne on the back and then grabbed her into a tight hug.

"It is *so* good to see you, Vernie." Tears suddenly filled Charlie's eyes.

"Hey! No need for that, Charlie. I'm finally here and I can't tell you how happy I am to see you and know that I will never have to leave."

Wiping her eyes, Charlie told her, "My God, what a sissy thing to do. I don't know what's the matter is, crying like a Goddamn girl. You are such a sight for sore eyes." And with that she pulled LaVerne back into another hug.

Pulling back once again, Charlie laughed. "Come on, let's catch up with your wagon and get you unloaded. You can bunk with me tonight if you want."

"I'd like that very much. We have so much to catch up on."

The two women turned their horses and rode up the trail. It only took a few moments to catch up with the wagon. As they neared Charlie's place Mr. Browning pulled up. Charlie rode up next to him.

"There, see?" She pointed at a fork leading away from her place. "That's the track that leads to Vernie's place."

"Lead on, missy. Looks like its rough going but these nags of mine have handled worse."

LaVerne followed Charlie up a trail she no longer recognized. It had been cleared and widened enough that a wagon and team could easily pass.

As she rode up alongside Charlie she asked, "Charlie, this doesn't look anything like the trail that was here." She grinned affectionately at her. "What have you been up to?"

"Nothing much." Charlie's cheeks pinked as she discounted all the work she had done in anticipation of LaVerne's arrival. "I just hitched up my team and drag and ran it up and down the trail a few times. Cleared a few saplings and now you have a road of sorts."

"Thank you so much." LaVerne was humbled by Charlie's thoughtfulness.

"No need to thank me. Neighbors help neighbors. I knew a wagon was going to have to get up to your place."

"Well, I *do* thank you. It is such a big help. I can't wait to get unloaded and show you all my treasures," she replied and then urged her horse into a trot.

Passing the wagon, it wasn't long before the two women rode into the natural clearing that would become LaVerne's home site. They dismounted and Charlie silently watched as LaVerne wandered from the site of her future cabin to where she planned for a garden, to the corner where her chickens and goats would be kept.

Suddenly LaVerne stopped and stared. She spied the stumps of trees cut close to the ground and there, in a neat pile, were at least thirty, near-perfect, straight twenty-five foot, long logs. She turned and stared at Charlie and then turned back to the log pile as if she expected that she was dreaming and they would disappear.

With tears running down her face, she turned back to Charlie. "You did this." It was a statement, not a question.

"Well, yes. But I had help. Stan and Milo came several days and helped me harvest the trees. Then word got out and other neighbors came to help too."

LaVerne walked to the stacked, lumber that had been stripped of its bark and reverently rubbed her hand along a log. She tried to swallow a sob. Charlie walked up behind her and placed a hand on LaVerne's shoulder. "There's no need to cry, Vernie. It's just my cabin warming gift to you."

"*Just* a house warming gift? You must've..." She couldn't finish the sentence she was crying so hard.

Charlie took her into a loose embrace and patted her back. "Well, I wouldn't have done it if I'd known you were going to cry about it," she laughed.

LaVerne laughed and that made her choke and suddenly she was bent over, hands on knees, coughing and sputtering. Charlie beat her back until she got herself under control. LaVerne straightened and smiled at Charlie who dug a rag out of her back pocket.

"Here. Mr. Browning won't know what to think if he sees you here five minutes and already blubbering."

"My God, Charlie. The amount of work this must have taken," she waved her hand in the direction of the logs. "I can't believe it…"

"Hallo! The house!" Mr. Browning yelled as he and his team entered the clearing. "Where do you want to unload?"

Vernie looked at Charlie. "What do you think?"

Charlie pointed to the proposed cabin site. "Well, you're planning on your garden there and that will have to get started right away. So why don't you unload on the other side of where the cabin will stand?"

"Good idea." LaVerne walked over to the wagon. "Right there, Mr. Browning." She pointed to the far right of the clearing.

Mr. Browning made a wide circle with the team and placed the wagon where LaVerne had indicated. The team was unhitched from the wagon and led to the creek for a much welcomed drink of water. LaVerne and Charlie began to untie the ropes that held the tarp in place. At the end of the wagon the chickens began a chorus of complaints anticipating another change was coming to their ordered lives. The roaster crowed indignantly and made the women laugh.

"Well, aren't you a handsome boy," Charlie told the rooster. "They can stay in the crates until you get your enclosure finished, Vernie. The goats can stay at my place until you're ready for them. But we should start on that tomorrow."

While LaVerne lifted down the chicken crates, Charlie removed the goats from their crates and, wrapping her arms around each goat, she lifted them down and attached ropes around their necks. She then led them to trees along the creek bed, tying them up, where they could drink and graze on the sweet grasses growing there.

Mr. Browning and both women made short work of unloading all of LaVerne's supplies, tools, and furnishings for the cabin. With three of them working together, they were able to drag the heavy, iron cook stove to the tail of the wagon and then slide it down two planks to the ground.

"That summa-bitch—pardon my French, ladies—is gonna have to sit right there until you move it into your cabin."

"No harm done, Mr. Browning. Thank you for helping me."

"Well, I'll just hitch up my nags and be on my way."

LaVerne reached into her pocket and drew out some money. "Sixty-five dollars is what we agreed upon, is that right, Mr. Browning?"

"Yes, ma'am. And if you ever need more supplies from the trading post, remember that I come up this way every few months and my rates are cheap."

LaVerne laughed and assured the grizzled old man that she would definitely use his services in the future. Mr. Browning backed his team into their traces and they were quickly harnessed. He turned, shook both women's hands, jumped up on the seat and snapped the reins, "Hi-yup, get along there, Tom!"

As the wagon moved to the edge of the clearing, LaVerne shouted, "Goodbye! Thanks again."

The women turned to each other and grinned.

"Let's get this mess sorted and covered. We'll lead the goats down to my place where they'll be safe overnight." Charlie said.

"What about my chickens?" LaVerne asked.

"I got a little trick up my sleeve," Charlie chuckled. "We'll throw a rope over a tree branch, tie the end to each crate and haul 'em up. They'll be safe enough until tomorrow."

"Is there anything you don't know how to do?" LaVerne asked Charlie.

"No, Ma'am," she said grinning at her friend.

🍂🍂🍂

The next morning, after a quick breakfast of bacon and gravy over cold biscuits, LaVerne and Charlie were back at her homestead. The first thing they did was lower the crates holding the chickens. Outraged at being hung in a tree, the hens were very vocal with their scolding. Charlie let them out and threw some grain to them. Claiming his territory, the rooster fluffed out his feathers and pranced about his hens, crowing loudly.

"I really don't know where to begin," LaVerne said.

"Do you mind if I make a suggestion? Or rather suggestions?" Charlie asked.

"No, please tell me where to start," LaVerne smiled and threw up her hands.

"We need to build your chicken coop and put up the fence for them and the goats. They can share the same enclosure. I noticed you brought a couple of rolls of chicken wire. Next, you should clear a space and get your garden planted as soon as possible. Another week and the ground will be soft enough."

"Okay. That's our plan." LaVerne paused, deep in thought.

"What is it?"

"Well, I was just wondering, do you have the time to help me? You do, after all, have your own place to keep up."

"Don't worry, I got my chores done a week ahead in anticipation of this. My morning chores were done before you woke up and I can see to my animals again this evening."

"I can't thank you enough. It seems like that's all I've been doing is saying 'thank you'."

"Will you stop? That's what friends are for. It's going to be so nice for me, you know, having another woman so close by."

Howler, LaVerne's new puppy, had discovered the chickens and how much fun it was to make them scatter. Last night, after they had bedded down the horses in Charlie's barn and put the goats in one of the other stalls, the two women had walked up to the cabin. As Charlie opened the front door five, six month-old puppies rushed out, jumping on them and whining a noisy greeting.

LaVerne had instantly fallen in love with the smallest of the litter. A male with one ice blue eye and the other, a yellow wolf eye, a sure sign that an alpha wolf had impregnated Moon, Charlie's husky. He might have been the smallest but he certainly was the loudest. As the puppies tussled for attention the little pup did his best to howl, but ended up sounding like a yodeler and not a very good one at that. Charlie had given LaVerne the pick of the litter but there was no question that 'Howler' was the dog for her.

"Howie! No! Leave those chickens alone!" LaVerne cried.

Howler ignored her and chased a hen into the bushes.

"Howler!" Charlie called. "Heel!"

The dog rushed over to her and sat down, grinning up at Charlie as if to say, 'see how much fun this is'.

"No! Leave the hens alone. Bad dog."

The puppy whined and lay down on Charlie's boots.

LaVerne laughed. "I'm going to have to learn how you do that."

"Just a firm, no-nonsense voice usually does it. He'll learn as he gets older."

"Now you try it." Charlie said.

"Howie, come!" LaVerne used a stern voice and to her delight the puppy jumped up and ran to her. "Sit. Stay."

The dog plopped his butt down next to LaVerne and looked up at her with adoration. "Good dog." She ruffled the hair on his head. "Now stay and leave the chickens alone."

Charlie unloaded her pack horse. She had some scrap wood boards left over from some project in the past, an extra shovel, tools, and a bag of nails.

"If you want to start mapping out the enclosure and begin digging some holes for the fence posts I'll bring everything over." Charlie told LaVerne.

"Great!" LaVerne found her new post digger in the pile of her supplies and carried it over. She pounded some stakes marking the four corners of the space and ran string from corner to corner.

"Charlie, do you think this is large enough?"

"Y could make it longer so the goats have more room." She advised.

As a hole was finished Charlie dropped a post into it and shoveled the dirt back in, packing it down. LaVerne went onto the next hole and began to dig. Charlie walked over and took the posthole digger from her.

"Let me spell you. Why don't you go and get one of those bales of chicken wire?"

In one corner of the enclosure they began to build the coop, taking advantage of the fence post as a corner support.

"We don't care if it's not pretty. The chickens will never notice. They just need something to keep them out of the weather and safe." Charlie explained. "I brought some cedar shake shingles I had left over. Makes a good roof."

"I was thinking, since the goats are going to be kept in here too, we could extend the roof out a little so that they have some cover too." LaVerne told Charlie.

"Great idea. See if you can find a couple of saplings that are fairly straight. That should work as supports for the extended roof."

LaVerne picked up the axe and wandered away to find the small poles that they would need. A few hours later the chicken coop was completed. Even though it was primitive, it had four solid walls with tiny windows to let in light and keep predators out. Boards slanted down from one of these openings to serve as a ladder for the fowl. They had cross-hatch pieces nailed at small intervals to ease the chickens' descent to the ground. On the side, a small door hanging on rope hinges, was fitted with a sturdy latch.

The roof line extended out another four feet to give the goats added protection from the elements.

When LaVerne got her barn built they would winter in there. Inside the coop, they had built two rows of square wooden boxes, laying nests, and lined them with fresh hay. It was finally time to enclose the whole thing in chicken wire including the top of the outside enclosure.

As LaVerne held the wire, Charlie nailed it to the posts. With deft movements she pounded the nail part way in and then bent it over to catch the wire. Smaller boards were nailed parallel between the posts for added support for the wire. When the last nail had been driven, the two women collapsed into the warm fragrant grass. The puppies, thinking it was a new game, clamored over them, licking their faces and making a nuisance out of themselves.

The women lay in the sun, silent except for bird song, the distant clucking of the hens and Howler's off key cry when he cornered something in the underbrush. LaVerne suddenly giggled.

"What?" Charlie asked.

"How are we going to get the chickens into their new home? You know what they say about 'herding chickens'."

Charlie laughed. "That'll be the day when a chicken can out smart me."

LaVerne sat up. "Show me."

Charlie rose and went over to the supplies that she had brought from her cabin. She lifted out a small burlap sack and untied it. Then, walking to a couple of hens nearby, she brought her hand out of the sack and sprinkled a thin line of feed and began to back up toward the coop.

The hens immediately began to follow Charlie. The other chickens hurried over to see what was being offered and joined the line of birds following the food.

Chuckling at the sight, LaVerne rushed over to the wood framed, wire gate they'd made, and opened it wide. Charlie, followed by nine hens backed into the chicken yard.

Suddenly the rooster noticed that his hens were not where they were supposed to be and crowing loudly, he scurried after his harem and into the yard. LaVerne swung the gate closed.

"Well, you sure made that look easy."

Tossing some more feed to the clucking crowd at her feet, Charlie walked over and let herself out of the gate. "One job down, six million more to go," Charlie quipped.

"Do you want to peg the borders of my garden and then call it a day? We'll still have some day light to get your chores done back at your place."

"Sounds good."

Sixteen

Over the next week LaVerne and Charlie worked side by side staking and clearing the garden area and laying the foundation beams for the cabin. Under where the cabin would be built they dug a root cellar, by hand, just deep enough that they could stand upright. Later they would build shelving for storage and racks for dried fish and meat. A heavy trap door would open from the outside and give access to steps leading down into the cellar. Below ground, it would be cool during the summer and above freezing in the winter.

LaVerne had erected an eight by six foot shack, with a dirt floor, that she could sleep in until her cabin was completed. A cot for her bedroll, a steamer trunk to store her clothing in, and a tiny table would be her only comforts until the cabin was ready. A fire-pit outside the door would be her only source of heat and where she would cook her meals.

Now that she had her livestock penned in it would be imperative that she slept there at night. During the long days, while they worked, just about every neighbor, within a five mile radius, had stopped by to welcome LaVerne and then stay for a few hours to lend a helping hand. They made quick work of digging out the cellar and before LaVerne knew it, they were dragging logs from the pile and the first wall began to go up.

Digging a shallow hole in the ground, to be used as a mixing bowl, Charlie hauled water from the creek and pour some on top of the loose dirt, creating a soupy mud. To that she added hay. Mixing it to the right consistency they had the chinking material needed for between the logs.

As each log was placed, a notch had been chopped in the new log so that it fit the last log. They shoveled on a thick layer of the chinking material on top of each log and then gently laid the next log on. Leveling everything as they went. The weather was perfect and before long the mud and hay dried to a hard weather-proof seal. It took two days for the first wall to climb to just above six feet tall.

It was evident to LaVerne that she had not brought enough bales of hay what with the chinking and the bedding for the chickens. But Charlie and other homesteaders had assured her that sphagnum moss from the forest floor made excellent insulation between the logs of her cabin.

ᒪᒪᒪ

Mid-morning, a few days later, two riders trotted into the clearing. "Hey, Charlie! Hallo!" They called. Charlie straightened from the back breaking work of stuffing moss between the logs and waved. LaVerne turned from atop a homemade ladder and smiled a welcome. This morning they worked alone, friends and neighbors having chores of their own to accomplish.

"Hey yourself!" Charlie called. "What brings a couple of old sodbusters like you around?"

The two men pulled up in front of the cabin site and stepped down from their horses. They both surveyed the progress the two women had achieved with the help of other homesteaders.

LaVerne came down off the ladder and walked to where they were standing.

"LaVerne," Charlie said. "Let me introduce you to your closest neighbors. This here is Stan Mills and the ugly one is Milo Robbins. Boys, meet your new neighbor, LaVerne Guyer."

Both men tipped their hats to LaVerne. Stan was in his forties, short and stocky and his ginger colored hair had begun to recede. While the word attractive never would be applied to him, he had a pleasant demeanor and folks trusted him immediately.

Milo, on the other hand, was a huge man standing six foot, four in his stocking feet. He was handsome with sandy-blond hair worn too long and kind, moss green eyes. Being extremely shy, he watched the world from half-lidded eyes.

"Where have you been? Most everybody else has dropped by." Charlie laughed. "I thought maybe you two got lost somewhere out there in the wilds."

"Naw, we just rode over to the summer pasture for a couple of days to check on things for when we move the cattle." Milo offered in a quiet voice.

Stan said. "Then we heard that you'd moved in, Miss LaVerne."

"Please call me Vernie, everyone does."

Stan squinted up at the new wall. "Looks like you got a fair start on your cabin, Miss Vernie." He turned to Charlie. "Could you use some help getting those last logs in place?"

"Oh, yes!" Both women spoke simultaneously. "Could you?"

"Sure thing. Just let us water the horses and then we'll get those last logs put up there. Ya got plenty of moss for chinking there, Charlie?" Stan said as Milo led both horses to the creek.

"Let's you and me grab another log, Miss Verne," Stan offered.

The men made short work of the remaining logs and the first wall was finished at last. LaVerne stood back and beamed with pride.

"Vernie, Milo runs a small saw mill. You have him to thank for strippin' the bark off these logs." Charlie explained.

"Thank you, Milo. You too, Stan, for helping Charlie harvest the logs and everything."

"Weren't nothin'," Stan told her.

"We should be able to come back tomorrow and 'hep you some more," Milo told LaVerne. "What'ya say, Stan?"

"I got me some of my own chores in the mornin' but I can spare the time in the afternoon." Stan replied.

"Thanks, boys. Vernie and I should have the second wall well on its way and we could sure use the help on the top part," Charlie told them.

"Well, then we'll be on our way," Milo said.

"I can't thank you enough for your help. If you need anything from me, please don't hesitate to ask." LaVerne told the men.

Milo blushed. "We heard you was musical, Miss Vernie. When you get settled in we surely would love some music."

LaVerne was delighted with how simple a request it was and so easy to grant. "Of course! The first chance we get we'll get together for a social. Do any of the neighbors play an instrument or sing?"

Stan slapped Milo on the back. "This here rustler plays a little mouth harp, but he would never admit it to a real musician like you, Miss Vernie."

Milo took a playful swing at Stan. "Cut it out, I don't play. I just fool around a little on my harmonica."

LaVerne liked how humble Milo was and smiled at him. "I'm self taught myself, Milo. There's nothing wrong with that. I'll look forward to our musical night."

Milo's blush deepened and he turned away to fiddle with the cinch on his horse's saddle. Stan mounted and turned toward the trail.

"See ya'll tomorrow."

Milo chose to lead his horse across the clearing after he bid the two women farewell. At the edge he mounted and waved to them as he disappeared down the trail.

"You won't meet two nicer men, LaVerne."

"Do they have families?"

"Stan's got a wife and three kids. Now that he's back, he'll bring them over by and by."

"And Milo?"

"A bachelor and a recluse. Runs his cattle and his lumber mill and pans for a little gold. I was surprised he asked about a musical gathering. He rarely comes to any of our socials."

"He's shy."

Charlie laughed. "Oh, so you noticed."

"How could one help but not notice. He's painfully shy and I felt bad for him."

"Did you like him?" Charlie asked and then held her breathe. She was terrified of LaVerne's answer.

"Of course. They both seemed like real gentlemen. And to pitch in like that without hesitation and without a word of complaint."

"But, did you *like* Milo?"

LaVerne looked up suddenly at Charlie and then blushed. "You mean did I like, *like*, him?"

"Yeah."

"No, not *that* way. I'm way too busy to get tangled up with some man, Charlie. Jeez, that's all I need!"

LaVerne walked away to admire her new wall. If she had turned back to look at Charlie she would have seen naked relief on her face.

"Come back to my place for supper." Charlie called after LaVerne. "You can get back here well before dark."

"Sure. I'll just wash up in the creek."

Seventeen

Later that night LaVerne pulled her cot over to the door of her shack. On mild nights like tonight she loved to sleep with the door open and her head sticking out just enough to watch the stars and the northern lights. Tonight swirls of red, green, and gold danced across the night sky. Silent and slightly eerie, they made for a spectacular show.

Earlier, at Charlie's cabin they had dined on venison steaks, red potatoes and a cabbage salad from Charlie's garden. Charlie had announced that the venison was to celebrate the first wall being completed on LaVerne's cabin. After supper LaVerne had played her guitar and sang some of her original songs. Just at dusk she set out back to her place, Howler trotting at her heels.

Now she lay staring up at the billions of stars in the midnight blue sky. Over the tree tops and off to the east ribbons of color churned and twirled across the sky. It was one of LaVerne's favorite sights. She sighed with deep contentment on all that she, with Charlie's help, had accomplished so far. The walls of the cabin were going up, casting a dense shadow against the forest. Her garden was planted; a root cellar was waiting for her to finish and to fill with food stuffs.

The sound of her chickens, muttering in their sleep gave her a feeling of deep peace. Howler yipped and jerked, under her cot, as he chased a rabbit in his dreams. *Does life get any better than this?* To make such a wonderful friend in Charlie and to have neighbors who cheerfully helped her at every turn? *And this land, this place!* Home was a pristine clearing in virgin forest with snow capped mountains to the east and south. A river, two miles wide, practically at her doorstep, teaming with fish. *Heaven!*

LaVerne drifted off to sleep as she thought about all the things that she was grateful for. Several hours later she was startled out of a deep slumber by Howler's crazed barking. He stood by the side of her cot and when she reached out to reassure him she felt the hair on his back standing straight up.

"Hush, Howie, what is it?"

LaVerne fumbled for the lantern that she kept by her side and quickly lit it. Her gun was lying within easy reach. Then she heard it. A low rumbling, guttural, growling in response to Howie's frantic barking. Inside the coop she could hear her chickens squawking and frantically trying to fly, hitting the insides of the structure. Her goats had set up a terrible din of cries. LaVerne swung her legs over the side of her cot and slipped into her boots in one fluid motion.

With her light in one hand and her pistol in the other, she stood and walked out of the shack and towards the enclosure where the animals were.

The growling had deepened and LaVerne thought she could hear the distinct sound of bones being crushed. Her dog whined.

"Howie, stay." She told him.

When she was half way to the enclosure and with her gun cocked and ready, she raised the lantern and the enclosure was bathed in dim light.

Crouched in a corner of the pen, his front claws holding down a dead chicken, was the largest wolverine LaVerne had ever seen, alive or skinned.

He growled and barred his teeth at the unexpected light and her, then went back to his meal. *The nerve of this monster! He doesn't care one whit about me, not afraid at all. He's killed my chicken, the bastard!*

Then rational thought took over. LaVerne knew that if she placed her shot well she would have a skin that was worth about fifty dollars on the fur market. She walked closer in order to get a clean shot. The wolverine raised his head and looked at her with vicious, coal black eyes. He bared his teeth and snarled.

LaVerne aimed, took a breath, let it out and then squeezed off a shot. The beast dropped where he crouched. Keeping the light and the pistol on the powerful animal she picked up a stick and let herself into the pen. She didn't have much experience with live or dead animals. Did they play possum? She moved just close enough to poke it with her stick. No movement. The bullet had caught the animal under the chin and it had died instantly.

LaVerne looked around. In one corner she saw where the wolverine had been able to pull back the chicken wire where it met the wall of the enclosure.

Going back to her shack, she gathered up a shovel, some baling wire, rope and another lantern. Howler whined and begged to be set free to inspect the carnage.

"Okay, Howie, show's over." The dog jumped up and wagged his tail. He rushed over to the pen and then ran back to her. "I know, I know. Very exciting night, huh?" she asked the dog as she struck a match to the kerosene wick of the lantern.

Returning to the pen, she hung the light from a nail left for that purpose. LaVerne then repaired the torn corner with extra pieces of wire. Picking up the half eaten chicken she walked over to the side of her garden and dug a hole deep enough that the smell of the bloody chicken would not attract other predators. As it decomposed it would make rich fertilizer for her garden.

She returned to the chicken pen and picked up the dead wolverine by its hind feet. Carrying her lantern with her, she walked to a nearby tree where she threw a rope over a branch. Hanging the second lantern from another tree branch, she tied the end of the rope to the feet of the animal and hauled it up.

Working quickly, she gutted it, throwing the entrails into the hole with the chicken. She had no idea if wolverine meat was edible but if it was, she didn't want the meat to spoil by leaving it overnight. It would cool overnight and hopefully someone would come by tomorrow and she would get her first lesson on skinning an animal.

Her calm actions seemed to sooth the goats and the chickens returned to bed, muttering under their breath. Howie trotted by her side as she walked to the creek to wash her hands.

"Time for bed, Howie. Good job guarding us tonight, boy."

Eighteen

The next morning Charlie rode into the clearing. She thought she had heard gun fire last night and was curious to find out if it had come from LaVerne. The first thing she saw was Milo standing very close behind LaVerne as she faced a tree. At the sound of the horse's approach LaVerne turned, bloody knife in hand.

Startled, Milo leapt back. "Whoa! Carful with that knife! It's sharp as a razor." Milo grinned up at Charlie. "Lookie at what LaVerne caught."

Charlie saw the pride of her first fur pelt shining in LaVerne's eyes. She motioned to the half skinned animal hanging nearby, "He was after my chickens last night and I shot him."

"A wolverine? My God, Vernie, do you know how dangerous they are?" Charlie asked.

"Yes, and now mine's dead!" LaVerne crowed. "Milo's teaching me how to skin it."

"Oh." Charlie swallowed her jealousy. "Looks like you're doing a good job for your first."

"She's doin' a fine job." Milo turned back to LaVerne. "Now let's get 'er finished up and curin', Vernie." He inspected the carcass. "You're ready to pull the whole skin down the body."

Charlie forgotten, the two turned back to the job at hand. Dismounting she let her horse wander off.

"Okay then, guess I'll forage for more moss for the cabin." Ignored, Charlie watched for a moment and then turned away.

"Careful now with the feet, Vernie. You don't want to pierce the skin. A little slit there and there. We'll make certain you've got any little bits of flesh or fat off the pelt, then we'll stretch 'er on a pole. Time will do the rest."

"What pole, Milo?"

Without answering Milo walked to the tree line and chopped at a dead spruce sapling. He bucked the limbs off and walked back to where LaVerne worked over her pelt.

"See here, Vernie? I'll break away all the bark off'a this here spruce and smooth it down with my knife," he explained as he worked on the pole. "Now turn your pelt right side to. The head goes to the thickest end of the pole, see? Then you gently stretch it down the pole tacking it in a few places as you go."

Milo dug into his pocket and produced some unique looking tacks.

"These here tacks won't harm the pelt."

Milo worked very fast and LaVerne watched his every move. Before long the beautiful pelt was stretched along the pole.

"Can I use the meat, Milo?"

"Sure can. It'll make a fine stew. Just cook it a long time to get rid of the wildness. I can butcher it for you if you like."

"I need to learn. Would you teach me?"

"Sure thing."

I'm going to throw up if I have to listen to much more of this, Charlie groused to herself as she dumped an arm load of moss on the ground next to the wall they were erecting. *Milo's said more words in a morning than he's said all year. Could he* be *any sweeter on Vernie?*

As LaVerne cut up the carcass Milo instructed her on where to sever the legs and split the backbone.

"Now, just wrap it up in sacking if ya got some and put it in a cool, dry place 'till you're ready to cook 'er up."

"Vernie," Charlie called. "You ready to lay some logs?"

"Coming!" LaVerne quickly wrapped the meat in clean cloth and stuffed it in the back of her shack. "Charlie, how about some wolverine stew tomorrow night? I'll start simmering it early in the morning," she asked as she walked over to where Charlie was working.

"Sounds good.   When you leave my place tonight grab some of my sweet onions and garlic to throw in with it."

"Can you join us tomorrow for supper, Milo?" LaVerne asked.

"Sure would like that, Vernie, but I gotta go into town and won't be back 'till late."

"Oh. Okay then, another time." She replied as she and Milo lifted a log and placed in gently on the thick moss that Charlie had laid down. They were careful to rest it in the saddle they had chopped in the log.

Over and over, Charlie stuffed the chinking and Milo and LaVerne worked in harmony placing each log until another wall was completed.

"Two down and two to go," Milo told the two women. "Won't be long now and you'll be moving into your own place, Vernie."

"I can't wait," LaVerne laughed. "That shack of mine is getting smaller and smaller."

"Well, look at it this way.   That shack will be your first out building. Or it's far enough away from the house, it could serve as your outhouse."

LaVerne blushed. "No, I want the privy to be on the other side of the clearing away from the garden and the cabin."

Charlie grinned. "You'll be sorry when you have to trudge through five feet of snow to get to it."

"Ain't that the truth?" Milo said.

"Oh." LaVerne was nonplussed. She hadn't thought of that.

"Before I forget, Vernie, after your walls have settled you'll want some windows. I can cut you some boards on my saw to frame 'um out, if you like."

"Oh, that would be wonderful. Thank you. Charlie told me you have a saw mill. How does it work?"

"It's just a small one but it does the job. I drive it with steam. Got water piped from the creek into the reservoir and then I fire up the boiler with a wood fire and presto! You got steam to drive the blade."

"I would love to see it in action, Milo. Maybe when you cut the boards for my windows I can ride over and watch."

"You bet. Anytime."

Charlie grunted something inaudible and walked off towards the creek.

"Well, I best be on my way then. If you and Charlie want to work on the other two walls, Stan and I can probably get over to help finish them off in the next couple days."

"How can I ever thank you for all the help?"

Milo blushed. "Don't you worry none 'bout that. Glad to do it," he said as he walked over to his horse and tightened the cinch. He swung up into the saddle and tipped his hat to LaVerne. "I'll see ya soon, Vernie. Bye, Charlie." He called but got no response.

Nineteen

LaVerne lay on her cot and reread her letter from her mother. The night was quiet with the exception of an occasional scurrying and squeaking from the underbrush outside her shack. Her lantern filled the shack with a warm glow.

'Dear LaVerne,

My word, child, I don't recognize my own daughter. Building your own cabin, starting a garden, digging a cellar? Who are you and what have you done with my baby girl?

As I wrote last month Lillas and Bill and sweet little Maxine are back in Seattle, after three dreary years in England. Bill expects that they will reassign him soon what with Europe being in tatters from the war.

Your brother, Gerald, is talking about going somewhere, I don't remember where he said, to fight the 'oppressors'. I wish he'd find a nice girl and settle down here. Your father really needs the help. None of us are getting any younger.

Your new cabin sounds snug. I know how much you must love it. Imagine all your neighbors coming to help. It put me in mind of our barn-raisings back when we were all settling this area. Everyone helping each other. My goodness I just realized that it was over twenty years ago!

Your story of the moose rubbing its antlers against the side of your cabin was so funny...your Pa liked to die he laughed so hard. At least you won't go hungry with a cellar full of preserved moose meat when you catch one.

Wonderful news! Your brother, Earl is getting married. Finally. She is a young thing but they seem to suit. She is quite beautiful and they turn heads when seen together. Your brother is not the most handsome of men but she seems to adore him for his sweet nature and stable personality. Ivah is pregnant, at last. Arthur is strutting around like he owns the world. They will make wonderful parents.

I haven't heard a word from you, La Verne, in over six months. My letters go unanswered. I'm about to send out the Royal Mounted Police...or is that Canada? Ha ha. I am very worried and hope you are writing and that your letters are just delayed. Well, my darling girl, I'll close for now.

Pa sends his love, as do I. Please come home for a visit soon.

Your loving mother

LaVerne brought the pages up to her lips and kissed the paper when her mother had signed.

Oh, Mama that darn mail service is impossible. She'd written many times but rarely did it go out during the winter months. The good news was her family would get a packet of letters from her when they least expected it.

Tears filled her eyes and she dashed them away with the back of her hand. *I miss you so much, you and Pa. But this is my home now and I know now this is where I was meant to be.* If only they could see the northern lights in the night sky. Green, red, and blue waves streak across the sky in a never ending dance. And the wild life was beyond a person's wildest imagination. Alaska made the Washington state wilderness look like a Sunday picnic. There was everything here to sustain the people. It just took an amazing amount of hard work, but she welcome it and was so happy.

LaVerne laid back on her cot, holding her mother's letter to her heart. Her eyes slowly closed, her breath evened out and in seconds she was asleep.

Twenty

LaVerne and Charlie finally laid the last log. LaVerne found the moss from the forest floor to be much more beautiful than the mud colored hay mixture they'd first used. The subtle greens and golds in the moss made her cabin blend with the forest. She was happy that they used it only on the back wall before they had run out of hay.

Now, with various neighbors helping, four, sturdy, six foot walls stood in the afternoon sun. Extra moss was crammed into the corners, where the logs met, for extra insulation. Tired but jubilant, they walked their horses back down the trail to Charlie's cabin. The dogs ran ahead, barking at nothing, infected by the human emotions of celebration for a job well done.

"We should be able to raise the roof as soon as our neighbors have a spare minute to help, Vernie." Charlie commented as they entered her yard.

"All I care about right now is a hot cup of tea and a hotter bath." LaVerne leaned her head down to smell herself. "I smell."

Charlie laughed as they walked their horses into the barn and removed the tack. While LaVerne brushed both mounts, Charlie got their feed bags ready and replenished their pails with fresh water.

In contented silence they finish with the horses and walked side by side to the cabin. Moon and her son, Howler, clambered in behind the women, afraid of being left out. Charlie walked to the stove and opening it, stirred the embers and stuffed it full of dry wood. She lifted the cover to the water reservoir and dipped her finger in.

"Water's still hot."

LaVerne was pumping water into the kettle and set it at the back of the stove to heat. "Can I call first dibs on a bath? I can't stand myself another minute."

"Sure." Charlie laughed good naturedly. "You know where the hip-bath is. Go and get it, will you?"

"Thank God for small favors! I owe you."

LaVerne went out the back door and soon returned with a tin tub that was higher on one end than the other. A person could fit in it if they kept their knees pulled up to their chest. She placed it in front of the fireplace and, adding more wood stirred those embers to life. The two dogs, groaning contentedly, threw themselves down between the tub and the fire.

Charlie had filled three large pails with water and they began to steam on the stove top. LaVerne moved to the far side of the cabin and, turning her back modestly, started to strip out of her dirty clothes. When she was naked she slipped her shirt back on until the water was hot.

Charlie topped off the heating pails with hot water from the reservoir and hauled the first one over to the bath tub.

"Let me do that, Charlie." LaVerne rushed over.

"Get the other one, will you?"

By the time they had filled the pails from the reservoir, twice, the water was hip deep, hence the name. Charlie unwrapped a bar of soap that she kept for special times. One of her little indulgences, it was French and milled in Boston.

"Here." She handed it to LaVerne.

"Oh, no, I couldn't. It's too fine."

"Nonsense. I keep a stock. We have few luxuries out here; this is one of mine." Charlie smiled.

As Charlie turned back to the stove to replenish the reservoir and the pails with water, LaVerne dropped her shirt and climbed in over the rim of the tub. She moaned with pleasure as the water rose about her body. She soaped the bath rag with the lavender smelling soap and hummed a tuneless song.

LaVerne's shoulders, now ribboned with muscle after months of labor, shimmered in the firelight. Her black hair was pulled up on top of her head with damp tendrils resting on her neck. Her beautiful profile glowed damp and pink from the heat of the water and the fire and Charlie found herself staring.

LaVerne glanced up suddenly. "What?"

"Nothing." Charlie turned away abruptly.

"I won't be long, then it's your turn."

"Take your time. You earned it."

"I'm so happy, Charlie. My cabin is almost a reality." She soaked the rag and squeezed the water over one shoulder. "Is there a bit more hot water?"

Charlie hauled one of the pails across the room and slowly poured the hot water into the bath, being careful that it did not hit LaVerne's skin. Starring at her nude form, she set the pail down.

"Can you reach my back for me?"

LaVerne handed the soapy rag to her and Charlie moved behind LaVerne. Keeping rigid control of her emotions, she washed her friend's back.

"Oh, God, that feels so good. You're a saint to let me go first," LaVerne laughed and turned to look at Charlie. She was stunned by the naked need on Charlie's face.

LaVerne just stared, unable to move or look away from such longing. With both hands bracing herself on the rim of the tub, Charlie slowly leaned in and kissed LaVerne's forehead and then her eyes that had shuttered closed when Charlie first leaned over. Charlie moved down and kissed the corner of LaVerne's mouth. Feather soft, Charlie kissed her lips.

When LaVerne didn't respond, Charlie pulled away a breath's length and LaVerne's eyes fluttered open.

"Should I stop?"

"No!--yes!--no--I don't know--didn't realize…" LaVerne stuttered and then was silent.

Charlie stopped her words with another soft kiss, this one longer. Finally LaVerne responded with a little gasp. Charlie's tongue darted at the opening but did not enter. LaVerne moaned.

Something gave way in LaVerne's heart. She was drenched in new feelings, alive and awaken like nothing she had ever felt. Following Charlie's example she kissed back, nibbled at her mouth, and raised a wet hand to hold Charlie's head so she couldn't escape.

Was this love, then, she asked herself. Is this what she'd been waiting for? Is this why she had felt different from everyone else her entire life? Surely this can't be right, can it? LaVerne's need engulfed her. *I should stop. Mama would never approve, never understand.*

Twenty-one

Sitting on the front porch of her recently completed cabin, LaVerne smiled as she gazed down at the newest letter from her Mama.

The roof had gone on two weeks ago with the help of all her neighbors. It had seemed more like a party than hard work. There had been a covered dish potluck at the end of the day with children and dogs running around and the women visiting and catching up on news. Milo had brought a wagon load of shingles, made at his saw mill, and had presented them to LaVerne as a cabin warming gift. In spite of LaVerne's protests and arguments, he simply would not accept any payment for them.

LaVerne sighed contently as she looked out over the clearing. Her garden was over two feet tall now and thriving. The smell of smoke drifted down from the chimney. Her chickens clucked and scolded as they pecked at the dirt in their enclosure.

The shack that had been her home for several months was converted into a wood shed. Taking down the front wall, she had used that wood to build an open, covered area that expanded the space another third. It was already half full of stacked wood and LaVerne tried to add to it every few days. Milo had taught her to spot standing, dead spruce which when felled would need no time at all to dry out and be ready to burn.

Except for the roof raising, LaVerne hadn't seen as much of Charlie as in the past. They were both uncomfortable about the bath and kissing evening. LaVerne didn't know what to make of it or the feelings it had stirred deep inside and had no one to ask about it. Yes, she had Charlie, but since it involved her she wasn't comfortable yet discussing it with her best friend. LaVerne sighed, completely nonplussed about the event. The one thing she knew for sure was she didn't want *anything* to jeopardize her friendship with Charlie.

The goats were tethered at the edge of the forest and they cropped the sweet grass growing there. Without looking down, LaVerne's hand found the soft ruff of her dog's neck fur and gave him some scratches behind the ears. Without waking up, Howler groaned and huffed in his sleep.

"Wanna hear Mama's letter, Howie?" She asked the dog.

Dear LaVerne,

Everyone is fine here at home. I finally received a thick packet of letters from you…I guess those dogs and their sled made it through the snow, at last.

Gerald left last week to join the royal navy in England. He says it's just a matter of time before the Germans become a real problem. I will never understand your brother's lust for a fight! He told me that America will never get into a war so far away and that he 'had to do something'.

Your sister Lillas is packing up the house in anticipation of Bill's next assignment. Just based on what my children are saying I sense that the countries in Europe have not learned their lesson.

I don't think I told you in my last letter; Gladys and Al were here for a week. They returned to Boise yesterday.

We had such a lovely visit. Al is staying out of trouble and is now a supervisor on the loading dock where he works. Gladys is nine weeks gone with their first child. They both seem very happy. I couldn't be more thrilled about another grandchild! Speaking of grandkids, your sister Violet's letters are strained and lack news of her children. I can't imagine what she is up to other than running the bar and dining room. And she never mentions Phillip anymore. I worry for them, I do.

Ivah and Arthur are building a new home in the Queen Anne district in Seattle. Two stories, all brick --sounds like a mansion to me. But Arthur can certainly afford it with his law firm doing so well.

Your Pa is well. He runs his crew and doesn't do so much of the actual cutting and clearing anymore which is a great relief to me. He is able to spend more time here at home.

Well, my darling girl, that wraps up our news from the home place. Write soon.

Love always, your Mama

Howler's head suddenly jerked up and the hairs on his back stood straight as he rose to his feet. A low growl stuttered to life in his throat.

"Easy, Howie, let's see who's coming before you go all manly on me."

Milo, astride his big roan gelding, Buster, rode out of the forest. He waved and yelled, "Hello the house!"

LaVerne stood and waved back. "Hello, Milo, welcome."

Milo trotted across the clearing and pulled up in front of the cabin. Dismounting, he loosened the cinch on the saddle, and letting the reins drag on the ground, stepped away from the horse.

Smelling water the gelding moved off toward the creek and the sweet grasses that he knew he'd find there.

"How ya been, Vernie?" Milo asked putting his boot on the first step of the porch.

"Can't complain--in fact, truth be told, I'm happy as a pig in slop, as my Pa always used to say." She laughed.

"Thought I'd stop by and let you know the new glass for that last win'der got delivered in town. They're holding for ya."

LaVerne's eyes gleamed at the thought of the last window being put in. "I'll probably pick it up next week when I go in to get the mail and some nails I ordered."

"I'm goin' in, in a day or two, just let me know what you ordered and I'll bring it out to ya."

"That's very sweet of you, Milo, but there's no need. I can go get it."

Milo blushed. "It ain't no trouble, Vernie, I'm goin' anyways. Besides, I like do'in fer ya."

"Well, all right, if you're sure it's no bother. In return please stay for supper; I've got a chicken pie in the oven. Only it's made with quail, not chicken. And it's made with my Mama's recipe for crust. Melt in your mouth crust and I'm not bragging."

"Sounds real fine, Vernie. Thanks."

"Come on in and see what I've done since you were here last."

Milo walked up the rest of the steps as LaVerne rose and together they went into the cabin. Milo held the screen door for LaVerne to enter. Just inside the door, Milo stopped dead in his tracks and stared.

LaVerne walked over to the oven and, grabbing a rag, opened the door a crack. A fragrant steam billowed out.

"Almost ready." She announced turning. "What's wrong?" She asked when she turned and saw Milo was still standing at the door.

"Nothin'--uh--nothin'. It's just you've done so much with the place. Looks like you've lived here for years."

LaVerne felt her face heat at the praise. She looked around seeing her home through a friend's eyes. Red checked gingham curtains hung at the windows. Several thick slabs of white birch had been used to make a long dining table. Charlie had helped with that. Benches on either side were made of black spruce. LaVerne loved the mixed woods together.

A rocking chair and an easy chair flanked the fireplace. LaVerne had lovingly laid every rock, with Stan's guidance, and it towered from floor to ceiling. The red in the curtains was repeated in a green, black and red afghan that LaVerne's mother had made and was thrown casually over the rocker.

The mantle displayed pretty rocks, a piece of driftwood the river had sculpted and reminded her of a mother and child. An oil lamp in red glass held the place of honor. A ladder, fashioned again out of black spruce led to the sleeping loft above.

Over Milo's shoulder she could see her rifle resting on a rack made from deer antlers above the door. It gave her a sense of peace and safety seeing it there.

Interrupting her thoughts, Milo continued, "You've done a fine job, making this a home, Vernie. A far cry from my bachelor digs. Spartan is my decoratin' theme." He chuckled.

Joining in his laughter, she pumped some water into a basin and put out fresh toweling. "If you'd like to wash up, Milo, while I set out some plates and spoons, we can eat."

Rolling up his sleeves, Milo moved over to the sink. Cupping his hands, he brought water up to his face and then lathered up his hands and forearms.

LaVerne glanced up as she set the table and was suddenly embarrassed by the domestic scene she and Milo had inadvertently created.

What in the world is wrong with me? He's just a friend stopping by in time for supper. Get a hold of yourself, Vernie! But she couldn't help but notice what a fine figure of a man Milo was. With his shirt sleeves rolled up to keep them dry while he washed, his muscled forearms were very nice to look at, no denying it.

Looking back she realized that this was the first time that she and Milo had ever been alone together. *That's what it must be, this odd sensation I have in my stomach. Just nerves.* It was awkward being alone with him, here in the cozy confines of the cabin. She forced herself to turn away, giving a huff of disgust at herself and her girlish imaginings.

As Milo dried his face and hands, he grinned across the room at her. "This is nice. Thank you for inviting me."

LaVerne ducked her head and continued to set out utensils and mugs of hot coffee, bread and butter. She mumbled something, "least I could do...you've been so helpful...think nothing of it."

My God! Vernie, what is wrong with you? Could you be any clumsier?

"Have a seat, Milo. I'll just get the pot pie out of the oven."

Milo sat down and tucked the cloth napkin into his shirt front. "That smells awful good, Vernie."

Using a thick towel, LaVerne lifted the hot pie plate out of the oven and brought it to the table. She picked up a large spoon with one hand and reached out for Milo's plate with the other. As the spoon broke through the rich crust the fragrant steam from quail, onion, celery, potato and gravy poured into the air. LaVerne heaped Milo's plate full and placed it in front of him.

"Oh, my word, Vernie, you sure can cook! This is wonderful," he told her around a mouthful of succulent meat.

Taking a smaller portion for herself, Vernie took her first bite and silently evaluated the crust.

"My Mama insisted that all us girls learn to cook. She always said it didn't matter what we did in life, we should be able to feed ourselves and our future families."

Milo raised his eyes to the beams above their heads in prayer, "Thank you, Mama!" He exclaimed.

"I'm glad you like it."

"Like is too weak a word--I love it!"

They ate in silence for awhile; the only sound was that of the fire in the stove settling as a log fell and the clank of their spoons against the bottom of the tin plates. Once again, LaVerne felt that undercurrent of domesticity. Milo was so easy to be around. So appreciative of anything she did for him. *We're lonely, that's all it is. It's nice--cozy, sharing a meal with a friend.*

LaVerne looked up to find Milo staring at her over his coffee cup. "Vernie, I got somethin' on my mind that I want to tell you…"

"Yes?"

"We haven't known each other all that long but I have grown to have a deep regard for you and--well-- I was wonderin'…"

Suddenly Howler charged out from under the table, barking and howling. As steps could be heard mounting the porch and crossing to the door, Howler's tail began to wag a mile a minute. The door flew open and Charlie walked in followed by Howler's mama, Moon.

"Vernie! Come see what I ca…!" She stopped mid-sentence and glared at the happy scene before her. "Oh! You got company." She frowned at the man. "Hello, Milo."

"Hey, Charlie. How ya doin'?"

LaVerne had risen from the table and crossed to Charlie. She pecked her on the cheek saying, "Are you hungry? You're just in time for supper. Quail pot pie."

"I don't want to interrupt anything."

LaVerne frowned at her friend. "Don't be silly. Sit. I'll get you a plate."

"I need to wash up." Charlie moved easily to the sink and, knowing the cabin almost as well as her friend, helped herself to soap and a towel. She walked to the table and sat down as LaVerne served her a helping of the steaming pie.

"What did you want to show me?" she asked as she sat down.

"I set some traps down by the beaver dam and caught two. They're on the porch. Beautiful pelts."

"Ooo…I've never seen a beaver up close."

"You'll get some good money for beaver pelts, Charlie." Milo said.

"Yeah, I know. They're in the top three for fur prices. But I'm not selling these."

She turned to LaVerne. "I thought that they'd make us each a swell hat for this winter, Vernie."

"Really?" LaVerne rose and crossed to the door. "I want to see them," she said as she left the cabin.

Charlie grinned at Milo, "Good grub, huh?"

"Yep. She's a damn fine cook."

"Don't ya think she's a little young for you?"

Milo flushed. "I don't know what you're talkin' about."

"Oh, I think you do." Charlie said as she mopped up the gravy with a chunk of bread.

With a pensive expression, Milo stared at the door that LaVerne had just disappeared through.

Twenty-two

A couple of evenings later, just before sundown, a group of men rode into the yard of Vernie's place. Neighbors were always stopping by so she wasn't particularly alarmed. But these men were laughing and loud. Before she stepped out on her porch, she took her rifle down from over the door and set it just inside.

"Good evening, gents, what brings you by?"

Two of the five men doffed their hats in respect while one man spoke. He wasn't drunk but LaVerne could now see they were well on their way.

"Good evening, Miss LaVerne. We haven't met yet," a couple of his friends giggled and leered at her, "but my name's Pete. This here is Bill, Jim, Steve, and Sam. We come here to let you pick which one of us you'd like ta' marry. No woman should be alone out in this here wilderness and we're all eligible bachelors. We're clean and we got most of our own teeth."

His friends laughed uproariously at the tooth remark.

"Mighty fine place you got yourself here."

LaVerne smiled. "Well, that's very generous of you. I'm flattered but I don't need a husband right at the moment."

"Now Miss LaVerne, don't be stubborn. We can't leave here without your decision. Maybe a few kisses would help ya make up your mind." Pete swung off his horse and almost fell in the mud, much to the delight of his friends.

Just then Charlie broke from the trees, pulling her horse up a few yards from the men. Her .12 gauge shotgun rested on the pummel of her saddle. She'd been clearing dead-fall from her branch of the trail and spotted the men as they rode past.

"Howdy, Pete, Bill. What brings you this way?"

Bill spoke up, "None of yourn beeswax, Charlie. Butt out."

"What's the homo doin' here?" one of the other men muttered.

Ignoring the slur, she drilled Pete with her stare, "What do you think Milo would do if he found out you was pestering Vernie? I think he would fire your ass from the mill. You too, Bill."

"We ain't pesterin' her. We come with a honorable proposal'a marriage. We're givin' her pick of all of us," Pete explained, remounting his horse.

"Whooee, thas' right! Pick me, Miss LaVerne. I'll give you lot'sa babies!" one of the other men shouted.

"No! Pick me!"

"Wait a goldurned second, I saw her first," Pete shouted.

Charlie calmly raised her shotgun and fired a round of buckshot into the air. Amidst dancing and rearing horses the men quieted down quickly and one fell off the back of his mount.

"Now apologize for bothering Miss LaVerne and be on your way. Shame on you acting this way and molesting a decent woman."

"We wasn't molestin' her, Charlie, we was proposin'!" Pete argued.

"Well the next time you get it in your head to try and get a wife, I'd suggest that you come by one at a time and sober. Now get! Before I pepper the backside of your britches with buckshot. And apologize on your way out." Charlie leveled the shotgun at them.

Pctc turned his horse to Vernie. "Sorry for the misunderstanding, Miss LaVerne. We didn't mean no harm." He aimed his horse at the trail and didn't look at Charlie. The other men followed, muttering their apologies.

Once the last of the riders disappeared down the trail, Charlie rode up to the porch and grinned at LaVerne.

"So many admirers, Vernie, how will you ever make up your mind?"

"Can you believe what just happened? I think they were serious--drunk but determined." She laughed.

"'The ratio of women to men in this country is very low. That's why many men marry native women because white women are so scarce."

"I feel bad for them. Their hearts were in the right place but they went about it all wrong."

"Liquor can make decent men do bad things, Vernie. Next time people who you don't know ride in, greet them with your gun. That could have turned mean."

"I *did* have my rifle ready just inside the door."

"Not good enough. No one will think the lesser of you if you walk out with a weapon on you. Promise me you'll be more cautious in the future."

"Oh, all right, I promise. But I don't think they were a threat to me." She smiled. "Can you come in for a cup of coffee?"

"No, I was in the middle of clearing my trail and now," she glanced up at the sky, "it'll be dark by the time I ride back. I'd best get on home. I'll see you tomorrow." She turned her horse.

"Good night, Charlie, and thanks for riding to my rescue, quite literally."

Charlie's bright laughter floated back as she disappeared into the forest.

Twenty-three

The Homestead
1923

The summer had flown by in a blur of preparation for the long dark months of winter. Sixteen to twenty hours of darkness was typical and it was imperative that LaVerne was ready. Her first garden had produced root vegetables which were carefully stored in her cellar. Wild berries were picked and preserved.

The wood shed was finally full and Charlie had assured her that eight cords should suffice for the entire cold season. Now everyone waited for the first snow fall when it would be time to hunt elk and moose. Late in September the salmon began their annual spawning run up the rivers of Alaska. One day Milo rode into her clearing and hailed the house.

"Vernie, hello! Vernie, where are you?"

Stepping from the barn she raised her hand in greeting. He trotted his horse over to where she stood.

"Want to see the salmon running?"

"Really? They're in the river?"

"Saddle up and we'll take a ride."

LaVerne hurried over to her brush corral and slipped a bridle and saddle on her horse. Walking to the cabin she said, "Let me just get some gloves and another coat."

Soon they were on the trail that skirted the village and were headed north along the shore of the Yukon

River. The day was perfect with the deciduous trees in full color against the emerald backdrop of the evergreens. About five miles upriver they came around a bend and LaVerne got her first look at a contraption she'd never seen before. She laughed with delight.

"What in the world is *that*?"

"It's a fish wheel."

"What does it do? It resembles a Ferris wheel from the carnivals that used to come to town back home, and now has fallen into the river."

The wheel turned slowly and methodically, water sparkling off the nets and dropping back into the river. LaVerne then spotted a huge salmon temporarily caught in the netting, then slipping into a trough which led to a large wooden box to one side. As she watched another salmon appeared.

"Milo! It's catching fish!"

He laughed at her enthusiasm, "yes, I know."

"How does it all work?"

"The river's current propels the wheel and as the nets go under water they catch salmon as they swim by. As you can see the fish fall into the trough and slide down and into the catch box."

"Oh! It's wonderful. Did you think of it?"

"No, no. It originates from Scandinavia. A big Swede, from Ohio, brought the idea here about twenty, thirty years ago. Wanna see what we do after we catch the fish?"

"Oh, yes, please."

Milo dismounted and dropped his horse's reins to the ground. His animal was trained to stay in the area as long as the reins dragged on the ground. LaVerne did the same, easing the cinch on Junie's saddle.

Milo walked out onto the far side of the fish wheel and grabbed two salmon by the gills, "Come on up to the fish camp and I'll show you where the work really begins."

They hiked half way up the hill to a small shack. There was a homemade table out in front. Off to the side was a drying rack with a roof to keep the weather off the curing salmon. About a third of the racks were already filled with fish. Milo plopped the two fish down on the table.

"First you take the guts out," he began to demonstrate, "and if it's a female we usually milk the eggs from her. They make mighty fine eatin'. Then you cut off the head. Running the knife up almost to the tail you cut the meat in half, long ways."

Milo emptied entrails and head into a bucket, "We'll dump all this into the river so it doesn't attract bears."

He then took a clean, debarked branch from a pile under the table and hung the two fish by the tail end.

"You wanna try?" he asked Vernie.

"I'd love to," she headed back down the hill to the wheel.

LaVerne quickly got the hang of cleaning and hanging the fish. They worked in companionable silence for a few hours, filling rack after rack of salmon. She helped steady the poles as Milo went up a ladder to hang the fish.

"This is why the racks are up in the air," Vernie observed, "to keep the bears and such away."

"Yep," He came back down the ladder, "let's take a break," Milo said.

Together they walked down to the river to clean their knives and hands. Milo went to his saddle bags and brought out a camp coffee pot, and a food sack. Back up at the shack he quickly got a fire going and put the coffee pot on to boil. They sat on the steps of the shack and watched the fire, the river and the fish wheel. A bald eagle circled the area where the wheel worked.

"Do the eagles steal your fish?" Vernie asked.

"Not so much. Too much suspicious activity what with the wheel turning and the noise and dripping water. They would much rather hunt out over the river. They're great fishermen."

Milo stood and, going to the fire, dumped some coffee grounds into the now boiling water. He moved the pot over to the hot rocks that ringed the fire pit so the brew could steep. Going into the shack he returned with mugs.

"No sugar, no milk for your java but the sandwiches should be good," he told Vernie as he set out the food.

"An impromptu picnic. I love it," she replied.

LaVerne saw Milo's ears grow pink. She'd managed to make him blush with the simplest of observations.

"Yeah, well--gotta feed my worker," he grinned at her. "If you'll unpack the food, I'll pour us some coffee."

They munched for a while in silence. Again, LaVerne marveled at how peaceful a man Milo was. She liked his silences. It made what he had to say so much more important because he didn't fill the air with bragging nonsense like so many men. She had two brothers that were like that and of course Pa.

"How much fish will you take, Milo?"

"As much as the river and the wheel will give us. Several hundred if it's a good year."

"So many. Why?"

"They are the main staple for the sled dogs in the winter when meat is scarce. Easy to store because after they dry on the racks, they'll freeze and last until the next run, next fall. When it's been a good year we share with the village. The women smoke and can the fish."

"There are other wheels on the river?"

"Yep. Joe and Elk-tail have one. Any of the elders in the village that are still strong enough to do the work have had them for decades. Stan and his partner have one. The biggest and heaviest job is hauling the wheels out of the river before the first freeze."

"Oh? Why do you have to take them out?"

"If they're caught frozen in the river, come spring and thaw the ice flows would crush them. We all get together and help each other haul 'em out."

LaVerne wadded up the waxed paper that had held their sandwiches and stowed it in the now empty food bag. She drained her mug of coffee. Standing she asked, "Ready to do a few more racks?"

"I'm game if you are. You're a hard worker, Vernie, that's one of the things I like about you." He looked away, unable to look her in the eye with the compliment.

"Why, thank you, Milo. I'm really enjoying myself today."

Near the end of the day as they packed up the horses and closed up the shack, Milo filled a bag with fresh salmon for LaVerne to smoke in her new smoke house.

"I know Audrey, Stan's wife, would loan you her pressure cooker if you wanted to can the remaining fish. I'll be bringing you more next week."

"I would love that. Mama always canned Chinooks at home. It's one of my favorites."

"We'll stop by their place and see if she can spare it for a couple of days."

Once in the saddle, LaVerne turned and caught Milo's eyes. "Thank you for today. It was wonderful."

Milo nodded without answering and clicked his horse into motion.

Twenty-four

Late in the fall, LaVerne awoke to a dusting of snow on the ground and temperatures hovered around twenty five degrees. The skies were gray but the snow had stopped sometime during the night. While cooking Howie and herself some breakfast she decided that she deserved a day off. She hadn't been back over the hill to the marshes and lakes where Joe had shown her the moose.

"That would make a nice hike, wouldn't Howie?" she asked her dog.

Howler whined and, grinning up at her, his tail beginning to pound the floor in anticipation.

"Who knows, we might even see some moose."

Howler gave a sharp bark and ran to the cabin door.

"Hold your horses, I gotta get some stuff together."

An hour later LaVerne stood on her front porch and looked over the pack she had prepared for a day's hike. She had packed an extra pair of socks in case she got wet crossing a stream or marsh. She had also packed a cold lunch of meat, a biscuit and a crab apple, some rope, gunny sacks, a knife and extra ammunition. Under her coat, which was a heavy insulated canvas, she wore a thick flannel shirt. Her corduroy pants covered a full set of long John underwear. On her head she wore the beaver cap that Charlie had made for her out of the pelts she caught.

Her Winchester rifle leaned up against the railing. She looked over at her snow shoes and discarded the idea of taking them. There was hardly any snow on the ground so they would be useless and just one more thing she would have to pack and carry. She remembered the trail over the hill well and, picking up her rifle, she struck off behind her cabin knowing that she would intersect the trail to the lakes.

"Come on, boy, let's find us an adventure," she told her dog.

By mid-morning LaVerne had walked down the far side of the hill and began looking for sign; scat or moose hair rubbed off on a tree trunk. Suddenly she found some prints in the soft spongy ground. Two large kidney shaped pads with little toe marks in the back. It was a sure sign that she was following moose. Excited she began to track the animal, barely noticing that snow had begun to fall lightly again.

This must be a big bull, she told herself, *eight or nine hundred pounds of meat, at least*. Charlie and Milo would be amazed if she bagged something that big. She mentally rubbed her hands together in anticipation. Another hour passed and the snow was coming down harder. Focused on a potential kill rather than on the weather, LaVerne skirted the marsh land still following the moose's track. She suddenly found some scat that was steaming, it was so fresh. Howler walked silently beside her like a ghost. The wind kicked up and was suddenly blowing horizontally, lashing LaVerne's face like icy needles. She pulled out her scarf and tried to cover half her face with it, just leaving enough skin exposed to be able to see.

"Now, Howie, where is this brute?"

Howler raised his head to the wind and whined deep in his throat.

"Do you smell somethin' boy?"

LaVerne had walked deep into the marsh land, her attention to the ground and looking for sign. When she finally looked up, she was surprised to find that she could only see a couple of yards ahead.

"Well, crap, Howie, the weather's gotten worse. We'd better hunker down somewhere until it clears some..."

As she spoke she stepped on a mossy rock and her leg went out from under her. Off balance because of the weight of her pack she fell and landed hard on her shoulder and hip. "Oww. Damn it!"

Howler stood over her and licked her face.

"Stop it, you funny dog." She laughed. "Lem'me up."

LaVerne slipped off the pack and started to get to her feet. She sat down again fast and hard and reached for her ankle.

"Oww." She told the dog, "My ankle's not acting right, Howie."

Grabbing her pack and her rifle she crawled to the base of a large tree, trying her best to get out of the wind and snow. Howler lay down beside her and whined.

"Yeah, I know, boy, we can't stay here for very long. It's only going to get worse."

Using the tree as support LaVerne tried again to regain her footing, only to have her ankle crumple under her once more. Digging in her pack, she brought out the gunny sacks to sit on so she wouldn't be sitting on cold ground.

"I don't want you to panic, Howie, you hear? Charlie said that's the first thing that will kill you here in Alaska is to panic. We just have to think this through."

Three hours later, at dusk, LaVerne sat in a white out blizzard--blowing wind and snow with the temperature dropping steadily. She had crawled under the low hanging limbs of an evergreen and sat with her back to its trunk with her knees pulled up to her chest. Her dog lay at her side. She held her rifle across her knees. She trembled from the extreme cold and was getting sleepy.

Suddenly Howie's head snapped up. His ears perked forward and he growled softly. "Shush," she whispered.

LaVerne looked in the direction of Howie's ears trying to see something in the howling snow. Out of the blizzard walked a huge bull moose, barely five yards away, oblivious to everything but the last of the sweet willow leaves on the bushes.

LaVerne slowly slipped her hands from her fur mittens and lifted her rifle. Moving carefully, she rested it against her shoulder. She knew that the moment the moose heard the noise of the bolt driving a cartridge into the chamber he would be gone. She would have to try to make it all one fluid motion; throw the bolt home, aim, and fire. She only had one chance. Trying to keep the noise to an absolute minimum she worked the bolt, took aim and pulled the trigger. The moose took two stumbling steps and dropped.

LaVerne sat there in shock. She couldn't believe her eyes and expected to see the moose jump up and run away. She was shaking with adrenaline, the onset of hypothermia and disbelief. Howie whined and licked her hands. She worked the bolt again, putting another bullet into the chamber. Safety off she drug her rifle, along beside her as she cautiously crawled out from under the tree and over to the fallen moose. When she got close enough she poked it with the barrel of her gun. *I killed it, with one shot!*

LaVerne sat there in the driving snow and stared at the body. *God, I'm so cold and now I've got to gut this brute.*

Leaving her rifle leaning up against the moose's antlers, she crawled back to her pack. She stuffed the sacks back in and dragged the pack out into the storm. When she returned to the moose, she pulled out her Bowie knife and quickly cut open the belly of the moose. Hot intestines and bloody organs gushed out into her hands.

That feels so good, she sighed. *My hands are freezing.*

Moments later she had dressed the moose and then a thought struck her. The inside of the moose was still hot and she was so very cold. Without hesitation she crawled into the cavity of the moose's belly and closed the top ribs and skin over herself. Sticking out her arm, she pulled snow towards the long opening, sealing herself in as best she could. She refused to think of the gore and blood that covered her.

I'm out of the wind and snow and it's so warm in here. I just won't think about where I am.

LaVerne could hear Howie snuffling around the moose. "Go lay down, Howie. Stay!" The dog obediently went to the back of the animal, which blocked much of the wind and, circling twice, made himself a bed in the now deep snow.

It was the most harrowing experience in her short life. LaVerne wasn't even certain if this was a good plan or if it would keep her from succumbing to the bone deep cold. But it was the only plan she had and, as she pressed herself deep into the animal's cavity, she prayed not to God, but to her Mama to keep her safe. She finally slept as the storm grew in intensity and the temperature dropped to ten degrees below zero. It was 30 degrees warmer in her macabre shelter. Her only hope was that Charlie or Milo would find her the next day.

.&.&.&.

Early the next morning the sky was clear as the storm had blown itself out sometime during the night. Howler jumped up, barking with joy. He could faintly hear voices calling LaVerne's name.

"Vernie! "Where are you?" Charlie's desperate voice called.

A long, shrill whistle sounded and Howler barked hysterically. Three horses rode up the trail. Black-eyed Joe, Charlie and Milo urged their horses toward the dog.

"Where's Vernie, Howie?" Charlie asked as she dismounted and stumbled toward the husky. "Where is she, boy?"

Milo lurched off his horse and, turning around, searched the area for anything that looked like a body. The only thing sticking out of the three feet of new snow were a pair of moose antlers. He knew the chances of finding LaVerne alive were slim.

Joe walked to the antlers and gave them a shake. LaVerne's rifle fell over.

"She's nearby, this is her rifle," Joe said.

Suddenly the snow on top of the gutted moose moved and fell down. The skin peeled back and LaVerne peered out. She was covered in blood but alive. Shocked, Milo and Charlie stood like statues as their friend crawled out of the cavity. Joe laughed.

Tears streaming down her face, Charlie ran to the other woman and knelt beside her.

"Vernie, are you all right? Are you hurt? Where are you bleeding from?" she cried as she cradled LaVerne in her arms.

"No, no--it's okay, Charlie. This is the moose's blood. I'm fine except for this damn ankle."

Milo suddenly laughed. "You spent the night inside that there moose?" He bent over and laughed some more. Joe laughed even harder.

LaVerne grinned up at him. "It's not so funny when you're in there, Milo!"

"Well, lemme tell ya, it probably saved your life, girl. What possessed you to do it?"

"I was so cold I would have slept with the devil if he had enough blankets."

Milo laughed again. "By the way, nice kill, Vernie. You must have eight hundred pounds of meat here."

LaVerne flinched as Charlie examined her ankle.

"Sorry. The good news is it's not broken. A very bad sprain and you won't be walking on it for awhile."

"We must get her warm," Joe said and began to gather wood.

"I *am* cold. Thank you, Joe."

The two friends helped LaVerne over to a stump where Joe prepared a fire. She could sit and watch them as they skinned and prepared the meat. Her dog sat at her side and laid his head in her lap.

"How'd you find me?" She asked Charlie.

"I dropped by early this morning to see what you were up to. The fire was out and your rifle was gone. The fire was so cold I knew that you had probably left yesterday. I rode over to Milo's and Joe happened to be there. We headed out and, on a hunch, Joe thought we should head this way. The blizzard had wiped out any sign of you on the trail. But as we came down the hill Joe found some of Howie's fur stuck to a bramble. It was then we were sure you had come here looking for a moose."

As they talked Joe started the fire directly in front of where LaVerne sat and it minutes it was merrily blazing. Charlie gathered more wood to keep it going while they butchered the meat.

"What were you thinkin'?" Milo couldn't help but ask. He'd been terrified that they wouldn't find her in time. "Walkin' out in weather like that?"

"It wasn't even snowing when I left my place. Then I got on a fresh trail and when I looked up the weather had turned--bad. Real bad. Then my ankle…" Two tears made tracks, through the dirt and blood, down LaVerne's face. "I couldn't walk and I was free--zing…" She stuttered to a stop.

The enormity of what could have happened to her suddenly overwhelmed her. She couldn't believe that she had been so stupid as to think she could go out for a day's stroll completely unprepared for any change in weather or conditions. If that moose hadn't wandered by the end of this adventure would have been far different.

Charlie laid down her skinning knife and crossed to her. She knelt beside her and hugged her close. "Shhh--don't think about it. You're safe now." She turned to Milo. "Stop scolding Milo. Things like this can happen to the best of us."

"Lucky for me you brought a third horse. If I could ride up behind you, Charlie," LaVerne sniffled, trying to compose herself. "We could pack most of the meat out on the spare horse. What do you think, Milo?"

"If we butcher it here we can pack it out on all four horses." Milo offered. "You ride Smoke if you think you're up to it, Vernie."

For the next hour Joe, Charlie and Milo worked like a well-oiled machine. They quartered the meat after they skinned it, placing it in cotton over-sized pillow cases that were a permanent part of Milo's saddle-bags. They then carefully wrapped the head in the hide.

The meat was equally distributed between the horses. The fire had done its job of warming LaVerne as the others worked.

"Ready to ride?" Milo asked as he stood over her.

Milo bent down and scooped LaVerne up like she weighed nothing.

"Yes." She wrapped her arms around his neck.

"I got your rifle stowed and I tied your pack behind your saddle," Charlie said.

Milo gently put LaVerne in the saddle and made certain that the one stirrup was adjusted for her good foot. Charlie had made a bush-splint out of branches and thick bark and had torn up one of the gunny sacks to secure it to her injured ankle and calf so her left leg stuck straight out from her seated position.

"We'll ride slow, we got all day. If you get tired, Vernie, just let us know." Milo told her.

"I just want to get back home."

"Maybe you should stay at my place for a few days, Vernie. You're gonna want to stay off that leg."

"Okay. Thanks, Charlie."

Joe taking the lead, they turned their horses and, at a walk, left the marsh land.

♪♪♪

Three hours later the riders rode up to Charlie's cabin. LaVerne was trying to hide how much her ankle hurt and how miserable and cold she was. Milo dismounted and hurried over to her, scooping her out of the saddle. He walked up the porch steps with his burden while Charlie, in front of him, opened the door.

They hurried into the cabin and while Milo set LaVerne on the sofa, Charlie swiftly crossed to the stove and stirred the embers of the fire to life. She piled on the firewood and soon it was blazing. Without being asked, Howie had followed them into the cabin and lay at LaVerne's feet. Charlie helped LaVerne remove her dirty, blood-stained coat and boots, while Milo squatted in front of the fireplace and lit a fire there too.

"You stay here and get Vernie settled in, Charlie. Joe and I will ride over to her place with the other horses and hang her meat. How does that sound?"

LaVerne smiled at Milo and Joe.

"That's a good idea," Charlie told him.

"Then I'd better get those nags back home. They've had a hard day of riding and packing. I'll be back tomorrow to check on you, Vernie."

LaVerne took his hand in both of hers. "Milo, you're such a good friend." She turned to Joe. "Thank you for finding me, Joe."

Milo blushed and patted her hands. "Weren't nothing. But you shor' did scare the liver outta all three of us."

"Get well, soon, Denigi."

LaVerne raised her eyebrows. Was Joe honoring her survival by calling her *Moose*? Joe smiled at her.

"Joe, please take the moose heart and have it for supper tonight, will you? I'll see you tomorrow."

LaVerne offered it because she knew, in Alaska the heart of any kill was a delicacy and considered a great compliment to receive it as a gift.

"Okay enough chitter-chatter. Get on outta here so I can get this wet, bedraggled girl into a hot bath," Charlie shooed the men towards the door.

"Get some rest, Vernie, We'll see to your animals while I'm over there." He said as he opened the door.

"Thank you."

As Milo left he heard Charlie fussing over LaVerne. He gathered up the reins on two of the horses and mounted his horse.

"Let's ride, Joe."

"A good ending to this day, my friend. Do you think little Miss knows how close she came to not surviving?"

"I don't even want to think about how it *could* have ended up." Milo shuddered.

Joe chuckled, "It will make a fine tale around the fire."

Twenty-five

LaVerne sat on the porch of Charlie's cabin. She was waiting for Charlie to return from doing the chores at her place. Milo had hung the moose meat from poles he had erected, high enough off the ground so predators could not get at it. It was so cold now that nature provided all the refrigeration one needed. When she got home she would cut choice strips and placed them on racks in her smoke house. They would smoke over a slow alder fire for a week. *There's so much work to be done and here I sit like a wounded duck. Damn the luck!*

Lying by her side Howler slept in the early winter sunlight. Near her chair and propped up against the cabin wall stood a pair of crutches. The day after they brought LaVerne home Milo had returned with them. He had fashioned them out of spruce and padded the tops with thick fur. Now a week later LaVerne was ready to give them up and she had begun to put a little weight on her ankle for short periods of time.

Howler gave a low woof and raised his head. His mother, Moon, bounded into the clearing and right behind her Charlie rode in. LaVerne stood and using the porch railing for support she hobbled down the porch to the steps.

Charlie rode up and dismounted, "Be careful. You shouldn't push your ankle if it's not ready."

"*I'm* ready!" She replied laughing. "I'm going nuts in this invalid role. How's my cabin? Are my chickens doing all right? Do the goats miss me? Did you build a fire in my stove to keep the damp out?

"Fine. Yes. Terribly. Yes." She chuckled. "I brought back a couple of moose steaks for our dinner. To celebrate your hobbling around."

"Charlie." LaVerne frowned at her teasing.

"Come, sit back down and I'll give you all the news." Charlie put her arm around LaVerne's waist and supported her as they walked back to the chairs.

They sat for a few moments, in silence, watching Howler trying to get his mother to play with him. Frustrated, he nipped at Moon's back leg. Instantly Moon had her son down on the ground, her sharp teeth displayed in a snarl. Throat exposed, Howler lay in a submissive posture and whined. Her point made, Moon licked his face and then walked away to lie in a patch of sun not far from the porch and her mistress.

"Women rule!" Charlie laughed. "Don't mess with us, Howie."

The young dog grinned at the two women as if to say it had all been planned and he wasn't embarrassed at all.

LaVerne laughed. "Oh, Howie, you are such a wuss." She turned to her friend. "So everything is fine over there?"

"Yes--and if it wasn't I fixed it."

"What happened?" LaVerne's voice rose in alarm.

"Whoa--nothing earth shaking. The chicken coop door was open. I latched it good and snug."

"Did I lose any chickens? What got in there?"

"No, I think it was just the wind. Hens and one ornery rooster all accounted for."

They sat side by side in contented silence. Charlie abruptly scooted her chair around to face LaVerne.

"You put the very fear of God into me with that moose stunt, you know."

"I know and I'm truly sorry. It could have ended badly, I realize that."

"It made me realize what life would be like if you had died." Charlie rubbed her face in frustration.

"But, I didn't Charlie. I'm right here."

"I know, but it gave me a serious re-think of what's important in my life. And you--you are so important to me." She stared at her friend. "So no more pussy footing around what we both know. I'm in love with you."

LaVerne cheeks pinked and she stared over Charlie's shoulder out into the yard. "I know," she whispered.

When Charlie couldn't stand the silence any longer she asked, "How do you feel about me?"

LaVerne's eyes slashed back to Charlie's face. "I love you too--you have been such a good friend. My feelings..." She stuttered to a stop.

"Yes?"

"I'm confused. I've never been *in love* with *anyone*. How can I be in love with another woman? And yet I have very deep feelings for you. Isn't that wrong--somehow?"

"Vernie, we each have to decide what is right and what is wrong. For me, who you love is never wrong. I believe that a person can't help who they fall in love with. But you're young and I can understand your confusion. You know I'll wait until you work it out."

"I know," she said.

Charlie rose and leaning down, she gently pressed her lips to LaVerne's forehead. She straightened and rubbed her hands together.

"Well, what do you say we get some spuds baking and prepare those steaks?" She walked down the porch and into the cabin.

LaVerne sat where she was and stared into space. *Is it wrong, this love I feel for Charlie?* She wondered about a husband and children? Could she love a man as much as she loved her friend? *I know that she loves me above all else. What would Mama say?*

Twenty-six

Back at her own cabin for a week now, LaVerne had finally been able to give up her crutches and use a stick as a cane. She only had a slight limp and her ankle hurt only when she over-taxed it. Walking out of the chicken coop after collecting the eggs, she paused when she caught sight of Howler, her dog. He had been gone for a couple of days which was not surprising or alarming. Just as she was about to call a greeting to the big dog he trotted back to the edge of the trees, whining.

LaVerne wouldn't have seen the other dog but for the splash of red. *Was that blood? W*hose dog was that? Howie had gone to the other dog and, licking its face, he laid down beside it. LaVerne could only see the dog's flank, that was obviously bleeding, and one ear. The minute she moved the other dog disappeared into the woods. She quietly let herself out of the chicken pen and walked slowly up to her cabin. Howie came bounding to her, dancing around her and barking. Then he dashed back to the tree line.

"Come here, Howie. Let's get some food for your friend."

Howie disappeared into the trees. LaVerne went into her cabin, set the half dozen eggs down and got a chunk of meat out of the cooling cupboard. After cutting it up she quietly left the cabin with a bowl filled with the meat. She went to where she had seen the dog and found some blood on the ground. She dumped the meat under a bush, hoping that the wounded dog found it before other predators got to it. Then she walked slowly back to her porch and sat down to watch.

Silently LaVerne surveyed the tree line, waiting to see if Howie would lead the other dog back. An hour later her dog broke out of the trees and barked at her. Then he dashed back out of sight. There was suddenly a slight rustling in the leaves and LaVerne was pretty certain that she could see the other dog. It had found the meat and was swiftly gulping it down. Howie stood by as if to stand guard.

The other dog stood for a second in profile and LaVerne realized, by her teats, that it was a female and she looked very pregnant. She was also certain this was no dog, but a wolf. *Is this Howie's mate? Did Howie bring her home to give birth?* How was she going to help a wild wolf? The slash on her flank needed attention.

Charlie rode into the clearing and called out to her. Howie and the wolf faded into the forest. LaVerne stood and put her fingers to her lips to silence Charlie's natural exuberance. She nodded and rode quietly to the porch. She dismounted and tied her horse to the post.

Whispering she asked, "What's going on?"

"I'm not sure. Come into the cabin and we'll talk," LaVerne told her. "Bring Moon in."

Charlie quietly called to Moon, "Heel, girl," walked up onto the porch and followed LaVerne inside.

"Howie has brought his mate home. She appears to be pregnant and wounded. I think she's a wolf."

"Really?" Charlie said.

"I fed her. But how the heck am I going to be able to dress her wound and not get torn up in the process?"

"I'm going into the village. I stopped by to see if you needed anything. I could ask Joe to come out to help you."

"Yes, would you? Joe will know what to do."

"Anything else you need?"

"Just my mail if there is any. I haven't heard from Mama in over a month."

"*Through rain, snow and sleet is just a myth...*" Charlie laughed.

LaVerne walked Charlie back out onto the porch and watched as she mounted and rode away.

ॐॐॐ

The next morning Black-eyed Joe quietly walked his horse into the clearing. The two had remained friends but rarely saw each other. Joe was kept very busy with guiding and tribal business. Instead of calling out to announce his arrival Joe softly mounted the steps and tapped on the door of the cabin.

"Hello, my friend," LaVerne said when she opened the door. "Please come in." Joe followed her into the cabin.

"How is the ankle, Denigi?"

"Much better. Would you like some coffee, Joe? Are you hungry? Please sit." She indicated a bench next to her table.

"Some coffee would be welcomed. No I am not hungry but I thank you." Joe sat down at the table. "You are done with the sticks?"

"Yes. I use a cane when my leg gets tired but I am almost completely healed."

"Mother Earth favors you. She sent the moose to protect you with his life and his warmth."

LaVerne turned from the stove with cups and the coffee pot. "How do you know that?"

"Everyone in the village speaks of it. They call you *tr'axa denigi*, woman of the moose, as you were reborn out of its belly."

"My goodness," she said as she poured coffee for Joe and herself.

"Charlie tells me that you have a new friend?" Joe asked.

"Ha! If you call a wounded, wild wolf a friend," she laughed, "then yes. Howler has brought me his mate and I think she's carrying puppies. I have left food for her several times and she does eat, even though I am certain my human smell is all over it. Can you help me treat her wound?"

Joe pulled a packet of waxed paper out of his shirt and laid it on the table.

"My shaman has sent herbs to help tukoni to sleep."

"Are they safe?"

"Oh, yes. Chamomile has been used by our people, as a mild sedative, for centuries. Mixed with healing herbs, we shall also make a poultice to place on the wound once she sleeps. The shaman has given me prayers to speak over you and the wolf as you heal her. Do you have a knife I can use and some meat?"

LaVerne rose and collected a sharp knife and some meat from the cooler and brought them back to the table. Charlie cut up the meat and then made slits in the flesh and stuffed the herbs deep into the meat, all the while muttering some Athabascan words.

"Now, I will wait here so that the tukoni is not alarmed by my presence. You take the meat to her as you have before and we will wait and see. Do you have your needle, thread and medicine ready?"

"Yes." LaVerne rose and walked to the door. "I hope this works, Joe, her wound is very nasty looking."

LaVerne went out onto the porch, leaving the door open, and looked around. She was happy to see that Howie was laying down at the edge of the trees. That would mean that his mate was not far away. She quietly walked towards her dog and Howie crawled on his belly to meet her.

"Where's your wife, Howie? Such a good dog to watch over her," she said as she leaned down to scratch behind his ears.

LaVerne squatted down, and not touching the meat, she emptied the bowl onto the ground just as she had done before. The whole time she spoke in a quiet voice hoping that the wolf would grow accustomed to the sound of a human voice.

"You are so beautiful. Howie is so lucky to have you for a wife. You don't need to be afraid. I will help you if you let me."

Howie walked over and licked LaVerne's face and then laid down next to her.

"Good boy. This is for your mate, Howie, not for you. Leave it alone."

LaVerne rose slowly and walked away, not looking back. When she reached the door of the cabin Joe was just inside watching.

"She went to the meat as soon as you crossed the yard, Miss Vernie. If we stand here in the shadows we have a clear view of her."

LaVerne had turned and watched. The wolf was clearly visible, gobbling up the meal.

"That's the most I have seen of her, Joe," she whispered. "She's truly beautiful. Look at that silver coat."

"Yes, she is favored by Mother by being brought here for your care."

"How long do you think the sedative will take before it works?"

"A little time as she will need to digest the meat. We shall watch over her. Do you have hot water ready?"

"Yes, always. I'm ready."

They watched and waited. When Howie's mate had eaten she laid down. Howie got up and, approaching her, licked her face. He then trotted out into the clearing, looked at the cabin and barked furiously. He immediately went back to his mate and laid down beside her.

"We must be certain that she sleeps but must not wait too long as her sleep will be short."

LaVerne walked to the table and gathered everything she would need to clean and close the wolf's wound. Waiting beside Joe, they watched Howie and his mate lying side by side under the bushes.

"It is time, I think. She has not moved for many minutes. Let me go first and be certain that she is asleep." Joe said.

LaVerne followed across the clearing. Howie raised his head and whined but did not move from the wolf to greet LaVerne. Joe broke off a twig of leaves and brushed the wolf's nose with it. The big female did not move even though her eyes were partially open.

"She sleeps. Give me a clean cloth and we will cover her eyes with it. This will make her feel safer and protect her eyes," Joe explained.

LaVerne sat on the ground next to the wolf's haunches and examined the wound. It seeped blood and pus. She uncapped a bottle of very warm water and irrigated the wound thoroughly. Blood and pus ran through the silver hair and onto the ground. LaVerne continued to pour the water over it until just bright red blood flowed and the pus seemed to be washed out.

With sterile needle and thread LaVerne quickly sewed up the deep wound. Off to the side Joe had used some of the warm water to make a wet poultice of chamomile and other herbs that would draw out any infection. When he saw that LaVerne had finished the last stitch he laid the steaming poultice on the wound.

LaVerne bound the wolf's flank and leg with clean cotton and Joe tied it firmly with lengths of rawhide.

"She may not allow the bandage to stay on her leg but there is nothing more we can do," Joe said.

The wolf made a sound part growl, part whine and thrashed her front feet.

"She is waking up, Joe."

"Yes, it's time we left her alone. If she remains calm she may leave the bandage in place. Let us go."

The two friends returned to the shadows of the cabin door and watched the tree line where the two dogs lay. Twenty minutes passed and suddenly the wolf jumped up and took a few steps. Staggering, she fled into the forest, Howie close behind her.

"Tukoni will return, Miss Vernie. Howler will assure her and she understands now that you are a safe food source. She eats for many, neh?"

"Yes, I am certain she is carrying Howie's pups."

Twenty-seven

For two weeks LaVerne had been feeding Howie's mate. It had been snowing, off and on, for over a week and LaVerne knew that hunting would be difficult for the wolf. She'd been pleased that the bandage and poultice had stayed on a few days before the animal had licked and gnawed it off.

Each day she would dump the meat a few feet closer to the cabin so that she would have to come out of the trees in order to eat. Whenever the temperatures allowed and she wasn't doing chores around the homestead, LaVerne bundled up in her coat and boots and sat on the porch letting the wolf become accustomed to seeing her and having her around.

This morning there was a major breakthrough. LaVerne had gone into the chicken enclosure with grain to feed the chickens and to collect the eggs. When she stepped out of the coop the wolf was standing in the clearing about four feet from the tree line. Ears pitched forward she stood waiting.

"Well, hello, girl," LaVerne spoke in the quiet soothing voice she always used when around the animal. "Are you hungry for breakfast?"

Turning her back on the wolf, she walked to the cabin. Leaving the door open she collected a portion of meat and went back outside. The wolf had not moved.

"We need to give you a name, girl," she said. "How do you like Tukoni? It's the Athabascan word for wolf. What do you think of it?" As she spoke, she walked slowly half way across the clearing and emptied the bowl of meat chunks into the snow.

The wolf watched but did not run away. "Come on, Tukoni, you have to come and get it if you want to eat," LaVerne told her and then turned away and walked to the cabin. This time, she sat on the steps and silently watched the wolf.

Howie ran out of the trees and approached his mate. With a snarl, Tukoni ran to the food and began to wolf it down. Howie, good natured as always, ran past her and up the stairs to LaVerne's side. Sitting at her side, tail thumping the boards, he seemed to be telling LaVerne how proud he was of his mate.

"Yes, I know, Howie. She is doing very well." LaVerne draped her arm across her dog and rubbed his neck. "If you two talk, you must tell her that she and her pups are safe here, will you?"

Howie licked her face.

Twenty-eight

LaVerne rode the trail into the village of Tanana. Even though the temperature hovered just below five degrees, it was a beautiful day with blue skies and sunshine. Howie trotted behind and his mate cautiously followed along the tree line several yards back. As they neared the village Tukoni faded into the forest. LaVerne thought the wolf was torn between being with her mate and the risks of being too close to humans.

Her first stop was at the village store and post office. She quickly filled her short list of supplies; salt, sugar, flour and coffee. The post office window was doing a brisk business and standing in line was Milo. She was happy to see him as he hadn't come around her place lately.

Getting in line, LaVerne called, "Hello, Milo! How've you been?"

Milo turned around and blushed. "Why Vernie, I'm doin' just fine. Nice day, isn't it?"

"Yes, beautiful. Are you riding back home any time soon? We could ride together. I haven't seen you in a couple weeks. We could catch up."

"Yes, ma'am. Getting' my mail. Got my supplies all loaded up. You?"

"Yes, as soon as I get my mail I'll be heading home."

The line had moved forward and the clerk handed Milo several envelopes. "Meet ya out front then?" Milo asked, the tips of his ears turning red.

"See you in a minute." LaVerne replied as Milo walked past.

After picking up her mail she was gratified to see two letters from her mother. LaVerne returned to the front counter and retrieved her gunny sack full of supplies. Stepping outside she found Milo waiting and he held out his hand for her sack.

"Let me secure that for ya, Vernie. Okay to put your supplies in the saddle bags?" he asked.

"Yes, thank you that would be swell."

While Milo distributed the weight as evenly as he could, LaVerne stuffed her letters inside her coat.

"Ready?" Milo asked her.

"As soon as I find Howie."

"I saw him trottin' outta the village a moment ago," Milo told her. "Odd for him not to wait for you."

LaVerne laughed. "He has a girlfriend. She's shy."

"Oh really? Lucky guy," Milo quipped, but there was under lying note of envy.

LaVerne mounted and they turned their horses down the street to where it would pick up the trail just out of town.

"Are we all still going on a caribou hunt?"

"How'd ya hear about that?"

LaVerne smiled. "Charlie. She can't wait. Says she loves caribou meat above all else."

Milo grunted. "Yes. Another month and they will start to move through our area. You're coming with us, right?"

"I wouldn't miss it!"

They rode in companionable silence until they got to the trailhead that led to Vernie's cabin. Milo dropped back to ride behind her single file. Howie

trotted down the trail to meet them and whined to
LaVerne.

"Where's Tukoni, boy?"

The dog barked and ran back down the trail and
cut into the woods. Milo rode up closer so that
LaVerne could hear him.

"Tukoni?"

"Yes, Howie's girlfriend."

"Tukoni's wolf in the native tongue, isn't it?"

"Yes, she's a wolf and about to give us some
pups."

"A wild wolf? You're kidding!"

"Nope. She's staying at my homestead and she's
taking food from me. But I haven't been able to
touch her yet."

"Good God, Vernie. Don't try to touch her,
she'll take your hand off."

"I don't think so. She's beginning to relax a
little around me. She sees that her mate trusts me
and she's getting used to having me around."

They rode on for a few minutes. Coming to the
fork where another track turned towards Milo's
home and mill, LaVerne stopped.

"Milo, come on up to the cabin. I left a stew
simmering on the stove and I don't know about
you, but riding in the cold always makes me
hungry. Stay for supper, why don't you?"

"Mighty pleased to, Vernie. Thank you."

LaVerne was happy to ride along, her face up to
the weak, winter sun. Once in awhile she could see
Howie through the trees and at his side was his
mate. It made her smile how protective her silly
dog was of Tukoni. He was, after all, going to be a
family man very soon.

Milo and she rode into the clearing and walked
their horses over to a brush corral that LaVerne had
built. The walls of the corral were made of any

deadfall that LaVerne could find; dead saplings, branches and twigs. The gate was framed out with boards and sticks and brush had been woven in and out of the cross pieces. Pieces of rope made primitive, but effective, hinges. Milo lifted the gate and opened it and LaVerne walked their horses inside.

While Milo unsaddled both mounts LaVerne got a pail of water from the creek for them. Milo rubbed the horses down with an old blanket and LaVerne gave them each a portion of oats. The horses taken care of, they lifted the saddlebags to take them to the cabin and let themselves out of the corral.

"I'll be right in. I just want to wash the worst of the dirt off at the creek," Milo said.

"Don't be silly. Come in and use my sink. I've got warm water and a soft towel. How can you resist?" she smiled at him.

"If you don't mind," Milo blushed.

Laughing, LaVerne slipped her hand through Milo's arm and together they walked up on the porch.

"Oh Lordy, I can smell that stew clear out here." Milo sniffed the air.

In the cabin LaVerne set out a towel and soap and then ladled a dipper full of hot water into a basin. She quickly washed her hands and then ladled fresh hot water for Milo.

"You want some coffee while I finish up supper? I thought I'd throw some biscuits in the oven. Won't take that long."

"Yeah, a cup of your coffee would go down real nice, Vernie. But let me make it."

After washing his face and hands, Milo stoked the stove with firewood. He pumped water into the coffee pot and added fresh grounds. They worked in contented silence.

I like this about Milo. He doesn't always feel like he has to fill the air with conversation. He's very comfortable to be around. He was not helpless around a kitchen and certainly did his part. LaVerne wondered if it was a result of being a bachelor all these years.

In no time at all she had rolled out the dough. Using a glass canning jar as a biscuit cutter, she placed sourdough biscuits on a tin sheet and slid them into the oven.

"What kind of stew did you make?" Milo asked.

"Moose. As flavorful as that meat is, I'm looking forward to a change in diet with a caribou."

"We could go squirrel hunting if you want something different."

"Ugh. I can't abide squirrel. I can't get the thought out of my head that I'm eating a tree-rat," LaVerne laughed.

"Have you ever tasted it?"

"No. My Pa and brothers used to go squirrel hunting all the time. They swear it takes just like chicken but I just couldn't put it in my mouth. Ick."

LaVerne had set the table and checking on the biscuits found them golden brown. She brought a plate of them to the table and a bowl full of fresh butter. Returning to the stove she ladled stew into bowls and set one in front of Milo and one at her place. She carried the coffee pot over to the table and refilled Milo's cup.

Sitting down across from Milo she began to eat.

"This is awful good, Vernie," Milo told her. "I could get used to this on a regular basis real quick."

LaVerne looked at him questioning. "You're welcome here any time, Milo."

Milo wiped his mouth on his sleeve and, laying down his spoon, he fished into his pocket. He brought out a velvet pouch, tied with a golden thread cord. As LaVerne watched, he opened the mouth of the little pouch and turned it upside down over his palm. A ring fell into his hand. LaVerne's eyes grew round.

"I tried to tell you a few weeks ago how I feel about you, Vernie. But we was interrupted. I been carrying this around with me, determined to speak to you again."

"Oh, Milo…" She was shocked but knew in her heart of hearts what was about to be said.

"No, please let me finish or I'll lose my nerve and never get it said. This ring was my mother's. I have come to care for you deeply and I was hopin' you might feel the same way." He grasped her left hand in his. "I wanted to ask you--that is--would you?" He visibly gulped. "Could you--care enough for me to be my wife?"

"Oh, Milo--I wasn't expecting--I don't know what--are you certain?"

"Yes, I'm sure as I can be. You don't have to answer right now. Think about it. I wouldn't ask you to leave your homestead. My old bachelor cabin ain't near good enough for you. We could live here and I would keep my place for the saw mill and my animals. It ain't that far away."

"I don't know what to say." LaVerne sighed.

"No need to say nothin' right now. But I would like you to accept this ring as a token of my sincerity--and…" he whispered the last, "and--my regard."

Milo slipped the garnet and diamond ring onto her ring finger.

LaVerne sat silent and numb. Why hadn't she seen this coming? His love was so apparent in his eyes if only she had looked. Is this *what I want? What about my feelings for Charlie?* The last thing she would ever want was to hurt this lovely, gentle man.

"Milo, dear, will you let me think about it? I'm just so surprised and honored but I don't have an answer for you tonight."

"Of course--take your time--think all you want." He blustered. "I'm just happy you agreed to think on it and accept my ring. I knew I was going to make a hash of it. I was sure you'd turn me down cold."

"You didn't make a hash of anything, Milo. It was the sweetest proposal I've ever heard."

He stood abruptly. "Well, I better get along home. My animals will be bawling and caterwaulerin for their dinner."

He took his bowl and cup to the sink. He turned to find LaVerne standing with his coat and hat in her hands. He walked over to her and she helped him into the coat. He gently took his hat from her.

"May I kiss you goodnight, Vernie?"

"I'd like that."

Milo didn't touch her but rather leaned in and brushed her mouth with his lips. Gently planting feather kisses across her bottom lip. He pulled back just enough to look into her eyes. "I'll be hopin' that your answer is yes, Vernie, and you make me one happy man."

He leaned in again with the second kiss. Once again there no race into passion. No attack or fevered assault. No beginning or end, just a tender loving kiss as fleeting as a butterfly. His tongue flirted with her closed lips until they softened, and on a sigh, opened. Shivers went up and down LaVerne's back and she found herself leaning in and returning his kiss. He pulled back and gazed at her. "Again." LaVerne whispered without opening her eyes.

Milo dropped his hat and wrapped his arms around her slender body. For several moments they kissed each other, Milo never taking more than was offered. He ended the embrace and stepped back. He laughed with pure joy as his picked his hat up off the floor.

"Good night, Vernie. I'll see you in a couple of days. Sleep well."

"'Night, Milo. Be careful going home."

Carrying his saddlebags, Milo stepped out on the porch and went down the steps. He crossed to the corral and, taking his tack from the rail, saddled his horse. LaVerne had followed him and now stood at the corral gate and held it open as he rode through. Milo touched the brim of his hat and LaVerne raised her hand in farewell. As Milo rode out of the clearing Howie followed barking and dancing around the horse's legs.

"Howie! Come here boy!"

When Milo reached the edge of the trees he turned in the saddle and waved at LaVerne, then disappeared down the trail. With Howie following her, she walked slowly back to the cabin, opened the door and retrieved her coat and scarf. She moved to her favorite rocker, sat and stared out at the silent clearing. Her chickens had roosted and she could hear their faint squabbling in the coop. Under the extended roof her goats had bedded down on fresh hay.

Those two nannies will need to be milked in the morning. She sighed. *What am I going to do about Milo's proposal?* What did she want? There was a strong appeal about him--steady, gentle, and he loves me. She sensed he'd make a great father. *And his kisses! Wow!* Her body still tingled with the controlled passion she'd felt with him. She then thought about Charlie. LaVerne knew it would hurt her if she married Milo. Would she understand? Would she still be her friend?

LaVerne's thoughts were interrupted by Howie's mate half crawling, half walking across the snow in the yard. Howie jumped off the porch from where he'd been resting at Vernie's feet and ran to her. He then dashed back to LaVerne and whined. Tukoni crawled a few more feet and looked up at her.

"Oh-oh, girl, is it time?" she asked the wolf quietly. A contraction hit and Tukoni whined and licked herself.

Off in a corner of the porch LaVerne had folded and stacked old blankets and soft sacks in preparation for this day. She slowly rose and crossed the porch. Taking the stack into her arms she returned to the steps, quietly talking to the wolf the whole time, as she slowly walked down them.

"It's okay girl. Your puppies are ready to meet the world. If you'll crawl under the cabin you'll be safe. I know it's not exactly a den but it's the best we can offer. Howie, tell her it's safe for her and her babies."

LaVerne got down on her hands and knees and scooped away the snow that had drifted along the corner edge of the cabin's foundation. Pushing the blankets ahead of her, she crawled through the hole and under the house. Howie followed her and then rushed back out to be with Tukoni. When she had finished making a nest for Tukoni, she scooted back out. Rising slowly she walked back up to her chair on the porch and quietly sat down.

Tukoni took a few more steps and lay down again. A milky liquid streaked with blood gushed from her hindquarters. The wolf bolted the remaining distance and disappeared through the hole LaVerne had made under the cabin. Howie followed and LaVerne heard Tukoni growling under the porch. Howie swiftly crawled out and, just outside the doorway to the makeshift den, he sat guarding the entrance.

"Well, Howie my lad, you'll soon be a papa."

Howie turned his head and looked up at LaVerne. She was certain he was smiling at her.

Twenty-nine

A week after Tukoni had given birth to six healthy puppies Charlie rode into the clearing. LaVerne was just coming out of the smokehouse where she had been replenishing the alder wood and checking the meat and salmon strips hanging over the low, smoky fire. Hanging from LaVerne's mouth was a deep orange piece of smoked salmon. Grinning, she tore off a chunk and called out to Charlie.

"Hey stranger. Welcome! Where have you been hiding?"

Charlie rode over to her and dismounted. She took the left over piece of salmon from LaVerne's hand and popped into her mouth. "Ummm…just about right. Another day?"

"Yes, I think so. I don't like it too dry."

"The summer fish wheels did well this year. Everyone I've talked to got more than enough, for the winter, to feed both dogs and folks."

"I have a surprise!" LaVerne's face lit up with pride. "Wait until you see. Come on, we'll put your horse in the corral. Where's Moon?"

"She's somewhere around. Got on a scent back in the woods and off she went."

After Charlie's horse was secured with fresh water and a portion of oats, LaVerne led Charlie over to the cabin.

"Be very slow and quiet. See that hole in the snow there? Peek your head around and look inside. Move very slowly and don't speak."

"What in the world?" Charlie asked as she crept up to the hole and slowly looked under the cabin.

LaVerne's wolf lay there sound asleep. Curled against her side and nursing were six tiny pups. Two black, two silver and two that looked like Howie and Moon. Charlie pulled her head back out and grinned. LaVerne motioned for them to leave and go in the cabin before they spoke.

Closing the cabin door, LaVerne took Charlie's coat and hung both garments on the hooks on the back of the door.

"I'll be damned. You did it. You got that wild beast to trust you enough to birth her litter right here under the cabin."

LaVerne laughed. "I think Howie helped a lot. Tukoni thinks we are her new pack."

"That's what you named her? Tukoni?"

"Yes, Athabascan for 'wolf'. Not very original but I thought it had a pretty, girlie sound."

Charlie tried the word on for size. "Tukoni, yes I like it. What does your wolf think of it?"

LaVerne grinned. "She's too busy with her babies to worry much about what I call her. My job, at the moment, is to bring her meat and fresh water every day and stay out of her way."

"You've got a good start on a dog sled team."

"You think so?"

"Sure, why not? You may never tame Tukoni but her pups will only know this life. As soon as their Mama will let you, start handling them. Blow your breath softly into their noses so they'll imprint on you. If she doesn't carry them off while they're still nursing you'll have a beautiful start on a team."

"I'll do it. I never thought that far ahead. Want some coffee?"

"No, thanks. I stopped by to tell you that the caribou have been spotted moving through. With so much extra snow this year they're moving early. We are packing up and going after them on Saturday. Pack your overnight gear and enough food for at least a three day hunt. I'll bring two of my pack horses. There's a hunting shack up there. We'll bunk together, if that's all right with you, since the rest of the hunting party will be men."

"That's fine. Who's going besides Milo?"

"Stan and Joe. He needs meat for his people and he's a great guide. They will each bring a pack horse."

"What about our animals while we're gone?"

"Joe's brother will stop by our places and feed and water them for us. He'll collect eggs as payment. He's very good with animals but I doubt he will want to come anywhere near your wolf. Will you be okay with it, if he leaves her meat outside the doorway to the den?"

"Yes."

"He's coming by both our places tomorrow to get instructions. You can tell him about Tukoni and her pups so there are no surprises and she can get fed while we're away."

LaVerne frowned. It was a terrible time to leave when the pups were so very young.

"What? You look worried. Don't be." Charlie reassured her. "Joe's people revere the wolf. It will give his brother status to be caring and feeding a wild wolf with a litter."

LaVerne brightened at Charlie's words.

Thirty

Joe, Milo, Stan and Charlie, rode into LaVerne's clearing, at dawn, leading five pack horses. LaVerne was standing by her porch steps tightening the cinch on Junie's saddle. On the steps was a stack of her gear and her Remington rifle.

"Good mornin', Vernie!" Milo said.

"Good morning, everyone."

As LaVerne looked on, amusement lighting her eyes, Charlie stepped down at the same time that Milo dismounted. Together they both walked over to LaVerne's gear and laughed at each other's identical intention of helping Vernie.

"Guess we had the same i'dear," Milo said.

"Four hands will get her stuff loaded twice as fast, I guess." Charlie quipped. "We'll load your gear on one of the pack horses, Vernie, and then we'll be ready to go get some Caribou meat. Did you remember extra ammunition?"

"Yes, I think I remembered everything. Looks like I'm prepared for a month instead of a few days."

"Best to be prepared," Milo told her. "We might be out there several days or a week, depending on the migration, the weather and our aim."

Gear packed and lashed down, LaVerne mounted her horse and they all turned northwest towards the foothills. They would cut straight through the forest, skirting behind Charlie's homestead and come out at the tree line of the Aeolia Hills. LaVerne learned early on that in the lower forty-eight these would be considered mountains. But given Alaska's soaring peaks, they were regarded as hills. When the Caribou began their three thousand mile trek they moved quickly to get to their birthing grounds by spring. So hunters had to be there in time or miss out completely. It was a hard, one day ride to a hunting shack but worth it if they wanted to be dry and warm tonight.

꙳꙳꙳

Several hours later, just at dusk, the five weary riders rode up to a rough, scraggly-looking cabin. It was tiny compared to the cabins back at their homesteads.   It held two sets of bunk beds, a primitive wood stove and a bench built in along one wall. The hunting shack also served as an emergency shelter for any who were lost or delayed along a trail. It was a staunch tradition that when you left a trail shack, such as this one, you left dry firewood inside, a few canned goods, dry beans, and candles for the next visitor.

The men created a hitch line for the horses. They removed saddles and replaced the bridles with halters, tying each horse to the line. Taking coarse blankets from the shack they rubbed down each horse until it was properly cooled. They had packed enough dry hay and oats to last the trip.

Meanwhile the two women opened up the shack, started a fire in the pot-bellied stove and aired out the straw mattresses. On one of the bunks Charlie rolled out her bedding. LaVerne rolled out her bed roll of blankets and furs. Glancing over at her friend, she then stared.

"What in the world is that, Charlie?"

"It's the latest thing. A bag you sleep in. They call it the Euklisia Rug. It's kept me snug in below zero temperatures."

"Where'd you get it?"

"I ordered it out of Boston. My brother wrote me about them. Best thing I've ever purchased."

LaVerne walked over to get a closer look.

"It unzips down the side so you can crawl in; then you zip yourself back up."

"I've never seen the like…" LaVerne marveled.

Soon there was coffee brewing, bacon frying, and gravy heating. Some camp biscuits were browning on top of the stove. With some luck they would be dining on caribou meat tomorrow night.

Outside, the men had moved on to erecting a large tent and starting a bon fire for extra warmth. The two women walked outside to tell them that dinner was ready. They filed in, and as Charlie dished up the food and LaVerne poured the coffee the men sat on the bench and the lower bunks to eat.

There was little conversation. They were all exhausted and they just wanted to eat and find their beds. Tomorrow would be equally taxing. There was no guarantee how far they would have to ride and then hike to find the migrating herds.

As soon as everyone had eaten their fill the men said goodnight and left the cabin. LaVerne and Charlie washed up the tin plates and cups and stoked the fire for the night. Stripping down to their long Johns, they crawled into their bunks. Charlie extinguished the kerosene lantern, the only light coming from the fire in the stove.

"Who owns this shack--sorry. Cabin?" LaVerne asked.

Charlie laughed. "Call it what it is, a shack. We don't know who originally built it. It doesn't belong to anyone in particular. You could say it belongs to all of us. It's used by anyone caught out here in bad weather or as a hunting shack. Did you see that paper nailed to the wall?"

"Yes. With all the names on it."

"It's a record of who was here and when. In case someone gets lost, the people trying to find them will know when they were last here in this shelter. We will also make our entry with the date, our names and when we left to hunt. Before we leave, we'll restock the firewood, leave kerosene, dry matches, and any non-perishable food we might have left over."

Silence reigned for several minutes with just the occasional crackle of the fire.

"'Night, Vernie. Sweet dreams." Charlie whispered, assuming the conversation was over. There was no answer. "Vernie?"

"Are you sleepy, Charlie?"

"I'm tired but not very sleepy. What's up?" Charlie asked.

"Can we talk?"

"Always."

"I need to tell you about something."

"You sound like it's serious."

There was no easy way to say what she needed to say to Charlie. LaVerne plunged in. "Milo asked me to marry him."

"What! When?"

"A couple of weeks ago."

"Did you give him an answer?"

"No, I asked him if I could think about it."

"Well, you need to turn him down. It's ridiculous," Charlie blustered. "He's much too old for you."

"I'm still thinking about it." LaVerne whispered.

Charlie flopped over on her side facing LaVerne's bunk as if she could see her better in the firelight.

"You're actually thinking of marrying him?"

"I want a family, Charlie. He's kind and gentle. Steady."

"You don't love him." She didn't make it a question; it was a statement.

"No--yes--not the way I..." LaVerne stumbled.

"Not the way we love each other, you mean."

"No--not the way I love you. You're the best friend I've ever had."

"So, in spite of how I feel about you, you might marry him?"

"I'm thinking it over--but, yes, I might accept him."

"My God..." Charlie whispered.

"Charlie, I don't want to hurt you. I love you. I don't want to lose you."

"You couldn't."

"You see, the thing is, when I am in doubt about my actions or decisions I try to picture what Mama would say if she was sitting right here with me. And she'd never say loving you--in *that* way--would be right. I doubt that she'd even understand. She's known the love of one good man her entire life. She'd want that for me--and children too.

The silence was deafening in the small cabin for several long minutes.

"I want you to be happy. I was hoping you'd pick me--love me." Charlie sighed. "You won't lose my love or my friendship, Vernie. But, please take your time and think this through. Marriage is forever and forever can be a long, long time."

Thirty-one

Before dawn, the next morning, after a cold breakfast of moose jerky, biscuits and camp coffee, the five hunters rode out. The slopes, where the caribou migrated across, were a five mile ride away. They would leave their horses at the tree line and would circle around, on foot, to some rocky outcrops above the herds. All of their heavy hunting rifles had a range of a half mile for accuracy but they hoped the caribou would travel closer than that.

They spread out when they reached the rocks and, finding semi-comfortable places, sat down to watch and wait. As the sun broke above the mountain peaks behind them a stunning and majestic sight revealed itself. Thousands of animals walked or trotted across the slope below them, stopping to paw at the snow looking for the lichen they fed on.

Leisurely the caribou stopped and started, but were always moving forward to their goal. Each hunter picked a particular animal to shoot because they would only have one chance; perhaps a second but that shot would be at a moving target. The moment the rifles fired the caribou would stampede and disappear.

They preferred to take bulls because most of the does would be pregnant.

LaVerne picked a young bull, rich with winter fat. He was in a group of four, about seven hundred yards away. The moment the animal turned broadside to LaVerne's position she fired. He dropped in his tracks. Four other rifles rang out. Charlie's first shot bagged a huge buck. Milo hit another one. Stan missed and Joe brought down a large doe. LaVerne immediately reloaded and took her second shot at another bull. It sagged to the ground.

Instantly following her second shot the valley rang out with the second attempt from the others. They tried for a second kill but the caribou were racing away from the danger.

The hunters looked over at each other and grinned and, gathering their gear, they hurriedly walked down the hill to where their kills lay. Joe went from animal to animal, and in his native tongue, thanked each animal for giving up their life so that the hunters and their families might have meat and survive the winter.

Standing over her two kills, LaVerne watched Joe. She then knelt down by each of her animals and whispered her own prayer. "You are a beautiful animal, little bedzeyh. Tsin'aen for your life, your meat and your hide. Nothing will go to waste as your sacrifice was great."

Getting to work, she quickly made a cut from the genital area of the animal up to above the ribcage. Entrails and blood gushed out.

"I can help you gut your second animal, Vernie," Stan said as he approached. "I missed my goldurned shot."

"Thanks, Stan, I appreciate it. I'm sure you'll have better luck tomorrow."

Joe walked up and threw down two leg traps. Surprised, LaVerne looked up. "What's this for, Joe?"

"We shall leave a bait heap of guts and maybe catch some fur. Wolverine, lynx, maybe wolf."

"Oh. Will you show me how to set it up?"

"Yes. This will be your first lesson in fur trapping."

Stan straightened up, hands red with blood. He called out to the other hunters. "Figure since I'm the only one who's empty handed, I'll go fetch the horses."

There was a chorus of laughter and agreement as Stan walked off.

Milo, finished dressing his buck, walked over to LaVerne. "That was some shooting for a gal on her first hunt, Vernie."

"Thanks."

"Where'd you learn to shoot like that?"

"My Pa and growing up with five brothers. They were always trying to outshoot me," she laughed at the memories of all the target practice contests that she and her siblings had growing up.

"That shot must'a been at least eight hundred yards. And you took down two. Your Pa must'a taught you good on how to sight a rifle." Milo didn't hide the note of pride in his voice. This was the woman who might be his wife.

"We weren't allowed to touch a gun unless we knew how to break it down, clean it, put it back together and adjust the sights. My Pa was strict."

Charlie walked up. "Nice shooting, Vernie." She turned to Joe. "Ya got a trap for me?"

Joe handed her a trap and she walked back to her kill. LaVerne suspected that Charlie didn't want to be around when she and Milo were together. The painful conversation of last night was too fresh.

Each hunter wrapped the heart and liver from their animal in clean gunny sacking and set them aside. The lungs and other organs joined the pile of guts and then a trap was carefully set with snow sprinkled over the trap to hide it. Joe supervised LaVerne's set and approved.

Stan arrived with all the horses in tow and the group slung the caribou over the backs of the pack animals. Skinning and butchering would take place back at the shack.

JJJ

Several hours later, back at the hunt camp, the horses had been tended to first. Each caribou had been hung by its hind legs from a tree and the hunters got busy skinning the animals. The meat was then quartered and left to hang off the ground and away from predators that might be looking for an easy meal. The overnight temperatures would freeze the meat thus preserving it.

Charlie and LaVerne sliced fresh Caribou liver and onions and were frying up enough for everyone. The coffee pot produced a fragrant and mouthwatering aroma and the men's bellies groaned in harmony as they finished up the last of the butchering.

Milo opened the shack's door and peered in.

"Sure smells good, ladies. When's it gonna be ready? We're about half starved out here."

"It'll be ready when it's ready!" Charlie snapped at him. "We'll call ya in when it's time. Now get!"

Milo, frowning at Charlie's tone, glanced at Vernie, then made a quick exit.

"It's not like you to speak to your friends that way, Charlie," LaVerne said after he had left.

Charlie turned and glared at LaVerne. LaVerne flushed and dipped her head, focusing on the frying meat.

The next morning the hunters set out again before dawn. With any luck at all they would bag more animals and help Stan get his caribou. There was no limit to what they could kill but they were subsistence hunters and LaVerne knew, from Joe's teachings, not one of them would dream of taking more than they needed for their families and the village.

In the case of Joe, who was hunting for an entire village, any meat that wasn't needed by the other hunters would go to the community of Tanana. They were also limited by the weight their pack horses could safely carry out.

Like the day before the men and women were in position as dawn broke. As the sun rose, mists swirled in the valley below. The caribou sprinkled the hill side and some were only visible by their antlers rising above the foggy mist. They waited and watched hoping the fog would thin enough to see their targets.

There was a sudden break in the fog and, on a silent signal from Joe, all the hunters took aim and fired. Three bulls and two cows dropped. The caribou that could be seen vanished into the mists below and the hillside was suddenly empty and silent.

The hunters walked down to their kills and set to work. Joe moved off to where they had hunted yesterday and checked each trap they had set the day before. He was satisfied to see that Charlie's trap had a wolverine in it. His own trap was empty but Milo's had a lynx and LaVerne's another wolverine. He quickly dispatched the two wolverine with his pistol. Fur was a vital part of earning extra cash for the homesteaders.

"Joe, if you want to go and get our horses, I will dress your bull," Milo suggested.

"Thank you, friend." Joe said as he turned in the direction of where they had tethered the horses. He stuffed the fur into a saddlebag. There would be time enough to thaw them out and dress and skin them back at camp.

"Stan, your luck was good today," LaVerne hollered over to him, as she gutted her bull. "I want you to take this one for your family. I have too much meat for just one person."

"Thanks, Vernie. I sure will be glad to take you up on that offer."

An hour later they were headed back to camp with heavily laden pack horses. It was a lot of work skinning and butchering five more animals. Most satisfying was the knowledge that they had not only filled their own larders with meat but they were assured that the entire village would eat this winter.

Charlie and LaVerne sliced off big caribou steaks and after browning them in hot fat, left them to simmer in their own juices for several hours. Par-boiled potatoes and carrots would be added later.

Since Joe was the quickest and best at preparing fur, he gutted and carefully skinned all the fur bearing animals while Milo and Stan butchered Joe's caribou cow. The men didn't mention it but they were all secretly pleased that the cows killed had not been pregnant.

By late afternoon the butchered meat hung in the trees, the fur was stretched on poles, and the horses were watered and fed. Hobbled, they were allowed to browse around the camp for whatever they could find to graze on under the snow.

Melted snow provided hot water and a way for everyone to wash the gore from their hands and arms. When they all had a tin plate heaped with tender caribou meat and vegetables they sat around the bond fire and relived the successful hunt.

"You're quite the sharp shooter," Stan told LaVerne. "If you ever get bored with homesteadin' you can start your own Wild West show like Buffalo Bill did."

LaVerne laughed. "Thanks, Stan, but I'll stick to this life. It suits me very well." She smiled warmly at Milo over the flames of the campfire but when she tried to catch Charlie's eye she found her friend concentrating on her dinner plate.

"Mother Earth smiled on our hunting trip. She saw her children helping each other and feeding her People." Joe told them. "She brought the herds back to us today so that there would be enough meat for everyone."

After they had each eaten their fill, one by one they trouped into the cabin to put their plates in the pot of hot water simmering on the stove. Charlie and Milo suddenly found themselves alone by the fire.

"I guess you're pretty pleased with yourself, huh Milo?" Charlie asked.

Milo turned to her. "What burr got under your saddle blanket, all of a sudden? You been growling at me for two days."

"I got just one thing to say to you. If LaVerne is dumb enough to accept you, you'd better be good to her every damn day of your life or I'll come gunning for you. And don't make the mistake of thinking that I'm joking with you."

Milo's eyebrows met his hairline in surprise. "So that's what's got you all riled up, huh? LaVerne told you I asked her to marry me."

Milo was met with stony silence.

"Listen, Charlie, I know you love her. I'd have to be blind to not see what's between you. But, I love her too. And I can give her children, God willin'. Can you?"

Tears of rage filled Charlie's eyes and just as she was about to tear into Milo some of the others returned to the fire with fresh coffee in their cups. LaVerne followed carrying two cups and handed one to Charlie.

"I noticed you let your coffee get cold."

Charlie swiped at her eyes and reached for the offered cup. "Thanks, much appreciated." But she couldn't meet LaVerne's eyes and suddenly rose to walk to the edge of camp and the tethered horses.

"So what's the plan?" LaVerne asked the group.

"Get a good night's sleep and head out in the morning?" Milo asked the group.

"At dawn I will ride back and check the fur traps I set today." Joe said.

"Good plan, Joe." Charlie had recovered her composure somewhat and returned to the fire. "We'll break camp, load the horses, replenish the cabin and by the time you get back we'll be ready to start for home."

With those words Charlie turned and walked off into the night. LaVerne gathered up cups and went into the cabin to start washing the dishes. Milo followed her.

"Need any help?" he asked as he walked in.

"Thanks but no. Charlie should be back any minute."

"I don't think so." Milo said as he picked up a piece of toweling and began to wipe the dishes dry as LaVerne washed them. "She ain't too happy with me right now, asking you to marry me."

LaVerne sighed. "Yes, I know."

"I just want you to know that I know you two have a special kind'a friendship and that I will never stand between you and that. I know that you love her. But I also know that there is no limit to how much we can love and I hope someday you will come to love me too."

"Oh, Milo…"

"No. You don't have to explain or answer. Just know that I will be good to you. We'll have a family someday and I will devote myself to you and any children we are lucky enough to have."

LaVerne placed her soapy hands on Milo's shoulders and leaned up to kiss his whiskery face.

"Thank you."

The cabin door suddenly swung open and Charlie stood there. She took one look at the guilty expression on LaVerne's face and turned around, slamming the door as she left.

"Oh dear."

"She's gonna have to get used to me being in your life, Vernie, especially if your answer is yes." Milo studied her face, "Is it yes, Vernie?"

"Yes, Milo, my answer is yes. I want to marry you."

Milo laid down the towel and gathered LaVerne into his arms. He kissed her sweetly and only when she responded did he deepen it.

Raising his head he told her, "You'll never be sorry, Vernie. I will love you forever."

And with that promise he kissed her again.

"Come on, let's tell everyone." Milo said as he grabbed her hand and led her to the door of the cabin and outside to the fire.

"Listen, everybody, I got an announcement to make."

Joe and Stan looked up expectantly. Charlie was glaringly missing from the group.

"Vernie just agreed to marry me!" Milo crowed.

Joe and Stan jumped up and strode over to Milo, each taking their turn at pumping his hand and pounding him on the back. Then it was LaVerne's turn and while Stan picked her up in a bear hug and twirled her around Joe was more sedate in his congratulations. He laid his hand gently on top of her head.

"Mother is pleased with your choice of a man, Miss Vernie. She will give you and Milo many children. You will not want for anything under his care. I am deeply happy for you both. "

Stan had returned to Milo. "You old dog. You finally getting' hitched? After all these years."

"Waitin' for the right woman," Milo smiled at LaVerne over Stan's shoulder. "I found her."

Charlie stood in the darkness by the trees and watched the celebration around the camp fire. Tears silently ran down her face.

Thirty-two

They had been gone five days. As they rode by each of their own homesteads they off loaded a share of caribou meat and hung it out of harm's way. Their last stop would be the village. They had enough meat left over to insure that no one in Tanana would go hungry this winter.

Now Charlie and LaVerne rode up the trail to their respective cabins. Since the night of Milo's announcement of their pending wedding, Charlie had been, for the most part, stoically silent. When they reached the final fork in the trail, Charlie stopped and turned her horse toward LaVerne's.

"Guess I'll see you later then," she said, not meeting LaVerne's eyes.

"Charlie--please don't leave me on that note."

"There's not a whole lot more to say, Vernie. You've made your decision."

"Yes--yes I have. But I want us to still be friends. I don't want to lose that. Can you try to be happy for me?"

"You won't lose my friendship, I told you," Charlie finally looked at LaVerne. "But I need some time. Alone. I'll see you in a couple of days." Wheeling her horse around she rode off, not giving LaVerne a chance to say anything more.

LaVerne sighed and rode on toward her own place. A quarter of a mile from her cabin her dog, Howie came tearing down the trail, barking a greeting. He jumped up with one paw on

LaVerne's stirrup and whined. Leaning down she gave him a good scratch behind the ears.

"Hey, boy, how are your pups doin'?"

Howie ran back up the trail and then back down again dancing around LaVerne's mare.

"God, it's so good to be home." She said to herself as she stepped down and opened the corral gate, then leading her horse into the enclosure.

Tending to the horse, she made certain that Junie's hooves were clear of any pebbles and that she had fresh water and a flake of hay. Carrying her tack, she let herself out of the enclosure and walked to the shed where she stored her saddle and bridle. Waiting for her, Howie lay outside the hole where the wolf and her pups were still denned up. *At least I hope that Tukoni has not moved her babies.* She'd check on her with an offering of some meat and fresh water.

LaVerne mounted the steps of her cabin with Howie on her heels. She was pleasantly surprised to find a low burning fire in the cook stove, just enough to keep the chill out of the house. Bless Joe's brother!

Leaving her coat and hat on, she got two tin bowls out. She pumped water into one and cut up some meat in the other. Retracing her steps she returned to the den entrance under the cabin and speaking softly, she poked her head in. There lying on the bed of old blankets was Tukoni. The tip of her tail beat a tiny tattoo on the ground.

"Hello there, girl. How have you been? I'm so happy to see you and your babies. Look how they've grown--I haven't been gone that long and they've doubled in size. You are such a good mama."

LaVerne continued to praise and talk to the wolf as she set down the meat and water nearby. She then lay down, facing Tukoni, and watched the puppies for a while. With a contented groan, the wolf lay back down on her side so that the pups had easy access to her milk.

An hour later LaVerne jerked awake. *Oh, for goodness sakes, I fell asleep under my cabin. Damn! It's cold.* She wiggled back out the hole and stood up, brushing straw, dirt and twigs off her coat. With a panting grin Howie looked up at her in approval.

"Yes, I know you like me to spend time with your babies, but it's too cold for me to sleep with them too," she laughed. "Come on. You hungry?"

Howie jumped up and followed LaVerne into the cabin.

Thirty-three

The cabin porch was festooned with cedar boughs trimmed in red ribbon and pine cones. A huge bon fire roared in front of the cabin and rough tables had been set up around the clearing. LaVerne and Milo had decided on a Christmas wedding and it was the morning of their nuptials. People were still arriving, most carrying a covered dish or pot of food and a wedding present.

A huge cauldron of Caribou stew simmered at the edge of the fire. Moose steaks were ready to throw into skillets to fry up and chunks of salmon were baking in Dutch ovens. Milo, visiting with their guests, had been banned from seeing his bride until she stepped out onto the porch for the ceremony.

Stan and Joe's wives and Charlie were in the cabin with LaVerne putting the final touches on her bridal attire: her best and only dress, fur mukluks that Joe had made for her and a new parka, trimmed in wolverine fur.

"Is the village pastor here yet?" LaVerne nervously asked.

Charlie went to the window, "Yes, he's out there talking to Joe."

LaVerne joined her and peeked out between the curtains, "My, oh my, that's quite a crowd."

"No one is going to miss a party."

"Charlie…" She turned to her friend and spoke quietly so the other women could not hear her.

"Thank you for being my maid of honor, in spite of how you feel about my marrying Milo."

"Who else but me? I just want you to be certain that this is what you want to do," Charlie replied.

"Yes, this is what I want."

"Then I'm happy for you--and for Milo too. He's a lucky man."

Stan's wife called out, "It's time, Vernie, if you're ready to wed that no-good scoundrel."

Laughing, the three women gathered around LaVerne and escorted her outside to the porch. Howler bounded up, a red ribbon tied around his neck. He grinned up at his mistress.

"You ready to walk me down the aisle, Howie?" she asked the dog.

Milo and the pastor moved to an arbor of twigs, pine cones and red ribbons that some of the women had created. The Reverend took his place at the back of it and Milo stood just inside. Joe, as his best man, stood at Milo's side.

The women walked LaVerne down the steps and across the clearing until only Charlie and Howie escorted her to join Milo. LaVerne passed her bridal bouquet of cedar boughs, pine cones and more red ribbon to Charlie. She brushed her lips across her friend's cheek before stepping next to Milo.

The Reverend began, "Dearly beloved and friends, we are gathered here in the sight of God to join…"

In addition to the normal words spoken at every wedding, LaVerne and Milo had decided that they wanted to say a few original words to each other. Surprisingly, it had been Milo's idea and spoke first.

"LaVerne Guyer, my beloved, you have done me the great honor of becoming my wife. This is my pledge to you: for the rest of my life I will dedicate myself to your happiness and wellbeing. When we are blessed with children I will love and care for them above all else. I love you so much."

LaVerne's last doubts fled before Milo's heart-felt words. "Milo Robbins, the first time you rode into my clearing to welcome me the thought that came to my mind was, 'he has kind eyes'. I wasn't wrong. Your kindness is always there at the forefront, not only for me but for the whole community."

The gathered friends and family mumbled their agreement. "You have shown me what it means to be truly cherished by someone. I'm not too good at words unless they're lyrics so I wrote you a song--a wedding song."

Joe stepped up and handed LaVerne her guitar. A sole harmonica quietly joined her as she sang.

I see the mountains
I think of your strength
I see the river
I think of your stead-fast-ness

I think of you--
I think only of you

I see the night lights
I think of your joy
I see a herd of caribou
I think of your loyalty
I see the forest
I know your love is forever

I think of you--
I think only of you

When the final lyric had been sung, there wasn't a dry eye in the clearing. Howie caused guests to laugh when he howled along with the higher notes.

At the end of the ceremony Joe stepped up and draped Milo and LaVerne's shoulders with a woven cloth that his mother had made. He spoke a blessing in Athabascan over their heads, praying for warm shelter, plentiful game, healthy children and peace all the days of their lives. And at that moment Charlie knew that she had lost the love of her life.

After the wedding party and guests had stuffed themselves with caribou, moose, salmon, casseroles and strawberry-rhubarb and apple pie, they men threw down some sheets of plywood and they danced until the moon set.

Thirty-four

LaVerne couldn't believe it. At Milo's suggestion their wedding trip was to visit her family in Washington State. They had left her homestead two days after the wedding and began the arduous trip by dog sled to Fairbanks where they stayed the night and visited LaVerne's old boss and her friends. Joe and his uncle had taken them and it had been high adventure traveling on the frozen rivers and making camp over night before they reached the outpost.

A train to the port city of Anchorage, they then boarded a ship that had taken them to Seattle. The final leg had been by train again to Olympia when Pa and Mama had met them. Retracing her steps that had taken her to her homestead, a few short years ago, gave her an eerie sense of déjà vu.

LaVerne was confident that her decision to marry Milo had been a good one. Milo was loving and steady. Their intimate life was good. Milo was a gentle and thoughtful lover. Without words he seemed to understand and accept that she had a special bond and relationship with Charlie. She liked and respected her husband and enjoyed his quiet company. She felt certain, that with time, she would come to love him with her whole heart.

Two weeks before they wed LaVerne had received a packet of letters from her mother. In them Mama explained how Violet and Phillip had lost everything; their house, his business. Violet had kicked Phillip out because of his gambling.

Mama was leaving for San Francisco in a couple of weeks…

My dearest daughter,

I have finally become accustom to not receiving any letters from you during the winter months. It's hard to imagine four or five feet of snow with temperatures in the minus zero range when our winters here in Washington consist of lots of rain, fog and temps around thirty on a very cold day.

But, happily last week I received a packet of three letters from you. You have become quite the pioneer woman, shooting wild animals for food, gardening, panning for gold, trapping fur. My goodness, is there anything you can't do?

My news is not so happy. Violet's husband, Phillip, has let his gambling get completely out of control. As a result they have lost their beautiful Victorian home and his two dry-cleaning stores. The only reason why they have not lost the bar and restaurant too is that it is in Violet's name. Smart girl, as it turns out!

About three weeks ago, your niece, Doris showed up here at the farm, alone. She looked like death warmed over and I have been getting her healthy with lots of sleep, good food and fresh air. She and her brother, Jackie, have had a rough time of it. Doris informs me that Violet is pregnant. Not by Phillip but by some sailor she met. What am I going to do with that girl?

I leave in a week for San Francisco to see for myself what Violet has been up to. Your sister has a lot to answer for. I plan on bringing the two children and your sister back here to the farm. And I do not intend to take no for an answer!

Lillas and Bill are back from England. Everyone, Ivah and Arthur, Gladys, her husband

Al, Lillas and Bill, Earl and his wife are all coming to the farm for a reunion once I get Violet and the children back here and settled.

Please! Please consider coming home for a visit. Bring Milo so that we can meet him. He sounds like such a lovely man by your descriptions, and so good to you.

Your Pa and the boys will be in and out so we will be stacked like cord wood but we always were, right?

I can't think that we would have this reunion without you and Milo. Please say yes. Always sending love, your Mama

Part Three

Coming Back to the Home Place

Thirty-five

LaVerne and Milo stepped off the train in Olympia and into the arms of her mother and father. There was much hugging and back slapping for the bride and groom and then they and their luggage were whisked off to Pa's car.

"My stars, Pa, what happened to the rest of your car?" LaVerne exclaimed.

"It's supposed to look like that, little girl," Pa chuckled. "You're looking at Mr. Ford's Model TT pick-up. They put in a bed for haulin'. Perfect for the farm."

Milo walked around the vehicle admiring everything about it, "this is really somethin', Mr. Guyer."

"First of all, best begin by calling me Pa or Levi, son. And yes it is that. One ton capacity with a heavier frame and rear axle. And it drives like a dream.

"Boys, you can play cars later," Mama playfully scolded. "We need to get these tired newly-weds home."

They all piled into the front seat after stowing the bags in the back flatbed.

An hour and several bumpy roads later they pulled into the home place. Two lovely women ran out the back door of the farm house and rushed to the truck. Milo stepped down and helped LaVerne out. Her sisters, Lillas and Ivah grabbed her and hugged her until she cried for mercy.

"Vernie, my God, it's really you! Look at you, all grown up," Ivah shouted.

"Your hair is so short, Vernie. And you've grown into a beauty--who'd a thought?" Lillas crowed.

"Daughters! Where are your manners? Let me introduce you to LaVerne's new husband, Milo," Mama said.

Lillas and Ivah immediately turned and hugged Milo like they'd been family for years. The tips of Milo's ears got red and he looked at LaVerne beseechingly.

"Okay, you two. Get off my husband," LaVerne laughed.

"Take the bags out of the truck and let's go inside, shall we?" Mama ordered.

Arm around the waist of her mother, LaVerne turned and they walked toward the house. "Where's Vi, Mama?"

"She's in Olympia getting some legal things done and sending a wire to her manager at the restaurant. She'll be back tonight."

"You know Vi, Vernie, business first, last, and always." Lillas quipped.

"I really dislike that nick name, Lillas. I gave you girls the prettiest names I could find and you girls shorten everything! Really! Vi instead of Violet. It's so--abrupt."

"Oh, Mama, you can be so Victorian at times. It's almost 1930. Language changes. Everything's faster. At home my friends call me Lil. Women are modern. It only took me five hours to get down here from Seattle--and I drove myself."

"I guess you're right. Anyway, back to Vi. She writes that Phillip will not stop gambling. She was afraid he'd gamble away the restaurant even though it was not his to use as collateral."

As they chatted they gathered around the huge kitchen table and Mama filled the tea pot with fresh, hot water and set it to steep.

"She would never let anything come between her and her restaurant--much less some man. She's a shrewd business woman," Ivah told them.

Milo looked at LaVerne and raised his eyebrows. She shrugged, "I told you…"

"But, he's the father of her children, for heaven's sake." Mama exclaimed.

"How will she manage with two little ones and no husband?" Ivah wondered aloud while she set out tea mugs, milk and sugar. "I can't imagine my life without Arthur."

"Ivah, there's pound cake in the larder and cookies in the tin. Get them out, will you?" Mama went on, "She says she has hired a girl to keep house and watch the kids while she runs the bar. During the slow times, she's taking in sewing and mending. Imagine! Mending for a bunch of women in the red light district. Whores!" She glanced at Milo, "Excuse my language."

"Mama! Such language! Whatever will my new brother-in-law think? You shock all of us."

Mama's children all laughed at her blushes.

"Well! That's what they are. And one of my daughters is associating with them! That's the kind of modern woman I can do without, thank you very much. She says not to worry...like I cannot not worry!" She scoffed.

"You know Vi, Mama, she always lands on her feet. She'll be okay," Lillas said.

"Well, I am just happy I followed my instincts and went and got her and Jackie. I wish you girls could have seen the state Doris was in when she suddenly appeared on my doorstep. She's had a hard time."

Mama brought the large tea pot to the table and placed a homemade cozy over it.

"LaVerne let's get your bags into your room and then we'll all sit down and have a long visit."

Milo jumped up and grabbed their bags. Following the two women down the hall he could hear Vernie's sisters begin to whisper.

"Isn't he just the most handsome..?"

"So tall and what a physique!"

Milo hurried to catch up with his wife and his new mother-in-law just in time to hear LaVerne scolding her mother.

"Mama! We *cannot* take yours and Pa's room. It wouldn't be right."

"Your Pa and I agreed. The newlyweds deserve the largest room and the most comfortable bed. Your Pa will bunk out in the barn with the other boys and I will sleep in one of the girls' rooms."

"But, Ma…"

"No buts, it's decided."

Milo followed them into a lovely, homey bedroom that smelled of beeswax and cinnamon. He piled their bags under the window out of the way. Besides the four poster bed there was a beautiful antique dresser with a pitcher and basin and next to it was a stack of fresh towels. A little vase sat to the side filled with green salal and red berries from the forest.

In the corner was a huge rocking chair with a homemade quilt hanging down the back. Milo was drawn to the fine workmanship of the carving and stroked his rough hands over the patterns.

"Levi made that for me before our first child was born, Milo. He carved every bit of it."

"It's lovely, Mrs. Guyer."

Mama crossed over to her new son, "Milo, if we are to get to know each other I can't have you calling me Mrs. Anything. You have your pick of Ma, like my boys call me, or Mother, or Mama. My last choice would be Mother Guyer."

Milo blushed, "I'd be honored to call you Ma…"

Mama hugged him tight for a moment and then led the way back to the kitchen.

As the three rejoined the family at the table Ivah was telling the rest of them a story. She hadn't changed much from her younger, hellion days.

"...just the other day, Arthur came home just as I was coming in from a day digging in my garden. I was in my shorts and covered with dirt. Arthur told me an important client was dropping by with some papers, so I said I would just hide in the kitchen and finish making dinner. About half an hour later, I heard the door bell and then a little while later, I heard the front door close.

Well, I'd heard so much about this particular client, I just had to get a look at him. He's a millionaire, you know. So--hang on to your hat--I got down on my hands and knees and crawled to the front dining room window so I could get a good look without being seen. Meanwhile, the important client was still sitting on the sofa in the parlor, watching me sneak across the floor."

Laughter burst out around the table.

"I heard a chuckle. I turned around so quickly I landed on my butt and there he was, sitting there grinning at me. It turns out that it was the paperboy who had come to the door to collect and the client hadn't left at all."

"Oh, my." Mama squeaked out between chuckles. "What did you do?"

"Well, we all had a good laugh and the client stayed for dinner."

"Your husband is a patient man." Mama said as she poured LaVerne and Milo fresh tea. "Cake, Milo?"

"Yes, Ma'am, don't mind if I do."

The kitchen door crashed open and a beautiful lavender-eyed beauty rushed in.

"I'm home! Is LaVer…" She spotted her sister and ran around the table. "Vernie! You're here. My God, you're all grown up!"

LaVerne had stood up as her sister crashed into her. She hugged her and began to cry. "Vi…I've been so worried about you. How are you? How're the kids?"

"Cut it out, Vernie! You're this tough pioneer woman and they don't cry. I'm fine. Better than fine!"

Milo rose and handed his red handkerchief to his wife.

"Hello, handsome, you must be my new brother-in-law." Vi stuck out her hand to shake his. "Well, Vernie, it looks like you done all right. Where'd you find this fine looking specimen?" She turned back to Milo. "Any more men that look like you up there in the wilderness?"

Milo blushed to his hairline.

"Lay off, Vi. He's taken and you're embarrassing him."

"Violet Marie, stop pestering the man and have some tea," her mother scolded.

Vi flounced into a chair and held a clean cup out so her mother could pour her some tea. "How's life in Alaska, Vernie? It took me some time to forgive you for sneaking away that night. You worried all of us terribly, especially Mama, until we got your first letter."

LaVerne opened her mouth to apologize or defend herself or something, but Mama stepped into the tension that filled the air.

"Violet, by-gones be by-gones. It's been years and we don't need to rake all that up. She's here now and on her wedding trip. That's what's important." She paused, "How did your business go in town?"

"Swell." She turned to her father, "Pa, I wanted your lawyer to look over the ownership and title papers to my building and make certain it was ironclad. The last thing I need is for Phil to come back around and try to claim an interest. Then I sent a wire to my manager, Clive, at the club."

"I'm impressed, Vi." LaVerne told her sister. "You're a success in your own right down there in the big city. A restaurant and bar. I don't know how you do it. Mama said in one of her letters that *the* Rudolph Valentino was actually in there one night."

Vi laughed. Nothing made her happier than talking about her bar. "All true. And you wouldn't believe what I saw. Turns out the Latin lover had a *boyfriend*."

There were gasps around the table.

"You mean like…he's queer?"

Ivah had always put a fine point on it, LaVerne remembered. Nothing subtle about her older sister.

"Ivah!" Mama exclaimed.

"I'm just saying what I saw--the night they commandeered my bar it was a party of around six men and no women and they were all dancing with each other," Vi giggled.

"Oh, my stars!" Mama said. "What kind'a place are you running down there, Violet?"

"The kind'a place that makes me money, Mama. I don't care who they are as long as they leave their money with me by the end of the night. I don't allow fighting and everyone knows that they have to act civilized at all times or they get the boot. It's a high class joint."

"What about your husband, Vi? Did he work there too?" Vernie asked.

Vi huffed. "No, up until a year ago he had his own thriving businesses in dry-cleaning. Then he lost it all in a card game or a bet on the horses--I'm not sure which. I wouldn't let him near my club."

"Where is he now?" Lillas asked.

"Don't know, don't care. I divorced him six months ago. It's final this time. He was gambling every penny I made at the restaurant. He just wouldn't quit."

"But, divorce, Vi? That's against everything we've been raised to believe." Lillas replied.

Vi turned on her sister, fire in her eyes, "Don't you judge me, sister-dear. We can't all have a quiet, boring lump like Richard!"

"How dare you? Richard is not a lump! You should talk, you're a *divorced woman*!"

Vi rose and started around the table toward Lillas just as if they were teenaged girls again."

"Now, girls, don't bicker. Sit down, Violet. Couldn't you reason with Phillip, dear?"

Vi sat in her chair and glared at Lillas. "I've reasoned with him for over fourteen years. He keeps promising he'll quit gambling and then some dog or horse comes along and he can't resist. I was sick of it."

"But, divorce?" Mama was clearly shocked.

"He lost our house, Mama. My beautiful home. One night some thug from the San Fran Family actually walked in, with his bim, and wanted a tour of *his* new house."

"What's a bim?" Vernie asked.

Vi ignored her sister and continued, "Phil had lost it to him in a card game. It took every political favor I could call in to keep the mob from the door of my club. They almost took it away from me."

"Oh, my." Mama whispered.

The rest of the family looked at Violet as if she had grown two heads or something. The mob? Politicians? Violet had traveled far from the gangly girl who played sports at the local high school.

"What's the San Fran Family, Vi?" LaVerne asked.

"The mafia, the mob," Vi scoffed. "You really *do* live in the back of beyond, Vernie."

"And what's a bim?" Lillas asked.

"His moll, his girlfriend, his piece of as…"

"Violet Marie!   That's quite enough of that language!" Mama cried.

Milo covered a laugh with a cough. LaVerne poked him in the ribs.

"So, where are the kids?" Vernie asked.

"What is this? The third degree?" Vi asked.

"Vi, for heaven's sake. Please watch your tone. Your sister asked an innocent question." Mama turned to Vernie. "The children are staying with my friend Judy, do you remember her?   She's got grandchildren about Doris and Jackie's age. They'll be back Christmas morning."

"Are you staying here now? Selling your business."

"Sell the business! The restaurant that I have put my life's blood into? Built from less than nothing? Grew it from a neighborhood speakeasy to the fine dining establishment it is today?   Really, Vernie, what a thing to ask."

"How are the children faring, with their dad being gone and all the upheaval?" Lillas asked.

"Jackie's like a little duck, everything rolls off his back."

"And Doris?" Ivah asked.

"Oh, you know her--well, I guess you don't. She's thirteen and hates me."

"Violet Marie, I don't know you anymore. Your children living with strangers--." She dribbled off as she realized what she'd accidently disclosed and hurriedly spoke again to Milo over Vi's outburst,

"Jesus Christ, Ma!"

"I don't know what you must think! I didn't raise my children this way."

"Mrs. Guyer--Ma--don't give it a thought. I know families can be complex. Perhaps I should go outside," He rose. "Yes, I'd like to look around." And with that, he fled out the door.

"Mama, why'd you blurt out my business like that to everyone?" Vi cried.

"I'm sorry, daughter, it just slipped out," Mama said.

"For Chrissakes, Ma!"

"Watch your tongue, girl. That's your mother you're swearing at," Pa scolded. "I think I'll join Milo." He rose and went outside.

"Well, now that it's out I'll tell you, missy, I never heard of such a thing. A child of mine abandoning her own children. I'm ashamed of you, Violet."

"What the hell are you two talking about? What strangers? Where did Jackie and Doris go?" Ivah was nonplussed.

"I had to farm out the kids for a little while what with Phil's trouble and the mob breathing down my neck. They're back with me now so no harm done."

"Well, that's a matter of opinion, Violet." Mama chided. "Doris had a rough time of it."

"Mama...don't say that. I got them back. It was only for six months."

"What did Doris and Jackie say? When you told them...when you left them." Tears glistened in her eyes. Lillas, the eternal mother, asked.

"Jackie was so sweet--he took my face into his little hands and said, 'Don't worry, Mommy. I understand. I'll work hard for Mrs. Daley. I'll be here when you come for me.'"

"Who's Mrs. Daley?"

"She's the lady who owns the farm where the kids were. Fresh air, good food, it was almost like a vacation for the kids." Vi said.

"Oh, my stars! And Doris?"

"Oh, well, you know teenagers. She's still hating on me."

"With good reason," Mama said darkly.

"What outrageous behavior, Vi, and all because of a building, a business?" LaVerne was shocked. "Dumping your kids because they were too much work? I knew you were selfish growing up, but it seems you've stayed that way. I'm ashamed of you!"

"Oh, shut up! You don't call sneaking away in the dead of night, scaring us all half to death, not selfish? You have no room to talk so just shut..."

"Girls! Stop it this instant!"

Vi and LaVerne's mouths slammed shut. When Mama used that tone, no matter how old they were, it was time to stop the latest sibling brawl.

"Besides, I've got some other, bigger news..." Vi gloated. She turned to her mother, "I'm pregnant, Mama."

"Oh, but that's wonderful. Does Philip know?"

"No! No, you don't understand. I've met the most wonderful man. It's his baby."

"I think I'm going to be sick," Lillas said.

"I don't understand. Philip's gone, and you're still married to him..."

"No, not any longer--I told you."

"...and you're having a baby with...with?"

"Yep. With Jay--William J. Woods. Oh, Mama wait until you meet him!"

"What in the world are you thinking, Vi?   Who is this guy?" Lillas almost shouted.

"None of your business. I'm having this conversation with Mama."

"You're right. I can't stand to hear any more of it. I'll be upstairs." She rose and stalked from the room.

"Now, Mama, don't look so shocked."

"But, Violet, I don't understand. When did all this happen?"

"About eight months ago. Phillip and I had this horrible fight about his gambling and I threw him out. He's been gone since then. I don't even know where he is. Probably hiding out somewhere until the mob stops looking for him."

"But, this man--this Jay person--where did you meet him?"

"Oh, he's been a regular customer at the bar for a long time. He always flirted with me, but then so do most of my customers. I didn't think too much of it. Then one night Phillip and I were arguing in the back storeroom and I guess they could hear us out in the bar. I came out to the front and my eyes were all red from crying, I was so mad! Anyway, Jay noticed and said, 'Come on, we're going for a walk'. He took me by the elbow, grabbed my coat and walked me out."

"Well, I never..." Mama murmured.

"Oh, Mama, he was so wonderful. We walked and talked for hours. He was so understanding and sweet."

LaVerne piped up, not being able to stay quiet another minute, "But, who *is* he? What does he do for a living?"

Vi turned to her sister, eager to brag about her new man, "Like I said, his name is William J. Woods, but he goes by Jay. He's in the Navy--a chief warrant officer. Oh, you should see him--he's this big Irishman, black hair and blue eyes--he's so handsome. And he doesn't gamble at all."

"And you're pregnant? Are you sure?"

"Yes, Mama. About nine weeks. We're so in love."

"But, how? I mean...you're married to another man."

"Mama, I'm not. I told you Phil and I are divorced. I know you don't want to hear that, but it's done and final. As to how? The usual way, Mama."

"Don't be crude, daughter."

"We went camping up in the Sierra Mountains and there was this beautiful full moon--you felt like you could reach out and touch it. We tried to be careful--I didn't have my diaphragm with me..."

"Violet, please!"

"Sorry. Anyway, I lay there in Jay's arms and we looked at the moon and you know what he said?"

"I dare not imagine." Mama sighed.

"He said, 'Vi, if we make a baby tonight, I hope her life is as beautiful as this moonlit night'. Her life, he said. He's sure it's a girl. It was so wonderful, I cried."

"Sounds just like an Irishman! Full of malarkey. I don't know, child. You're thirty-nine--is it safe, you having a baby at that age?"

"My doctor says it's a little old but I'm healthy and the baby is doing fine."

"And what kind of father will this Jay person be--you met him in a bar."

"Where else would I meet someone? I'm at my bar working sixteen hours a day. I didn't meet Phil in a bar and he gambled our lives away!"

"Well, what's done is done. What are your plans? Does he want to marry you?"

"Of course he wants to marry me! What a question. He has shipped out for two months --maneuvers, or something. When he gets back we'll get married. It'll all work out, you'll see, Mama."

Lillas walked back into the kitchen, wearing her coat and hat. She crossed to her mother and kissed her forehead. "I'd best start back, Mama. I don't like to drive alone at night."

Mama patted her arm, "I know, dear. Be careful, won't you?"

"Well don't you want to know the dirty details, Lilla'? Aren't you the least bit curious about my illicit affaire?"

"It might surprise you, Vi, but no, I don't want the details. To board your own children out and run off with some sailor? And now you're pregnant? My God, what were you thinking? Have you completely lost your mind?"

"You were listening!"

"I was not."

"Were too. How did you know Jay's a sailor?"

"Your voice carries..."

"You were listening to every word, you big snoop."

"Girls..." Mama said in a warning tone.

"But, Mama--she's always so sanctimonious! With her perfect husband, her perfect daughter..." Vi complained.

"I am *not* sanctimonious. Mama." Lillas whined.

"Girls! Stop it this instant!"

♈♈♈

Later that night Milo and LaVerne were cuddling in bed after a mutually satisfying bout of love making.

"Well, my darling husband, are you ready to head for the hills after hearing all about Vi's business? Vernie asked.

"Your family is really something, Vernie." Milo chuckled. "Has your sister always been like that?"

"She's always been the star in her own little show. Things come to her easily and she just expects everything to go her way. I'm certain Phil's antics and lack of responsibility was a shocking reality check for her."

"I can't approve of her ditchin' her kids like that. What mother does that?"

"I'm so ashamed you had to hear that story. She's really gone too far. I will be surprised if Mama doesn't take another layer of skin off her."

"Your other two sisters seem to have pretty normal lives. Any skeletons there that I should be warned about," He laughed.

"No, Ivah and Lillas are the calm responsible sisters. Ivah's always been a prankster but she doesn't hurt anyone." LaVerne thought for a minute," I hope I'm somewhere in the middle."

Milo kissed her forehead. "Definitely."

"I guess one could argue that I'm as wild as Vi, running away to Alaska and making a life there."

"Have I told you lately how glad I am that you are and did?"

LaVerne snuggled deeper under the covers and hugged her husband, "No you don't tell me often enough. Are you happy that you married me and my crazy family?"

Milo kissed her long and deep. Raising his head just far enough to speak, "I am beyond happy,

LaVerne Robbins. I'm the luckiest man alive and now I'm going to show you, *again*, just how happy you make me."

Thirty-six

It was a wonderful Christmas week of visiting, eating, exchanging gifts and helping Mama and Pa around the farm. Milo pitched in as if he had been a member of her family for years. The other sisters and their husbands studiously avoided the topic of Violet and her out-of-control life. Everyone seemed to be in silent accord that they didn't want the week riddled with family squabbling. Lillas and Ivah had returned with their husbands and Lillas' daughter early Christmas morning, after spending a few days back home in Seattle.

Vernie's brothers would be home, from cutting trees in Forks, just in time to celebrate the holidays with the family. The morning before Christmas Day LaVerne was in the hen house collecting eggs. Her mother was in the kitchen starting breakfast for those who were left at the home place. Milo and Pa were in the barn building a birthing stall for a couple of animals that would be delivering in the spring. As LaVerne came out of the chicken coop she heard her mother calling her.

"LaVerne! Come quick! I think your song's on the radio! Levi! Milo, come here!"

LaVerne dropped the empty feed pail she'd been carrying, and holding the basket of eggs, in both arms, ran across the yard.

Pa and Milo burst from the barn, looking around frantically. They hadn't heard what Mama said, only that she was screeching at the top of her lungs.

"Grace, what in the world is all the hullabaloo? What's wrong, woman?" Levi yelled as he rushed across to her side.

"Hurry! Come in, LaVerne's song is playing on the radio!"

LaVerne and Milo met each other half way to the door and grinned at each other. Milo's smile told her that he hadn't doubted for a moment that someday her song would be playing.

"Can it be true?" she asked.

"One way to find out. Hurry before we miss it."

As they all pushed into the kitchen Violet was stumbling down the stairs in her nightgown and robe. "What's all the noise about? You woke me up."

Ignoring her, Mama crossed to the radio and turned up the volume. LaVerne's lively tune and lyrics were clearly being sung by the great Johnny Horton. "North to Alaska, the rush is on…."

"Oh my stars! It's yours, isn't it LaVerne?" Mama asked.

LaVerne had sunk into a chair, a dazed look on her face. "Yes…"

"I knew it would happen! Vernie, you're a star!" Milo crowed.

The family stood silently listening to the remainder of the song.

Violet poured herself a cup of coffee and slammed the pot back on the stove top. "I don't see what the big deal is--its just one of Vernie's ditties being played on a local station."

Mama frowned at her daughter, "That's very ungenerous of you, Violet. If the song reached us here in Olympia it only follows that it is being played on big city radio stations. LaVerne has always supported your successes and yet you feel the need to…"

Violet jumped up and headed for the stairs, "Well, excuse me for breathing..." bursting into tears, she ran up the stairs.

"Let her go, Mama, it doesn't matter what she says. Vi will always be Vi." LaVerne said.

"Well, daughter, I for one am damn proud of you and your music. And Johnny Horton! How'd he get your song?"

"It was several years ago, Pa, he ended up at the Fairbanks Trading Post with his producer. We played together one night at one of our musicals. He liked my music and asked if he could take *North to Alaska* back home with him. Of course, I said yes."

"Did he pay you for it, Vernie?" Her father asked.

"No! My goodness, Pa, its Johnny Horton. I was so honored that he wanted my song."

"Well, he should pay you for it. I'm certain it's a big hit and that means he's making money off'n it." Levi persisted.

"She'll probably have a letter from them when we get home, Levi." Milo suggested.

"If you hug those eggs any harder, we'll have chicks by afternoon," Mama said as she relieved LaVerne of the basket. "Boys, get washed up and grab a mug of coffee. Breakfast's about ready. LaVerne call your sister."

Vernie walked to the foot of the stairs and called out, "Vi, breakfast is ready!"

"I'm not hungry!" Vi shouted back and slammed her bedroom door.

Unfazed, LaVerne turned back to the room, "More for us," she cried merrily.

Thirty-seven

LaVerne stood on the train platform and watched as her mother tried desperately to hold back tears. Milo and Pa stood mute, uncomfortable by the public display.

"Mama, don't cry. You'll start me off and then our men will run away."

Her mother gave her a watery laugh, "Oh so true. It's just that I know I won't be seeing you for years again and I hate that. Are you certain you have to live so far away? What if you and Milo start a family? I'll never get to see my grandchildren." She glanced at Milo hoping for some support from him.

"I'm sorry, Mama, our life is in Alaska. We love it there. We've made our home there. Besides, we talked about this--you and Pa are going to come to visit. You'll love the fishing, Pa. And Milo and I have promised to come back within five years."

LaVerne embraced her mother. "Please don't be sad. We had such a lovely time and Christmas was so special what with most of the family home."

Christmas Day *had* been wonderful. Instead of turkey, Pa had shot two pheasants and a goose which Mama had roasted, along with a huge ham from the smokehouse. Fresh vegetables from the cellar, wild cranberries from the forest and pumpkin pies made from Mama's pumpkin patch.

After dinner they had all exchanged Santa presents; that was, one present per person. There was much laughter and groans of dismay as family members stole each other's gifts back and forth.

As they all relaxed in front of a roaring fire, they heard music coming from outside. Opening the kitchen door they found a wagon full of hay bales, and people, drawn by two huge dray horses. The carolers serenaded the Guyer family for several minutes. Laughing and waving they turned the horses and drove off to the next farm.

Now the time had come for LaVerne and Milo to begin the long journey home.

"Don't forget the picnic basket I packed for you," Mama said.

"No chance of that, Ma," Milo told her, "Those ham sandwiches on your home-made bread already have my mouth watering."

A shrill whistle was blown from further down the track. "We should board, Mama," LaVerne's eyes filled with tears.

Mama grabbed her baby-daughter and hugged her tight. "Come back home, soon." She turned to Milo, "Take care of my girl, won't you Milo?"

"Yes, Ma'am, with my life," He kissed his mother-in-law on the cheek and then turned to Levi. "It was a pleasure to spend some time with you on the place, Levi. It was a little hard being away from my homestead so working by your side made it a little easier." Milo knew that the man would understand that sentiment.

"Take good care of yourselves," A sudden sheen sparkled in the older man's eyes as he embraced his youngest child. "Don't be a stranger and keep writing your wonderful music." He whispered against LaVerne's ear. "You've got yourself a fine man there, Vernie."

Two hours later LaVerne woke from a nap and peered out the window of the train compartment they had been assigned.

"Where are we?"

"We should be coming into the Seattle Terminal before long," Milo told her.

"That far? How long did I sleep?"

"Coupl'a hours. It was an emotional visit, seeing everyone."

Milo's insight always amazed her. He didn't say much but when he did, he was always spot on.

They would be retracing their steps on the return trip home. Boarding an Alaska Steamboat Company's ship, they would sail to Anchorage and then change to the Alaska Railroad for the trip to Fairbanks. Within days Joe would meet them to carry them back to the Tanana Valley and home.

"Are you eager to get home?" LaVerne asked.

"While I enjoyed your family immensely, particularly your father and your mother, I am anxious to get back. I never thought I'd say this, but I miss my own chores. I'll bet the pups are big."

Vernie sighed with contentment. "I want to be home too and see Howie, Tukoni, and the babies. My chickens, my goats--our house." Milo smiled. "What?"

"That's the first time you've called it *our* house."

"No it isn't--is it?"

"Yep."

"I'm sorry--I always think of it as our place."

"I know. It was just nice to hear it...*our house*."

"Milo," she smiled sweetly at him, "Even before you let your feelings be known whenever we were in my cabin, setting the table, dishing up dinner, making coffee, cleaning up after--I always thought to myself how comfortable I was being with you. I felt so peaceful and--somehow--safe."

"Really?"

"Really."

A week later they were docking in Anchorage and, after spending an uncomfortable night in a hotel, they boarded the train to Fairbanks. Milo had wired Joe that they were on their way but there were no guarantees that the telegram, after arriving at the trading post, would make it to Tanana. They would just have to wait and see. Three hours out of Anchorage, there had been a heavy snow fall and the tracks had been blocked. Every able-bodied passenger had manned shovels and cleared the obstruction from the tracks. Luck was not with them when they finally stepped down from the train at sunset. The platform was empty except for the departing passengers. The door of the depot suddenly opened and Ma Powers stepped out. When she spotted Vernie and Milo she rushed over.

"Vernie, as I live and breathe, you're back. And how's my favorite bridegroom?" She hugged both of them not pausing in her dialogue. "Joe got delayed and won't be here until tomorrow. He just got your telegram yesterday late, so he couldn't leave Tanana. But the good news is I got a big, empty room, freshly made up, for ya at my place."

"Oh, Ma, it's so good to see you. I'm so happy to be home. Thank you for putting us up."

Milo turned to check that they had all of their luggage off the train and began picking up bags.

"Milo, let me help," LaVerne walked quickly over and picked up two smaller bags.

The three of them began the short walk to Ma' boarding house.

"How'd you find the lower forty-eight? Busy and noisy, huh, Milo? Your family well, Vernie? Any new babies?"

"It's different that's for sure," Milo replied.

"Yes, Ma, family is all fine. No new babies but my sister Vi is expecting in about seven months."

"You don't say. She's the one down in San Francisco living it up as I recall. That right?"

"Yes, that's the one. However, she's divorcing her husband and having trouble juggling all the balls she's got in the air."

"I don't abide divorce, Vernie, I gotta tell ya. Vows before God are sacred. And her expecting his baby--my word, child, I never did hear of such a thing."

LaVerne was quiet. She wasn't about to get into that story with Ma Powers.

Milo tried to divert the conversation, "Ma, how's business at the boarding house?"

"Well, now let me tell ya. While ya was gone I had me a line crew here to stay. Rowdiest bunch you ever did see. I had to take my skillet to a couple of 'em before they settled down and knew I meant business about my rules. When they wasn't workin' they was drinkin'. That doesn't set kindly with me."

"Well, Ma, if anyone could straighten out a rough crew like that, I'd say it would be you."

"Damn right! Excuse my French," she exclaimed. "Here we are," Ma tramped up the steps to the front door of her establishment. "Milo just dump those bags here in the entry and we'll have us a nice cup of tea before you settle in."

LaVerne and Milo exchanges glances. "Ma, I am so tired from the train. Do you think it would be all right if we went to our room, washed up, maybe rested before dinner, got some fresh clothes on first?"

"Oh, my stars, child. Where is my head? Of course you're exhausted from that terrible train ride. Milo! Grab those bags again and follow me!"

Ma led the way up the stairs and turned back to the front of the house. LaVerne knew, from her previous stay here, when she first arrived, that this was where the best and largest rooms were. She watched as Ma threw open the door to the bedroom she'd prepared for them.

"I hope you'll be comfortable in here."

It was charming. A large four poster bed took pride of place. A homemade quilt, in festive colors, covered the linens. On top of that was a huge bear rug. Ma bustled over to the bed and began beating and fluffing the pillows. Lace curtains and heavy drapes covered the windows that looked out over the front porch and at the mountains in the distance. There was a fireplace, with a fire laid, and several comfortable chairs about the room.

"There's fresh water in the jug. Fresh towels. If you need a bath Milo can haul the tub and hot water up." There was a question in her words.

"No, Ma. Maybe later after dinner. I don't want to make any extra work so I'll just bathe in the kitchen like old times, if that's all right?"

Ma walked up to LaVerne and cupped her cheek in her hand, "You just rest, child. That's a long, long trip you had. I must say, from the looks of you, marriage agrees with ya." She turned to Milo, "You keep it that way, boy!"

"Yes, Ma'am."

As LaVerne grinned at her husband, Ma waddled out of the room. "I'll ring the bell like always when supper is ready."

꧁꧂

The next morning Joe and his brother came ripping into town amidst flying snow and sled dogs barking and yelping with glee that they had reached their destination. LaVerne ran down the steps of the boarding house and was knocked on her back by eighty pounds of gray fur and hysterical yelps. As she lay helpless in the snow a pink tongue washed her face.

"Howie!" She wrapped her arms around her dog's neck and laughed and cried. With Howler laying on top of her, she gazed up at her friend, Joe. "You brought Howie," she said through tears.

"Welcome home, Mrs. Milo!" Joe grinned and pulled her to her feet and straight into her friend's arms.

"Joe! We're finally home!" She said as she hugged Joe tight.

"I see, Miss Vernie. We are happy to have you back!" Joe said. He turned to the man who had closely followed LaVerne. "Welcome home, Milo. You were missed." He shook his friend's hand and slapped him on the shoulder.

"Joe! You old varmint! You are a sight for these sore eyes! How's the village? How's your family? How did our homesteads fare?"

"Milo! Look! He brought Howie to me."

Her husband squatted down and gave the dog vigorous ear rubs. "How ya been?" He asked the dog. "How's your family?" Howie grinned at Milo, his second favorite human in the world.

As they all walked up the stairs and into the house Joe gave them a brief run down on what had been happening while they had been gone. "The village is quiet, ice fishing has been very good this year. My family is well, thank you. Your places are doing well. All livestock accounted for," he grinned at LaVerne, reading her mind as to what would be her first concern.

"And the dogs? The pups?" She couldn't help but ask.

"All good. The young ones continue to grow and grow. Howie was lonesome for you, he kept roaming around the cabin looking for you, I believe. The wolf, Tukoni, stays close to her pups but has left a couple of nights now that they are eating meat. She is restless. Howie is an excellent father and babysits when she leaves."

LaVerne and the rest of them chuckled at this. "I can't wait to get home. When can we leave, do you think?"

"The dogs will need a few hours of rest and food. We could probably leave midafternoon. The sun will begin to leave us around three. That means two more hours of travel after that, at the most. We will camp along the trail and then put in a hard day the following day. Or we can leave tomorrow and have two easy days."

"I vote to start back today. I want to get home. But I will concede to wiser heads." Smiling, Vernie looked around at the men. "What do you think?"

"I have to admit, I want to go home. If the dogs won't be too stressed, I'd like to start today." Milo said looking at Joe.

"My dogs are used to long days on the trail. With some rest they will be ready to go. We shall leave at three."

"Wonderful! Thank you Joe," Vernie said.

"Excuse me, I will leave now and help my brother with the dogs."

As he left the room and then the house, LaVerne walked to the front window of the parlor where they had been talking, and watched the goings-on outside. Joe's brother, Elk-tail, had built a fire in the yard and was cutting up frozen fish. A big pot was steaming over the fire and he threw the chucks of fish in to it. Joe walked over to both teams of dogs and began unclipping them from the sled line. Elk-tail had run a hitch line from two trees, while Joe had been in the house, and had spread a nest of hay for each dog.

Joe walked each dog over to a bed and clipped their harness to the line. The nest of hay would keep them insulated from the ground's cold. Next Joe took tin bowls from the sled and, going to the outside pump, filled the bowls with fresh water. As soon as he placed them on the ground next to each dog, they lapped greedily at the cold water.

Through the window Vernie saw Elk-tail speak and Joe laughed. Ma suddenly appeared from the back of the house and walked to the fire. Speaking to the men, she dumped a large bowl of meat into the broth simmering there. Both Joe and Elk-tail called out their thanks as she returned to the rear of the house.

Milo crossed to LaVerne and, placing his arm around her waist, watched the two brothers working in perfect accord. "He's a good friend,"

"The best! I feel like he's another brother to me," LaVerne replied. "He's so generous with his time and effort for us."

"Yes, he's been my friend for years and I value him. I'd do anything for him, but he asks little in return."

"It's his way," she turned and put her arms around Milo's neck. "That's why I love it here so much. Folks help one another and expect nothing in return."

Milo kissed the tip of her nose. "Well, we should be packed up so we're ready when Joe says we can leave."

Ma walked into the room, "Joe said you're leaving in a few hours, so I packed up some food for the trail."

🐾🐾🐾

Hours later LaVerne found herself in a cocoon of furs, tucked in one of the dog sleds. Some of the bags were packed, at her feet, in the front of the sled. Milo rode in the other one in similar comfort. Both mushers yelled an encouraging, 'Hike! Hike!' and the dogs surged forward down the trail and out of the small community of Fairbanks.

For miles LaVerne reveled in the frozen world around her, the not-quite-daylight but not-quite-darkness that was the Alaskan winter. Every tree they passed was a study in symmetry with their coats of snow. Along the trail LaVerne saw the animal prints of martin, weasel and rabbit. The dogs performed effortlessly to the mushers' commands to go right, 'Gee!' or left, 'Haw'. They lived to do a good job and make Joe and his brother happy. Suddenly they hit the Woods River, making travel much easier as they flew off the bank of the river and onto relatively smooth ice.

It was full dark when they finally stopped. They quickly unpacked and lit Kerosene lanterns so that they could see to make camp and tend the dogs. All four people worked in perfect harmony. Elk-tail ran a string-line between trees to clip the dogs' harnesses to. Joe unloaded a bale of hay and began throwing down a nest for each dog. Milo made a large camp fire that would accommodate a large pot of fish stew for the dogs, and cooking the camp dinner.

When Elk-tail had fed the dogs that morning he had cut up extra, for their night meal, so it was easy to fill a pot with snow, the chucks of frozen fish, and put it to boil. LaVerne unpacked a large canvass tarp that she spread out before the fire. Next she brought their bedrolls from the sleds and piled them on one corner of the tarp. The moment the tarp was down Howie flopped down, tired from the long run he had

had next to the sled dogs. Next she opened the food box and began setting out utensils, skillets and pots, and tin plates.

"Vernie, you will find moose steaks in the food box. Also canned beans that I bartered for at the post," he called.

"Wonderful, Joe!   That sounds like a perfect welcome home dinner."

A short time later each dog was tethered to the line, cozy in their beds of hay. As soon as the fish, in the stew, was thawed Elk-tail ladled it into bowls and he and Joe went down the line, serving the dogs. Once they had eaten the bowls would be reused to give them fresh water. The well-being and comfort of the dogs always came first. Before the people ate or rested the dogs had to be cared for.

Soon steaks were sizzling in the skillets and beans simmered over the fire. Laverne had managed to make camp biscuits without the use of a Dutch oven but Joe and Milo couldn't resist teasing her about their odd shapes. For the most part they ate in silence, weary beyond words from the winter trail they had traveled over for hours.

A camp coffee pot burped and bubbled over the fire. At the end of their meal the four laid back against their bed-rolls and sipped the savory brew.

"Joe, how about a story from the People?" LaVerne asked.

"Ah. Elk-tail is the real storyteller in our family. Perhaps he will tell you about a bear hunt."

Elk-tail sat up a little and stared into the fire for several minutes. Then he began, "long, long ago, a Koyukon Athabascan man and his son had been out hunting one winter day. On the way back to camp, they discovered a bear hole. The older man stuck the end of his long bear spear into the hole, hoping to wake the bear up and make him leave his hole. He poked and poked, while his son stood nearby with his own spear ready to stab the bear as it came out of the hole.

The bear started growling. The man felt him moving about--he was going to come out! As the big animal emerged angrily from his den, the two men panicked. The son lunged at him with his sharp-pointed spear. His father followed with another stab at the bear. There was a struggle--and the bear fell down, and slid back into his den. The two men were horrified. They knew that after a bear has been killed, its forepaws must be cut off, and its eyes must be burst. Although the bear was dead, its spirit, or yega, could still harm the men if these things were not done. The man and his son tried to remove the bear from the hole, but it was already dark by this time and the bear was very heavy. They could not pull it out.

The men returned to camp. They felt very worried because they had not followed the rules. The bear's yega would be angry. Days and weeks went by, and nothing bad happened to either one. Finally, they forgot about the dead bear in its den. A year later, the son went blind. The people in his band said he had gone blind because he had broken a rule. He had failed to burst the bear's eye after he killed it."

"Oh! Poor bear. Poor boy," LaVerne cried.

Thirty-eight

Before sunrise the camp was broken down and the sleds were packed. The dogs were fed partially thawed Cariboo meat and fish heads. Well rested, they were eager to get back on the trail. It would be a long day and every advantage had to be taken of the short daylight hours.

With cries of Hike, Hike!, from the mushers, excited yipping from the sled dogs and Howie howling his best song, they were off. The first leg of their journey would be five hours up the Woods River to where it met the Yukon. And then another two hours north to Tanana. If they made the trip in one day, they would arrive at the homesteads in pitch dark.

LaVerne knew that Joe's argument to stay in Tanana tonight was the safest choice, but she was eager to get home to her homestead. She also knew that it would make it a longer day for both mushers since after they dropped LaVerne and Milo off they still had to return to their respective homes and settle the dogs in. She sighed. That would be very unfair to her friends.

The decision was ultimately taken out of their hands. Three hours into their trip it began to snow and in no time it became a blizzard with winds creating a white-out.

"Gee! Gee!" Joe and Elk-tail called to their dogs and the sleds veered right off the exposed ice of the river and headed for the tree line. Deep in the woods the wind was cut in half and the trees sheltered them from the blinding snow. While Elk-tail and LaVerne settled the dogs, Milo and Joe found and cut small, straight pine trees. Assembling six and tying them at the top they spread the bottoms on the ground forming a cone shape. The 'tipi' was then covered with the tarp they had slept on last night. Next they went under large fir trees and found plentiful dry boughs to cover the cold ground inside. They dug a primitive fire hole in the center of the dwelling floor and got a fire started. The joined poles at the top created a small hole and allowed the smoke to escape.

All four unloaded the sleds for what they would need for the night. Then the sleds were tipped on their sides to somewhat protect the remaining provisions and gear from the wind and snow.

Nestled around a warm fire, LaVerne asked, "Where did that come from? The sun was shining this morning."

"You know what they say about the weather in Alaska. If you don't like it, wait fifteen minutes," Milo chuckled.

Their dinner consisted of cold beans, day old biscuits, and hot coffee. Exhausted by the storm, the frantic work to build a shelter and dealing with the sled dogs, no one wanted to bother with cooking. The men were soon in their bedrolls, snoring. LaVerne lay by the fire, Howie next to her side, she marveled once again, at her life. This was everything she'd dreamed about when she was growing up on the farm.

She'd been too busy to even realize that she was an Alaskan woman now and a successful homesteader. She'd met and married a wonderful man and could look forward to many years with him. She had made life-long friends in Tanana and Fairbanks.

At dawn the next day LaVerne poked her head out of the shelter. Sun light, breaking over the nearby foothills, bathed three feet of new snow in a pink glow. She crawled out, coffee pot in hand, and scooped and packed snow into the pot. She quickly crawled back into the tipi where a fire blazed. Breakfast would be camp biscuits and hot coffee. Milo was rolling up bedrolls and the other two men were with the dogs.

Howie looked beseechingly at his mistress.

"Yes, I know you need breakfast too," LaVerne grinned at him. "Let's go see if Joe has a chunk of fish for you," she said as she led the way back out into the snowy morning.

Howie followed her and ran to Joe who was throwing fish to his dogs. He sat a few feet away and whined.

Joe turned, "Howler, you must be hungry too," he threw the dog a choice portion. "That will have to do until we get home, boy."

Howie caught it mid-air and ran under a tree to enjoy it in leisure. LaVerne turned and headed back to the shelter. She saw that someone had tipped the sleds back up to their upright positions and cleaned the snow off them.

"The sleds are ready to load, Milo, as soon as we eat," she said as she checked the biscuits. "The biscuits are ready too."

"Call the men, will you Vernie?"

She opened the canvass flap and called out, "Joe! Elk-tail! Breakfast is ready."

Dishes and coffee pot were scrubbed clean with snow and packed away, sleds were loaded, and with dogs clipped onto the sled lines, they were on the trail again within the hour. They left the tipi poles standing in case some other traveler needed a quick shelter.

Four hours later the dogs began to bark and yap. "Haw! Haw!" the mushers called but the dogs knew the trail to the left, up over the river bank and home. Snow flying, dogs crying, they roared into the village and people came from their houses and cabins to greet the returning newlyweds and the two members of their tribe.

Two elders walked to the sleds. "Welcome home, Denigi-tri'axa, Mr. Milo. The Mother saw you safely back."

The second elder spoke, "Please honor us by sharing a meal. In celebration of your joining and your return from your travels. We know you are eager to return home this day but perhaps in a week or so?"

"We would look forward to that, Tok'adi, and are honored to be invited. Thank you."

"Father, we will continue our journey now to the homestead of our friends." Joe told the elders.

Amidst cheering and clapping, Joe and Elk-tail turned the dogs and headed for the trail out of town and toward LaVerne and Milo's cabin.

ᴥᴥᴥ

Tears shining in her eyes, LaVerne feasted on the sight of her homestead. Smoke spiraled from the chimney, the rooster crowed and made LaVerne laugh. The goats ran to the fence closest to the new arrivals and bleated in welcome. And best of all six happy puppies bolted out from beneath the cabin and ran to her. She had done what Joe had advised and when they had been newly born, she had blown softly into their noses so they would bond to her.

Now she jumped out of the sled and sat down in the snow. The pups clambered over her, whining with joy, nipping her fingers and licking her face.

"Oh, I know," she cooed to them, "I'm finally home and you are here and I love you."

Four of the pups were all wolf with the same coloration as their mother. The two males looked more like Howie with gray fur splotched with light brown and black. One pup had a blue eye and a brown one just like his daddy.

LaVerne continued to cuddle and kiss the puppies. Joe and Elk-tail grinned at the nonsense as they unpacked Milo and LaVerne's things and placed them on the porch. Milo had walked over to the enclosure, holding the goats and chickens, and saw that one of their friends had fed the livestock and thrown fresh hay down for the goats.

"That's everything, Vernie, Milo," Joe called. "We will be on our way."

LaVerne jumped up and, with puppies and Howie following at her heels, crossed to the two men. "How can we thank you?"

Milo joined them as Joe said, "No thanks is ever necessary. We do for each other, it is our way."

Joe, jumping on the back of his sled and shouting 'Hike!' followed his brother's sled back down the trail to the village and home.

LaVerne turned to Milo, "What good friends we have, Milo. What a good life we've been blessed with."

Milo put his hands on LaVerne's waist and pulled her close. "What a *wife* I've been blessed with," kissing her long and deep.

Howie and the puppies seemed to object to this and began baying and yapping. LaVerne and Milo broke away, laughing.

"Okay, okay, we'll stop with the mushy stuff! Quiet!" Milo told them.

Arm in arm they walked up onto the porch. LaVerne opened the cabin door and was met with the savory smells of a stew simmering on the wood stove. "Oh! Another surprise, Milo.   Dinner is waiting for us." *This had Charlie's hand all over it.*

LaVerne stopped so abruptly, just inside the door that Milo ran into the back of her. She was staring at the back wall of the cabin. There was a door that hadn't been there before they went away. LaVerne whirled around and stared at her husband.

"What did you do? That's wasn't there before!"

"Just a little surprise for my bride. Go on...open it." He said as he dropped the bags where he stood.

LaVerne rushed across the room and tore open the door. Inside was a new room, a bedroom all furnished with their bed, dresser, chair, and a window that looked at the forest and garden outside.

"Milo! How can this be?"

"Before we left for your family's farm I picked out logs to be cut around my place. Then while we were gone I had my men add the room. Charlie supervised the moving in with the furniture and such. Do you like it?"

"Like it? Like it? I adore it! No more crawling up into the loft. No more bumping your head on the rafters." She crossed to him and flung her arms around his neck. It was lucky he was standing by the bed as, with the force of her attack, they lost their balance and tumbled onto it.

"How convenient," she giggled.

"Get off me woman! All I can think about right now is that stew in the other room."

"Rain check?" she chuckled.

"You bet."

"Have I told you how much I appreciate and love you?" She kissed his chin.

"It's been too long," he smiled.

"I love you. I can't believe how thoughtful you are. Our bedroom on the first floor--it's a rare luxury!"

LaVerne untangled herself from Milo's body and stood. Milo followed her and they walked out into the main room.

"Umm, smells wonderful. Is that Cariboo or moose? I'm starving after that skimpy, trail camp breakfast."

LaVerne crossed to the stew pot and lifted the lid. Stirring with a spoon, she found a chunk of meat. "Come here and test taste it, hungry bear."

Milo hurried over and, first blowing on the steaming meat, took it from the spoon, a few dribbles of gravy seeping down his chin. LaVerne laughed and wiped his mouth on her sleeve. "What's the verdict?"

"Cariboo. My favorite. Bless Charlie."

"How do you know it was her?"

Milo answered with a look. No one else would get the cabin ready like this. A fire, stew bubbling on the back of the stove, the table set with a vase full of cedar boughs and red berries. He walked over to the table and lifted a clean terry cloth. Underneath was Charlie's signature blueberry muffins.

"Yep. Definitely Charlie," Vernie chuckled.

"You want to unpack tonight or wait until tomorrow?" Milo asked.

"I'm so tired all of a sudden. Let's just get out of our wet coats, boots and relax. Would you light a fire in the fireplace?"

Milo glanced at the hearth. "Since Charlie also laid a fresh fire for us it only involves lighting a match. Anything else you need, my love?"

LaVerne's eyes suddenly filled with tears and spilled down her cheeks. She hiccupped as she tried to swallow a sob.

Milo rushed to her side. "Vernie, what is it?"

Leaning into him and hiding her face in his shoulder she gasped, "I don't know...it always touches my heart when you say that: *my love*. How in the world did I deserve you? You are such a wonderful man and I have grown to love you so."

Petting her back, Milo nuzzled her neck with his face, "Ah, Vernie, I'm the one who's lucky. I never dreamed you'd accept my proposal and marry me. I say thank you every day to the heavens above. Never leave me. Please?"

Vernie pulled back just enough to look into Milo's eyes, "Why would I do that? I love you."

Milo got very somber, "I know how much Charlie loves you." He gestured around the cabin with his arm, "Look at this place. It looks like a lover welcoming back someone they can't live without."

"I know. But, Milo, dearest, I don't feel the same way as Charlie does. Yes, I love her very much but--as a *friend*. I've explained that to her. I love *you!*"

He kissed her deeply and then, "I will work every day of my life to deserve your love."

"You don't need to *earn* it, my love, it just is."

Milo kissed her hair, her eyes, her nose and then her mouth, "Thank you for loving me. I am so happy."

Cupping his cheek in her palm she asked, "How about we get comfortable and have some of that wonderful stew. And I'll make some coffee."

"Good plan. And if you're not too tired, I would love some of your biscuits. I appreciated your effort on the trail but those lumps of dough were pretty bad."

"Hey! Beggars can't be choosy! Is that why you ate four of them?" LaVerne said, "And what about Charlie's muffins?" She asked as she pulled the Dutch oven from a shelf over the stove and began to heat it."

"Let's save them for tomorrow. I love your biscuits with stew. Great for sopping up gravy."

"Goat milk biscuits coming up."

LaVerne mixed up the ingredients of flour, baking powder, baking soda, butter, salt and enough sweet goat milk to hold it all together. Her mother had taught her that just the right blend of milk and flour was what made them tender. She kneaded the dough only five times and rolled it out an inch thick. With a glass canning jar that she kept for this purpose, she cut perfect sized biscuits and, after oiling the Dutch oven, placed them in the bottom. She sealed the lid and placed it toward the back of the stove.

"The biscuits will delay dinner a bit," she informed Milo.

"They're worth it," Milo began to hang their wet outerwear, gloves, hats and boots on a rack. Using a pulley system, he pulled the rack up into the rafters of the cabin. He washed his hands at the sink and began making the coffee to go with dinner. Pumping fresh water into the pot, he placed four scoops of coffee grounds into the water and set the pot on the stove to boil. Once it had boiled he would pull it off the heat and the coffee grounds would settle on the bottom, leaving a clear, strong brew.

About the time that Vernie knew the bread would be ready, she ladled hot stew into two bowls. She smiled at Milo's domesticity. It always pleased her when he jumped in and helped. Her Pa wouldn't know the first thing around a kitchen. "Ready to eat?"

"You bet. Are the biscuits ready?"

"Would you check them please?"

Milo opened the lid and peered in. "They're golden brown. Look ready to me."

"Set the oven aside so they don't cook anymore. We'll have left-overs for tomorrow. Will you get the butter out of the larder too?"

A moment later they were seated at their table eating in silent contentment. LaVerne appreciated the fact that Milo was a quiet man. He never felt the need to fill every silence with chatter like some people did. She concentrated on Charlie's stew. She still hadn't mastered her recipe. Chunks of potato, bits of carrot, and just the right amount of cabbage floated in the rich gravy. The Cariboo was so tender it fell apart in a person's mouth.

LaVerne reflected on Milo's words about her friend and the obvious love she demonstrated for Vernie. *Does Milo believe me when I say I don't return that particular kind of love?* She must remember to reassure him with words and actions so he would have no cause to doubt her love for him. She glanced over and smiled at the good man she'd married.

Milo looked up from buttering another biscuit, "What?"

"Nothing. I was just thinking how extremely happy I am at this moment."

"I hope to make you happier. There's another surprise out in the barn--after dinner."

"Milo! You're spoiling me. Stop it. No--don't stop, I love it!"

Half an hour later they waded through the snow drifts, thirty feet to the barn. With the help of neighbors LaVerne had finished the small structure last summer. The walls were milled boards from Milo's saws and LaVerne loved the weathered patina that was changing their look from freshly milled boards to a beautiful gray aged wood.

Milo rolled the large door to one side and stepped in to light a couple of lanterns. The barn was fairly empty, for now. Bales of hay for the goats, homemade wooden bins for animal feed. LaVerne's and Milo's horses nickered sleepily from their stalls.

In the middle of the dirt floor, sitting up on wooden blocks, sat the most beautiful dog sled LaVerne had ever seen. It was so evident that it had been made with loving hands--Milo's hands.

The runners, cut and then bent were made from hickory wood. The bed slats were made of ash. Stanchions, top rails and driving bar were of birch. The rawhide lashings were precisely woven and tied for extra strength. The sled wasn't too long or heavy but just right for a woman who would be learning for the first time how to be a musher.

The different woods, polished and oiled, glowed in the lamp sight. She crossed to it and caressed the different woods. It was the most beautiful thing LaVerne could ever imagined. She sighed and turned to her husband with tears in her eyes.

"Oh, Milo, it's lovely. You made it for me." It wasn't a question.

Milo was always slightly embarrassed if praised or he found himself the center of attention. He coughed gruffly, "With your first litter of pups already here, you have a sled team. Seemed only right that you should have a sled."

"But I don't know how to drive a team," LaVerne almost wailed.

"Joe will teach you. He's the best around. And I'll be near to help you."

LaVerne hugged Milo and then returned to her sled, lovingly running her hands over the beautiful wood and sighed repeatedly.

"I have no words. It's gorgeous. Can I sleep in it tonight?"

Milo chuckled, "If you want."

"How did you find the time?"

"Before we wed, those nights I stayed at my place, filling orders of lumber I was working on it. I already had most of the types of wood that I needed so there was no time lost seeking out the right trees. So--it'll do?"

LaVerne turned back to him, her eyes filled with love. "Do? Do! Oh, I can't wait. When will the pups be old enough? How do I train them? When do you think Joe can train me?" She laughed and ran to Milo, jumping into his arms. "You are the best man I've ever met!"

Her momentum knocked them both off their feet and they landed in a soft pile of hay and cuddled.

"The pups should start training right away. Howie's probably too old but we can see what he thinks about it. At first it should be play time for the pups. Likely as not, Joe will have your dogs run free alongside his sled team to show them how much fun it is. After they are accustomed to a harness you start them out by dragging around a light chunk of wood."

LaVerne rolled on top of Milo's body, kissed the end of his nose, "I can't wait! How can I ever thank you?"

"Oh, I can think of several ideas," Milo grinned at her as he lazily ran his hands down her back.

"Milo! Not here in the barn! It's freezing cold."

"Race you to the house!" He pushed her off and sprang to his feet. "Don't forget to douse the lanterns," he called as he disappeared out the door.

LaVerne rose more slowly never taking her eyes from the handmade sled that her husband had built for her. She took a few more minutes to admire the craftsmanship and then, lifting the mantles, blew out the lights.

Thirty-nine

The next morning Howie and the pups began to bark and howl, signaling someone was coming up the trail. When they recognized the visitor their howls turned to happy yips. LaVerne looked across the table at Milo.

"I'll see who it is." He rose from the breakfast table and walked to the door.

Grinning from ear to ear Charlie was just throwing her braking anchor for her sled into the snow, when Milo stepped out onto the porch. Most of her sled dogs lay down where they had stopped and the puppies began crawling all over the older dogs.

"Hallo, the house!" she called. "Welcome home! I saw your smoke and figured you got in safe and sound."

"We was just havin' breakfast. Come on in and have a cup'a coffee and a muffin," Milo said.

LaVerne hurried across the room, when she heard Charlie's voice outside, and met her at the door, hugging her friend close. "My God! I missed you," she told Charlie.

"Missed you too. How was your trip?" Charlie replied and broke the embrace. "Was the trail from Fairbanks decent?" She asked Milo.

"It was good but we ran into a storm."

"Typical, right?" Charlie chuckled.

"It was wonderful to see my family and the farm again. The whole clan was there. We had a wonderful Christmas. But I don't want to travel again any time soon, I was that homesick," Vernie told her friend.

"Glad to hear you found the family well. How's the wild sister, Violet?"

"You don't want to know. She's completely lost her mind," LaVerne scowled.

"We can't thank you enough for the welcome you prepared, Charlie. The stew, the muffins, which I demolished this morning, by the way, the fire laid --everything you did."

"It was nothing. Two days on the trail during the dark months of winter, it's a tough journey. I wanted you to be able to relax when you first got home and not be faced with a bunch of chores and cooking."

"Well, regardless, it was much appreciated," Milo told her.

"Did the storm delay you? I thought you were a day later than you said you'd be."

Vernie snorted. "Delay is an understatement. It was a white-out blizzard. It hit at dusk and we had to camp an extra night on the trail. Thanks to Joe and his tipi design for a shelter we were pretty comfortable. But trying to set up camp in the dark was exhausting. But, you know Alaska weather, the next morning it had blown itself out."

They sat around the table nursing their mugs of coffee and caught up on news of what had been happening while they had been gone and stories of their visit to the lower forty-eight. LaVerne avoided talking about Vi. She was just too exhausting.

Charlie grinned fondly at LaVerne, "Ready to see your wedding gift?"

LaVerne looked blank, "But you gave us a lovely gift already what with getting the cabin all warm and snug for our return. We loved it."

With a sly smile Charlie rose from the table, "Come on outside and see my real gift."

LaVerne followed her friend with Milo trailing behind. Charlie ran down the steps and went straight to her sled and team, then veered to the back where another sled sat in the snow.

When Milo had come outside he hadn't noticed Charlie had been towing a second sled behind hers. It was not unusual for a musher to have two sleds behind the dog team, especially for larger jobs like hauling firewood or the meat from big game.

Milo stopped at the bottom of the stairs. The second sled looked new and was festooned with ribbons and shells. LaVerne stared at the sled, then at Charlie, then glanced back at Milo.

"Well, say something!" Charlie chortled. "Do you like it? I made it for you--and Milo--for your future dog team. It's made of hickory, mostly, and should last you for years."

Milo silently turned and, walking back up the steps to the porch, returned to the cabin.

LaVerne's eyes filled with tears at the pain she was about to inflict on her friend. "Oh, Charlie, I don't know what to say..."

"You don't have to thank me. It was such fun building it for you."

"And I love it but--it just that--well--Milo--he..."

"Milo what?" Charlie asked nonplussed.

"He built me a sled as a wedding present; it's in the barn."

Charlie's face suffused with an embarrassed blush, "I see." She fled back to her own sled and lifted the anchor that kept her dogs in place. She regarded Vernie with a deep pain in her eyes, "How could I have been so stupid? Of course we would think of the same gift, something you would love and can use. I'm sorry. Of course you can't accept mine. I'll see you later."

And with that she released the brake and yelled at her team, "Hike! Hike! For Chrissakes, go!" She screamed at her team.

Her team of dogs surged to obey her command and within seconds they had disappeared from the clearing.

"Charlie!" LaVerne called after her but they were long gone.

LaVerne turned to speak to her husband and realized he had disappeared into the house. She mounted the first step to the porch and paused. How had she become the one at fault for hurting the two most important people in her life? Charlie was crushed and Milo was feeling threatened and she didn't know what she could do. She continued up the steps and opened the door to find Milo washing out the coffee mugs, scrubbing them like his life depended on it. She removed her parka and hung it by the door. Moving to the stove she asked, "Is there any coffee left?"

Milo silently handed her a clean mug and went back to drying the dishes and putting them away. LaVerne pour herself a fresh cup, crossed to the table and sat starring at the hot liquid in her mug.

Milo sat down across from her. "Have you decided which sled you'll keep?"

LaVerne's head snapped up. "How can you say such a thing? Of course I want yours! I love it. But that doesn't change the fact that I had to hurt my friend."

"She had no business making you such an expensive and personal gift," Milo voice raised in frustration. "I'm your husband. She's got to come to terms with that."

"Milo, I'm sorry you've been put in this position. I would never choose anything or anyone over you. I love you. But she's my friend and she's been very good to me. I hated hurting her."

"I know, I know," he groaned. "But you have to make the lines clearer, Vernie. You're her friend, but you're *my wife*."

"I know and I will. I'll go over there in the next day or so and talk to her. Please don't let this upset you. I'm so thrilled with the sled you made for me. I will always remember how you listened to what is important to me and support the things I want to do."

Milo, slow to anger and quick to forgive, laid his hand on hers, "I always will, you know. I love you more than life. I guess I just worry about the influence that Charlie has over you."

"Milo, Charlie's so-called influence doesn't reach as far you might believe and certainly doesn't impact my marriage or how much I love you. Can we forget it, please?"

"Of course. 'Nough said. Ready to hit the morning chores? Then I've got to go over to my place and the mill for a few hours."

LaVerne jumped up and held out her hand, "Come on, husband, let's get some work done."

Forty

When Milo returned late in the afternoon, he was driving his sled and dogs, his horse tethered to the rear. LaVerne was just walking out of the goat and chicken enclosure when they arrived. Her puppies bounded out from under the cabin and rushed to greet Milo's dogs.

Milo threw his sled anchor down and stepping on it, crushed it deep into the snow covered ground. "Hi, wife!"

"You brought your team." LaVerne walked over and began petting the dog team.

"Yeah. Let me put up Buster and then maybe you would help me make some straw beds for them."

"Certainly."

While Milo led his horse to the corral and got him settled with a little feed and some fresh water, LaVerne hauled a hay bale from the barn. They met on the side of the clearing where Milo had put up a string line, weeks ago, for when sled dogs were in the yard.

"You know, we're going to have to clear some more land for your dog team. Build them houses and drive stakes, as soon as the ground thaws."

LaVerne grinned at him, "I can't wait! But why did you bring your team over?"

"We're a little late starting your dogs' training. What are they? Three months old?"

"Closer to four. Why?"

"They should have started running with a team around age eight to ten weeks. So, if you're game, we'll take them for a run tomorrow. We'll start them out just running free next to my team. Then over the next few days, we'll get them accustomed to a collar and harnesses. By the end of the week, we'll have them hooked up to a light chunk of wood and let them drag it around the yard here."

"Oh, that sounds like so much fun!"

♪♪♪

The next morning they awoke to a perfect winter day. The sun was shining with not a cloud to be seen. The temperature hovered around two degrees above but with no wind to drive the wind chill down, it was pleasant.

LaVerne and Milo hurried through the morning chores and breakfast. While LaVerne packed a lunch, Milo hooked up his team. Amongst much excited barking and howling, he improvised rope collars for the puppies. They could sense something monumental was about to happen and they ran around the clearing yipping and crashing into each other. Their dad, Howler, stood watching the preparations. Their wolf-mother had left the den under the cabin, before sun-up. She wanted nothing to do with whatever was about to happen.

Milo had packed his sled with emergency supplies like bedrolls, an axe for trail clearing, a rifle, extra furs and some food for the dogs. He didn't plan on going far but he knew from bitter experience that you should never trust Alaska's weather.

As soon as LaVerne came out of the cabin Milo helped her into the sled, covered her with furs, and they were off. Amidst yelping from the puppies and Milo's cries of 'Hike!' they shot out of the clearing, and onto the trail behind the cabin, like a cannonball. The pups thought it was great fun and raced along with the sled team. Howie, not to be outdone, ran up beside Milo's lead dog and kept pace with him.

A mile up the trail the dogs slowed and looking up ahead Milo saw that the trail was blocked by deadfall. He began to shout, 'Whoa' but his dogs, well trained, had already begun to stop. Milo threw out the sled anchor and stomped it into the snow.

"What is it?" Vernie asked.

"Dead trees and branches blocking the trail," Milo answered.

"Let me help. I could use a stretch," she said as she scrambled out of the basket of the sled.

They made quick work of it--Milo chopped the fallen trees and Vernie pushed and shoved them aside, while the puppies played tug-a-war with smaller branches.

"Okay, that should do it," Milo stowed the axe in the sled and helped Vernie settle back into her nest of furs. "Ready?"

She nodded and Milo, lifting the anchor, yelled, "Hike! Hike!" and they were off again.

They crossed a couple of smaller rivers with little worry about the ice being too thin. Milo knew that the dogs would slow and sometimes resist the order to cross bad ice. It had been a very cold winter but he still kept a sharp eye for the telltale sign of safety and blue ice which meant it was thick enough to cross. An opaque, green appearance meant thinning ice would require that he inspect it before they crossed or find another location on the river.

Five miles out they came to the moose lakes all frozen at this time of year. A little shiver crept down Milo's spine when he remembered how close he'd come to losing Vernie to a sudden blizzard.

He leaned over so he was close to her ear, "Wanna stop and eat? Give the dogs a break?" She nodded.

Milo directed the dog team left to a stand of large pines, "Haw! Haw!" And a few yards later, "Whoa!"

Once stopped the puppies broke away and explored the immediate area, pouncing on each other and tumbling in the deep snow.

"I'll get a fire started. We won't be here long enough to unharness the team; they'll be fine right where they stand."

Vernie noticed the dogs had already, lain down in the snow, their thick undercoat of fur protecting them from the cold. She piled out of the sled and began to gather their lunch and furs to sit on.

Milo crawled in under the large evergreen trees and began to break off dry, dead branches. LaVerne walked around the immediate area and began to gather deadfall that was dry and would make a good fire.

Within the hour the fire was hot and LaVerne had a coffee pot, with melted snow, heating on the coals. She sat on furs, laid near the fire, and she unpacked the thick sandwiches she'd made for the trip. Milo had watered the dogs and given them each a frozen chunk of salmon from the stores he'd brought with them.

He came over and flopped down next to her, his feet toward the warmth of the fire. "Hey, wife, those sandwiches look mighty fine."

She handed him two and then threw a handful of coffee grounds into the campfire pot. "Coffee'll be ready shortly."

Howie came over and lay down on the edge of the furs, looking for scraps from their lunch.

"Good dog, Howie," Milo murmured. "He seems to have taken a liking to the lead, did you notice that? Maybe I'll try him out with my dogs and see how he does. You might have a natural there."

Vernie ruffled her dog's head and rubbed his ears. "He likes to be in charge. Even though his mate," she grinned at Milo, "is wild, he's still the boss when it matters."

"Just as it should be, *wife*." Milo chuckled.

She snorted at the implication. "Coffee's ready. The *wife* will pour you some."

She loved that about her husband. Most people might see a big, silent, lumbering man who wasn't very interesting. But she knew differently. He was kind, very woods smart and had a subtle, slightly sarcastic sense of humor.

She lay back with her head on his leg and stared into the fire. In that moment her life couldn't be more perfect. She looked upside down at Milo, "My life with you is perfect. Thank you."

He leaned over and placed a light kiss on her nose, "Your welcome."

They were quiet as they ate their meal, listening to the forest around them. LaVerne had almost dozed off when Milo spoke.

"I saw a lot of tracks on this trail. What do you think about running a trap line up this way?"

LaVerne sat up. "Why?" She wasn't so sure she wanted to kill furry, little animals for their skin.

"It's a great way to supplement our cash and it's interesting to see what you catch. I've always enjoyed trapping. Haven't done it in a few years because my mill keeps me so busy."

"Won't we wipe out the species around here? It doesn't seem fair."

"No, we don't take so much that we threaten the numbers. The important thing about trapping is that you let the area 'rest' so that you don't put so much pressure on it. Take martin for example: they breed like mice. Ermine too. They're all from the weasel family so it's unlikely that you could wipe them out. But we'd be careful to not let that happen."

"I'm willing to give it a try."

"That's my girl. Well, shall we pack up and get these dogs home?"

LaVerne reluctantly rose and poured the left over coffee on the fire. Even in winter time it was not a good idea to leave a burning fire. Milo lifted and shook out the furs, much to Howie's disgust. He'd been comfortably snoozing there since they had stopped. The sled dogs stood up from their naps, and began to bark. The puppies, sensing that a new adventure was about to unfold, joined them by yipping and jumping up.

The sled was quickly packed and LaVerne stepped in. Milo called to the dogs and they bounded back down the trail.

Part Four

A Homecoming
Of Two Hearts

Forty-one

The next morning LaVerne left Milo to the morning chores. She wanted to ride over to Charlie's and clear the air after the fiasco of the two sleds. When Milo was finished around their homestead, he was going over to his mill to get some work done.

LaVerne rode into Charlie's yard and hailed the house. As she tied her horse at the bottom of the porch she glanced over and saw a pile of broken wood. It was what was left of the sled that Charlie had so lovingly made for her. She sighed with regret. Her friend came out the door.

"Hi."

Charlie didn't look like she had been sleeping well. Dark circles lingered under her eyes and she looked worn out, "Hi. How's married life?" She turned and went into the cabin, leaving the door open.

LaVerne followed, hanging her coat and hat on a peg by the door, and sat at the table.

"Coffee?" Charlie asked standing by the stove.

"Yes, I would like some. It's cold out there today."

Charlie poured two mugs and brought them to the table, setting one in front of Vernie.

"So. We're reduced to discussing the weather, are we?" she sighed.

"Don't be like that, Charlie. It was a terrible thing that happened--you and Milo making the exact same gift for me. But you have to understand that I couldn't accept yours, lovely as it was. Why did you destroy it?"

"Why not? I certainly didn't need another sled and I sure didn't want a reminder around of what a fool I am."

"I'm so sorry. I would never intentionally hurt you--you must know that. I feel somehow to blame for it all."

"The whole thing--it's not your fault. That you couldn't love me, that you didn't want to make a life with me, that you married that man…" Tears choked Charlie's voice.

"But I *do* love you, just not that way. I'm sorry."

"I'll get over it--eventually. But I don't think I want to stand by and watch you build a life with Milo. I'm thinking of going back to Boston."

"What! But, but," Vernie sputtered, "You hate big cities. What about your place here? What about your dogs? What about me?"

"Vernie, you can't have it both ways. I haven't decided anything definite but I am considering that as an option."

"I'll really miss you--miss our friendship," she whispered.

"You'll get over it."

Vernie and Charlie sat in awkward silence for many long minutes.

"Well, I best get back," she rose, "Chores, you know."

Suddenly they heard shouting outside above the din of excited barking from Charlie's dog team. Vernie recognized her husband's voice but had never heard it filled with anger and fear like it was now. She jumped up and ran to the door, quickly followed by Charlie. Opening the door they found Milo standing at the back of his dog sled, every line in his face carved in relief by his paleness and expression of fear and grief.

"Milo! What is it?"

"Elk-tail and his uncle are missing. They've been gone for two days. Hurry! We have to help with the search."

"Oh, my god," Charlie murmured. She turned to just inside the door and grabbed gloves, hat, heavy coat and gun belt. She shoved Vernie's outer wear at her and hurried down the steps. "What can we do?"

"They want you and your dog sled. As soon as you get hooked up, go to the village and they will tell you where they want you to search."

Charlie was already moving to her dog yard, "I'll be there as soon as I can."

"What about me, Milo?" LaVerne asked.

"I'll drop you at our place and you can saddle up. Then head straight for the village and see where the elders want you to search. Don't go out on the ice, on horseback, travel the shoreline. Promise me."

Vernie ran to the sled and hopped in. "I promise."

"I mean it, Vernie. You don't know how to read the ice. Stay off it!"

"I *promise*!"

"Hike! Hike!" Milo shouted to his dogs and in no time they were on the trail to their cabin.

As they stopped in the clearing Milo didn't bother with the anchor. He paused just long enough to let Vernie out. "I'm not going back to the village. They assigned me down river to where the Woods River flows into the Yukon. Will you be okay?"

"Yes. Go! I'll meet you at the village and if one of us isn't back, I'll meet you here at home."

"Be sure you're back at the village before dark."

Milo fiercely pulled LaVerne to him and kissed her. "Take care and be cautious of the ice."

"You take care too. I love you."

"Love you. See you tonight," and he was gone.

LaVerne raced into her cabin and got some extra outerwear. Gloves, a fur hat, an extra pair of socks just in case her feet got wet. She took her rifle down from its rack over the door and stuffed some extra cartridges into her pocket. She hurried back out and crossed to the corral.

A forty minute ride found her in the village where she saw people clustered on the porch of the main lodge. She dismounted and, as she tied her horse up, Joe was just coming down the steps. LaVerne walked into his arms.

"Slatsiin, thank you for coming. Your husband has already headed south."

"Joe, what happened? Where do you think Elk-tail is?"

"My uncle and brother were going out to run their trap lines. They were to return no later than yesterday. They have not come back."

"I'm certain they are fine. Maybe the fur was so good they were delayed. Milo found Charlie too..."

"Yes, she has already been here and has gone up river to help search."

"What can I do to help, Joe?"

"If you will ride along the shoreline on this side of the river, south. Look for any sign of a recent camp."

"I will." LaVerne said, turning back to her horse.

"Be careful and leave yourself enough daylight to return to the village, Miss Vernie."

LaVerne rode for several hours scanning from the shoreline up to the line of trees where a camp most likely would be pitched on the trail. Nothing. Winter daylight hours were very limited but she would ride back to the village at dusk every day. As the days pasted the atmosphere in the village was tenser and less optimistic. Too many loved ones had been lost under the ice to not anticipate the worst.

ມ.ມ.ມ

Vernie did not see Milo for three days. The search parties only returned to the village for food and some rest and then went back out, searching farther and farther up and down the Yukon. People who kept the search organized said that Milo had not returned yet. Knowing her husband, he was probably camping on the trail or in a hunter's shack so he could take full advantage of what little daylight the searchers had each day.

On the fourth day LaVerne was about to leave the village for home when an exhausted and bedraggled Milo arrived. His dogs ran in half-heartedly and were strangely quiet. There was something in the basket of Milo's sled, covered with a tarp.

Milo halted his team in the circle of bystanders, found LaVerne in the crowd and shook his head at her. He looked so grim that tears sprang to her eyes before even hearing the dreaded news.

Joe came down the steps of the lodge and walked to where Milo waited.

Milo gently placed a hand on Joe's shoulder, "I'm sorry, my friend. I have terrible news. I traveled up the Woods and found some bad ice. Elk-tail's sled was hanging submerged in the water, caught on some ice. His dogs were still attached to the sled--drowned. I followed the current down river about a mile and found your uncle washed into an eddy near another patch of bad ice. There was no sign of Elk-tail." Milo motioned to the sled, "I have brought Big Bear home to his people."

The women who had gathered around began to wail and the men stared at the ground.

"Thank you, slatsiin, for returning my uncle to his family. You should go home now and get some rest. We will care for my mother's brother in our way."

"We can search more, tomorrow, Joe, if you wish. I am willing to go out again."

"No, my friend, they are gone. Elk-tail will not be returning."

LaVerne walked up to her husband. "Let me take you home, Milo. You need rest and hot food." She turned to her friend, Joe, "I am so very sorry for your loss, Joe. Please let us know if we can do anything more."

"Thank you, slatsiin. When the ground is thawed we will lay Big Bear to rest so Mother can reclaim his spirit. We will hold a potlach in his and Elk-tail's honor. It would please me and their family if you and Milo would come."

"Of course. Please tell your mother how sorry I am."

The village men carefully lifted the body from the sled, leaving it covered with the tarp. It would be wrapped securely and stored in the communal ice house, until the spring, when a proper burial could occur.

Milo had turned his dogs and with LaVerne mounted and riding by his side they left the village and headed up the trail leading to their homestead. They rode in silence as neither one of them had words to express their sorrow at the tragic loss of Elk-tail, whom they considered a good friend.

They were soon pulling into their yard. The cabin looked dark and cold. No cheerful smoke came from the chimney, no lights shone a welcome. The goats scolded and the chickens clucked, not at all pleased with being left alone.

"If you'll see to your horse and the livestock, I'll get the dogs settled in."

"Yes of course. Let me just start a fire in the house and then I'll right out."

Without answering Milo walked away and began unclipping his dogs and walking them, one at a time, to the chains near their houses. He then removed their harnesses. LaVerne ran up the steps and into the cabin. She made quick work of starting a fire in, not only the cook stove, but the fireplace. Returning outside she led her horse to the barn and stabled her. Removing her saddle and bridle, she placed a light halter on her head. She pumped some fresh water into a bucket and gave the animal some grain. Taking the saddle blanket she rubbed down the horse's gleaming coat. She had mucked out the stall just that morning and had laid fresh hay on the floor.

Next she filled two buckets, one with chicken feed and one with food for the goats. She carried them into their enclosure, and while goats butted her in the legs and chickens pecked at her boots, she made certain that they were fed and had plenty of fresh water.

She glanced over to see how Milo was doing with the dogs. He was crouched down by his lead dog, Jake, with his face buried in the dogs' neck. He wasn't a man who let his feelings show but Vernie knew he was grieving deeply. He'd known Elk-tail and his family for many years. Letting herself out of the enclosure she went back to the barn for some fresh hay for the dogs' beds. After the grueling three days of searching they deserved every comfort.

LaVerne had locked the pups in a stall in the barn so they wouldn't be tempted to follow her or Milo during the days of the search. Now, set free, they bounded over to greet the team of dogs and Milo. She hoped that their joy for life would distract and cheer him. Sensing that something was terribly wrong with his mistress, Howie stayed close to her, following wherever she went. Leaving the dogs to weave their magic with Milo, she returned to the cabin and began a simple supper of leftover stew, fresh biscuits and coffee. She was exhausted and longed for her bed.

Forty-two

The long winter months were busy ones with chores around the homestead, making certain the livestock were kept warm and safe, and training Howie's pups to grow up to be a sled team. To that end, LaVerne and Milo developed and lengthened his trap line out around the moose lakes. It was a good run for Milo's team and the puppies thought it was great fun.

After only a few weeks of the young dogs running free beside the sled team Milo set up his sled to pull LaVerne and her sled behind him. She quickly learned the feel of her sled and how, when she moved her weight, her sled would respond. Periodically they would stop along the trail and clip the pups' harnesses to LaVerne's sled, three at a time. They were eager for the work and settled into the routine. Milo frequently set them free so they always saw it as an exciting adventure.

Howie had shown such potential that he was now second dog behind Milo's leader. Every other day they would run the trap line, harvesting the fur, setting fresh bait and scent, and checking traps.

One day they were on the trail, checking the line. Stopping at the first set Milo's dogs set up a terrific racket, lunging toward the trap site that was fifty feet off the trail. Milo set his anchor and walked into the trees.

"Stay here, Vernie, until I see what's what." Shortly Vernie heard him cursing. She laid her sled over to guarantee her novice sled dogs wouldn't pull out her anchor and run away and then walked quietly in to join Milo.

"What's the matter?"

"A damn wolverine has gotten my trap. All he left me was a little martin fur and one paw. Look at all the sign, tracks everywhere. Som'ah-bitch. Worse thing to have happen is a wolverine on our line. They'll come back again and again until we can catch 'em."

"Oh, no."

"Let's go on and see if he's found our other traps," Milo sighed.

Three miles and six sets later they found that every trap had been raided.

"God-damn-it! These varmints will ruin a trap line!"

"What can we do?"

"Set a trap for him and hope he ain't that smart. A lynx trap is heavy enough to get 'em and I got two on the sled."

Milo quickly replaced the martin trap with a sturdy lynx trap and baited it generously.

Milo explained to Vernie, "when trapping for any species in the weasel family the set's located at the high end of a thick branch leaning at a twenty-five degree angle against a small tree. The trap for this predator will be set on the ground against a large tree with sticks strategically placed to guide them into the bait. Then we toss a little loose snow on it to camouflage it." He explained it all as he set the lynx trap for the serious menace to his line.

On down the trail they found the next three traps had suffered the same fate. The last four were undisturbed. Milo turned sleds and dogs around and they returned to the beginning of the line. He set the second trap for the wolverine hoping to catch him before he could do more damage to his line.

"Well, we might as well call it a day. It's getting late," Milo sighed.

"We'll catch him tomorrow, you'll see," Vernie assured him, hoping she was right.

Forty-three

The next morning before dawn, Milo left Vernie sleeping and, using his dogs and sled traveled to his mill. Finding everything in order and running without a hitch he stopped by the village to get a few supplies. He also wanted to pick up their mail so he sat at the back of the store, near a pot-bellied stove, and chatted with Joe and a couple of elders, waiting for it to be sorted. Relishing the heat from the stove, Milo leaned his chair back against a wall and gulped his first cup of coffee of the day,

"How's your new trap line doin', Milo?"

"Pretty good until a goldurned wolverine started raiding it."

"Hmm…wolverine is a fierce competitor." Joe replied.

"You got that damn straight. Until I catch him, I won't be catchin' much fur. I put out a couple 'a lynx traps and will hope for the best."

"Wolverine fur gets good money," one of the elders joined in.

"Yeah. Don't much care for the meat but the dogs like it."

"That was a nice team of dogs Charlie had," Joe casually remarked.

Milo's chair slammed back to rest on four legs. "Whad'ya mean, *had*?"

Joe looked over with a frown, "She sold 'em off. I wisht I could'a afforded them. But she was asking a high price and every one of her dogs was worth it."

"When was this?" Milo asked.

"Late last week. I thought you knew. She left. Had a buyer in Fairbanks so drove her team that far. Her homestead's for sale. She went back east somewheres but can't remember the name."

"Boston." Milo said.

"Yep. That's the one. I overheard her leaving a letter for Miss Vernie. The post mistress's got it."

"Well, I'll be damned. What a goldurned crazy thing to do. Vernie's gonna hate that news."

"She didn't know neither?" Joe asked.

"I don't think so. We've been so busy this winter what with the fur trappin' line we haven't seen her as much as we usually do." Milo crushed his hat on his head and stood, "well, I'd best collect that letter and the rest of our mail and get on home. I'll be bringin' Vernie some painful news about her friend."

"Safe travels, slatsiin," the men called to Milo's back as he hurried away.

᎑᎑᎑

Before Milo returned home, he swung by Charlie's homestead, not quite believing that she was gone. He didn't want to cause his wife pain from the news and it not be true. Maybe it was a mistake. But as he drove into the yard he could tell—there's always a certain feeling, he thought, when a place has been sitting empty, devoid of people and animals. Different from when someone is just gone from home for the day or out on a hunting trip. The homestead had a cold and lonely feel to it already.

No smoke came from the chimney and there was a snow drift on the porch. Undisturbed snow layered the steps to the cabin. Charlie's live-stock was missing and the corral was empty. She was truly gone. He didn't know if her leaving was better than existing with her present in their lives every day. Now he had to live with a ghost--perhaps, even a perception on his wife's part, that of a lost love. Milo, shaking his head, turned away and headed for home.

When Milo drove into his yard he found his wife play-training her dogs. They had their harnesses on and were chasing her and each other dragging a chunk of firewood around. Vernie looked up at his arrival and grinned. She and the entire pack ran to his sled and gave out generous wife-kisses and doggy kisses.

"We missed you! How is the mill doing? How are our friends in the village?"

"Help me with the dogs, will you love?"

He knew she was studying his face, suspecting he had something on his mind.

"Sure. Did you eat? Are you hungry?"

"No I didn't and I'm not very..." Milo didn't finish his sentence and began unclipping dogs and walking them to their designated spots in the yard. "Could you get some chunks of salmon out for them?"

They both worked silently getting the dogs settled. LaVerne took the harnesses off her dogs and threw the chunks of wood back in the woodpile. She followed Milo toward the cabin.

"Did you get the flour? We're almost out."

Milo turned midstride and returned to his sled. He grabbed the wooden box used to store food stuffs and carried it to the cabin. Anything to delay giving his wife the news. He was well aware of the special bond the two women had and that Charlie was in love with his wife. He'd tried to be understanding and LaVerne had gone to great lengths to assure him that it was him she loved. But when the three of them were together he felt like the outsider.

Vernie held the door for him and then she and Howie followed him inside.

"What's wrong, Milo? And don't tell me nothing because it's all over your face."

Milo set down the box and removed his coat, hat and gloves. Vernie hung them by the door with her coat.

"Sit down, Vernie. It's not good news."

Vernie sank onto the bench by the table, "God, don't tell me someone else has been lost to the river. I couldn't bear it."

"No, no! Sorry. I didn't mean to scare you. But it is a loss and I'm so sorry I am the one to carry this news to you."

"Milo you're scaring me. What is it? Just spit it out, please."

"Charlie's gone."

Vernie paled at his words, "Gone? Whatever do you mean? Dead?"

"No! Christ, I'm making such a hash of this. She left her homestead, sold her dog team in Fairbanks and went back to Boston. She left you a letter."

"No, she didn't. She couldn't have…" Vernie rose and dashed to the door to grab her coat. Hand on the door's latch, she stopped at Milo's next words.

"Joe saw her. I went by her place just now to be certain the news was true before I told you. The place is empty. No livestock, no nothin'. Nobody's been there for at least a week."

Milo reached inside his shirt and pulled out a thin pile of mail. He put it on the table and, riffling through it, found an envelope with Charlie's distinctive handwriting. He held it out to Vernie.

Silent tears streaking her face she crossed to him and took it.

Letter in hand, she walked through the bedroom door and closed it softly.

"Vernie, I'm sorry."

Forty-four

LaVerne sat on the edge of the bed and stared at the letter. She still couldn't believe that her friend would leave without a word. The feeling of loss stunned her. Kicking off her boots and holding the letter to her heart, she crawled under the quilts. How could this be true? Her best friend in the world, outside of family, left without telling her.

Yes, they'd tried to talk about the sled fiasco and how marriage had changed their friendship but the disappearance of Elk-tail and his uncle had inter-erupted that. They'd never talked again. They'd seen each other briefly over the past weeks and conversation had been congenial. LaVerne assumed that the sled-thing had blown over. How could she have been so wrong? She wept again for the loss of Elk-tail and now her friend.

Exhausted LaVerne finally slept and a couple of hours later Milo's voice and the dogs barking brought her back to harsh reality. She sat up and leaned against the bed's headboard. Slitting the envelope, still in her hand, she took out the single sheet of paper.

My dearest Vernie,

If you're reading this then you know I am gone. I'm sorry because I know this will hurt you but I don't think you ever realized how much I was hurting. I lost you and then had to stand by while you chose another and married him. Your happiness was so evident it was another arrow to my heart.

You can't help how you feel and I can't help my feelings for you. It is just the way of life. But I have a choice and I'm taking it. You probably already know that I have returned to my family in Boston. I told Joe before I left. I am hoping the old adage of out of sight, out of mind is true and I will find some peace.

I left Moon with Stan in the hopes that you will take her. She would be so unhappy in a big city and so happy to stay with her son and his puppies. Please do me this last favor and give her a home.

I want you to be happy and I wish you and Milo a long and prosperous life together.

I leave you with Robert Service. It is how we began and appropriately how we shall end...

"—just Home and Love! It's hard to guess
Which of the two were best to gain;
Home without Love is bitterness;
Love without Home is often pain.
No! each alone will seldom do;
Somehow they travel hand and glove:
If you win one you must have two,
Both Home and Love..."

Alaska will always be my Home and you will always be my Love.
Charlie

Fresh tears coursed down Vernie's cheeks as she stared across the room. The dogs outside suddenly set up a loud din. In their voices Vernie could tell someone was coming down the trail to their homestead. She heard Milo shout a greeting. Stuffing the letter into the pocket of her pants, she rose and went out into the kitchen. Pumping some water into the sink she dashed water on her face and tucked in her shirt. She then crossed to the door where she took down her coat and hat, and putting them on, she walked out onto the porch.

There stood Stan, his sled and dogs and...Moon. Vernie ran down the steps to Moon and, kneeling in the snow, threw her arms around the dog. It took everything in her not to cry again. Howie jumped on both of them in his excitement to see his mother.

"Of course, we'll take her," Milo was saying to Stan. "If that's what Charlie wanted we'd love to have her. Come on in for coffee, can you?"

"I will another time. I have to get into the village for a few things and the mail. Then back home, hopefully before the storm hits. How're you, Vernie?"

"I'm just fine, Stan. How's your family? Have you seen Elk-tail's mother lately? Is she doing better?" She rose and tucked her hand through Milo's arm and into his pocket where she found his big, warm grip.

"Family's doing good, thanks for asking. Edna is doing better. She is very stoic but the loss of a son--it doesn't bear thinkin' about." He shook his head. "I can't imagine the pain if I lost one of mine."

"Are you sure you don't want a cup of coffee to warm your trip?" LaVerne asked.

"No. I best be on my way. Just wanted to bring Moon over like Charlie asked me to do. Too bad about her going back home. She'll be missed."

Neither LaVerne nor Milo answered him. They watched as he turned his dogs and headed back down the trail.

"I could use some of that coffee," Milo told her.

They walked back toward the cabin followed by Howie. Moon sat in the snow, shivering and whining.

"Come on, girl, you live here now," Milo said.

Without hesitation Moon bounded after them and up the steps into the cabin. After taking their outerwear off and hanging Milo's coat, hat and gloves on the drying rack, Vernie got down mugs. She took some cold biscuits, honey, sugar and goat's milk and brought everything to the table

Milo sat down and watched her. Moon lay under the table, across his feet.

"I thought you might be a little hungry. Dinner is a couple of hours away. Did you eat lunch?"

"No. Didn't want to bang around the kitchen while you were sleeping."

"Yes, I'm sorry about that. I must have been more tired than I thought."

"Grief and loss will do that to a person."

Not meeting his eyes, she poured scalding coffee into both their mugs. She sat down across from her husband and took the wrinkled letter from her pocket. She opened it, smoothed it out and placed in front of Milo. She kept her hands busy dipping sugar and pouring milk into her coffee.

"You don't have to show me that," he said.

"I want you to read it. There hasn't been any secrets between us so far and there won't be."

He pulled the letter to him but left it lying on the table as he read it. LaVerne watched him frown as he got to the end. He picked it up and put it on her side of the table. She didn't miss the gesture for what it was. He didn't want it near him.

She met his eyes, "Milo, this was her way of saying goodbye. I can't help what the letter says and I can't help her feelings for me. I hope I've shown you every day that it is *you* I love…"

Milo raised his hand to silence her. "Vernie, I'm only going to say this once and then we'll forget about it. I've understood from that day when Charlie tried to warn me off you…"

LaVerne was shocked and took a breath to speak.

"No. Please let me finish. I knew she was in love with you. Not many people around these parts know about her preferences. And I wasn't completely sure until I saw her with you. Her love came outta her like a beacon. I respect you and your strength of character. You chose me and you promised to love and honor me. That was good enough for me.

I have always loved you, from the first day I set eyes on you. And I think you have grown to love me. I know too that it must'a been hard for her to see us together. God knows it would have been hell for me if it was the other way around and I'd a'prob'ly taken off too. You've given me no doubts about your loyalty to me, as your husband, and that you only loved Charlie as a friend."

He paused, smearing honey on a biscuit but not eating it. LaVerne watched in silence.

"But I'm done living with Charlie's feelings and her presence in our daily life. And I sure as hell *will not* live with her ghost. You have to put this in the past. I think I've been more understanding than any man might be but it's done, I'm done. If you can do that we won't speak of it again. If you can't then I guess I will have to re-think some things."

A long silence ensued with the only sound in the cabin being the crackle of the fire, Moon's dreaming grunts under the table and the clink of spoons in mugs. Milo looked up and met her eyes.

"Milo, my love. You have been so patient. That's one of the many reasons I love you so much. Charlie was a good friend but, on my side, *only* a friend. I didn't--don't love her that way. I love you. I promise you, you will not have to live with the ghost of Charlie. I want a life with *you*. To love you forever and, God willing, to have a family with you."

She took his hand in hers and brought it to her mouth, kissing his rough knuckles. "Are we okay?"

Milo brought her hand back across the table and rubbed his cheek with it, "More than okay, Vernie, my love."

LaVerne had to get them back on track and on with their life together, "We should see to the livestock and dogs before it gets too dark, don't you think?"

Smiling Milo stood, "I'll start feeding the dogs if you want to feed your goats and chickens."

Moon jumped up and woofed at Milo.

"Looks like you got yourself a new dog," Vernie laughed at Moon.

"She's a good girl," Milo said scratching the dog's ears.

Howie rose from his bed in front of the fire and walked to Vernie's side. Not to be out done by his mother, he gave a half howl that broke the tension in the room and set both humans to chuckling.

"Yes, Howie, we love you too," Vernie told him.

Forty-five

The next morning a storm that had howled all night had finally blown itself out, leaving three feet of new snow. LaVerne cooked a big breakfast while Milo scraped off the porch and steps. She'd packed a food sack as they planned to run the trap line today. Chores done, they'd hurried through the morning meal and were on the trail by sunup.

As they loaded the sled, Milo had told her, "I think it's a good idea to bring Moon along so she can acclimate to her new home and the other dogs who she doesn't know. And they can get used to the new member of their pack."

"Good idea. She's so even tempered she'll do fine."

Howie was in harness behind the lead dog and the puppies would pull LaVerne's lighter sled behind Milo. The first trap, where Milo had set the lynx foot-hold trap was undisturbed but the bait was gone and the area was full of wolverine tracks.

"He's a smart one," Milo said as he returned to the trail where LaVerne waited, "Came around the back of the trap and stole the bait right out from behind the set."

The next three traps had been ravaged. Sprung traps with sign of ermine and martin fur. The wolverine had been busy. The next few traps had been raided of their bait but no sign that fur had been caught. The sleds and dogs approached the site where Milo had set the second lynx trap. The dogs went crazy and focused on the trees where the trap had been set.

"Whoa! Easy, boys!" Milo yelled. "Quiet down!"

Milo had brought his .22 gauge rifle with him beside his sidearm. With a wolverine in the neighborhood a man couldn't be too careful. Now he anchored his sled securely and glanced back at Vernie.

"Stay here until I call you. The dogs know something is at the trap or in it. You got your pistol?"

LaVerne patted her side and nodded. "Can I come with you?" She whispered.

"No. I'll call you when I knows it's safe. But keep a sharp eye out. Those varmints are sneaky."

Milo walked slowly and quietly into the trees. He came within ten yards of the trap and stopped. He took the safety off of his rifle. What he saw through the trees was devastation. All the branches around the site had been chewed up. Even some of the saplings had been attacked. There was no snow around the trap, the wolverine had fought so hard. Just churned up and raw soil. A large black and gray shape was lying on the ground.

Milo started forward and the wolverine exploded into life. He whirled around and snarled at Milo, all the while yanking on the foot trap that had him bound. If he got loose there was no doubt that he would attack. He raised his gun and fired one shot. The animal dropped dead. Not trusting the sly beast he walked slowly to the body and poked it with the end of his rifle. Nothing.

"Vernie," he called, "you can come in now."

Milo squatted beside the beautiful animal and gently dislodged his paw from the trap. The fur was pretty torn up due to the animal trying to escape.

LaVerne walked into the clearing and stared. The wolverine was huge. She was shocked by the damage he had done to the area but was happy for

Milo that he had finally caught the villain who was tearing up his traps and fur.

"Pretty, huh?" Milo held up the animal. "One foot has been mangled but the fur'll still get a good price. If you'll take him, I'll get the trap. We will need to reset somewhere else.

They walked back to the dogs and Milo showed them the catch. It was partly to reward them for setting up the alarm and partly to train them that they shouldn't bite or touch the animal. Storing the animal in a game bag, they continued up the trail.

They had three more traps to check and, with the wolverine problem eliminated, each trap held a martin. Milo kept on up the trail and extended his line another two miles, making sets as they went. They came to one of the half dozen moose lakes and stopped for some hot coffee and lunch.

Milo started a fire and put the pot on to boil. LaVerne got out their food sack and a bag of snacks for the dogs. She spread a fur out by the fire and Moon immediately plopped herself down. Howie, as part of the sled team today, whimpered to join them.

"Nope, dog. You're working today so no house privileges for you." He poured hot coffee for them both and they munched on sandwiches.

"How 'bout fresh trout for dinner?" Milo asked.

"What? How? Where?"

"It's early. We could do a little ice fishing before we head for home. Save some of the meat from your sandwich for bait."

"Oh, I'd love some fresh fish. But we don't have any poles or gear with us."

"I always carry hooks, a couple of sinkers, and line. That's all we'll need."

LaVerne quickly stowed the leftover food in the sack and, shaking the fur free of snow and twigs, she put both back into her sled. They left the coffee pot simmering on some hot rocks, for later when they came off the ice and wanted something warm to drink.

Shortly they were walking out onto the ice of the small lake. Milo began to break a hole in the ice with his axe. A foot down he hit water and proceeded to clean out the ice that that fallen in the hole. He baited a line for LaVerne so she could start fishing. He showed her how to 'jig'; little upward jerks of the line every few minutes. Six feet away he cut himself a similar hole and threw his line into the water.

Suddenly Vernie squeaked and jerked her line out of the water. A beautiful rainbow trout flew out of the hole and lay flapping on the ice.

"Milo, look! I caught one."

Milo was grinning at her across the ice when his line went taught. He set the hook and yanked his line from the water catching another trout.

"Do you need me to bait your hook," he called.

"No. I think I've got it. Nice fish by the way, but just a little smaller than mine."

"Oh, so that's the way it's going to be, is it? Okay, I'm up for a challenge. Biggest fish doesn't have to wash the dinner dishes and gets to sit by the fire and be waited on." He laughed.

"Done and done! Hope you like washing dishes," Vernie plunked her line back in to the hole.

Nine gorgeous rainbow trout later they decided that was enough for their dinner and enough left over for a special treat for the dogs. After comparing sizes, LaVerne had caught the biggest fish by two inches and was looking forward to being spoiled that evening. Milo fashioned a stringer out of a thin willow branch and they returned to their fire and the dogs.

As they finished their mugs of hot coffee Milo teased her, "No fair. You had beginners' luck going for you."

"What do you mean? I've been fishing with my Pa and brothers since I could hold a pole."

"Have you ever ice fished before?"

"No."

"There you go--beginners' luck. I call foul."

"You're still doing the dishes and cleaning the fish."

"If you say so, wife. I think I'll clean them here instead of the cabin. Get me an empty sack, would you?"

LaVerne went to the sled and grabbed a sack for the fish. Milo was fast and had already started gutting and cleaning the third fish.

"You want more coffee before I throw it out?"

"Sure. Warm up what I have here." He handed his mug to her.

"Eww, Milo, fish guts on the mug." She set it down in the snow and poured the hot brew into it. LaVerne then threw the left over coffee on the fire to help put it out and finished by kicking snow on the hot embers.

She stood watching Milo and marveled at how efficient his movements were. In no time all nine fish were gutted and in the sack. Milo scrubbed his hands in the snow, drying them on the top of the bag. He quickly donned his gloves.

"Ready?"

"Yes, my love. Let's go home. Should I let the puppies loose?"

"Down the trail a bit you can. We don't want them to get into the gut pile here."

"Oh, right," she turned and looked at them. Four little faces, two with masks of black against silver fur stared at her, ears cocked. "Look Milo. They are wondering what the next adventure will be. Aren't they cute?"

Milo grunted, "They're shap'in up real nice. Doing a good job in the harness and obeying you for the most part. Cute? Yeah I guess so."

LaVerne laughed. "Milo you know you can't hide your tender heart from me. I see you with Moon when you think I'm not looking. Admit it, you think the puppies are cute and beyond."

Milo grunted and continued to check the dogs and sled line. As he checked the pups he ruffled the fur on each of their heads and murmured things like, 'good dog' and 'good boy'.

"It's a good trail back." Milo told her, "Let's unhook your dogs and sled from mine and see how you and the dogs do. What do you think?"

"I'd love that. It's time to see if I'm a true musher or just a follower," she laughed.

"I'm going to have you go in front of me so I can keep an eye on you. Remember if the sled starts to tip over just throw yourself clear. The weight of the sled will stop the dogs."

Milo moved to the edge of the trail to let Vernie go ahead. As she pasted she grinned across at him, yelling, "Hike! Hike!"

Her dogs surged by and Milo quickly followed. In the thrill of the first solo run, Vernie forgot all about unhooking her dogs to let them play. They were so eager to work for her and she reveled in it.

🐾🐾🐾

Two hours later the two teams rushed into the home yard. "Whoa! Whoa," LaVerne called. Her dogs slowed and stopped. Barking and yipping they turned to her as if looking for approval. She stomped the anchor into the snowy ground and walked up the line, praising each dog excessively. The recipe for creating a great sled dog was a strong bond between dog and human, good food and water, shelter and lots of praise for a job well done. Positive reinforcement was the key. A sled dog was never punished.   Like an athlete, they were in training all year long.

All the dogs were taken to their individual houses and chained. Milo checked the hay inside each dog house for dryness. Vernie scrubbed their bowls with snow and filled them from an open spot in the creek. Milo got a fire going, in the fire pit, and put a big pot of stew on to boil. The stew included fish parts, chunks of frozen caribou, and cut up potatoes. The liquid from the stew would rehydrate the dogs too.

Chores done, they were just about to go into the cabin, when the dogs began to bark excitedly. Turning Vernie and Milo saw Howie's mate, Tukoni, standing at the edge of the trees. Howie sprang off the porch and ran to her, whining in welcome. Moon followed closely behind.

The two bitches sniffed each other rear and front and, in a flash, began to fight. Snarling and biting they were evenly matched but Moon, being the alpha bitch older and heavier, quickly had Tukoni pinned to the ground.

Milo had jumped off the porch anticipating what might happen. He grabbed Moon by the collar yelling, No, Moon! Heel!" Moon immediately obeyed and backed off, letting go of Tukoni's ruff. The wolf leapt up and ran into the forest with Howie on her heels.

"Is she hurt, Milo?" Vernie asked.

"No, a little bite to her ear. It's already stopped bleeding. Not much more than a scratch."

"I hope Tukoni's not injured."

"I didn't see any blood on her and look," he indicated the ground, "no blood on the snow. Always a good sign." He rubbed Moon on her flanks, "What were you thinking girl? That's a wild wolf you tangled with."

Vernie crossed to the husky and squatted by her side. She wrapped her arms around Moon's neck, "Protecting us, literally, from the big, bad wolf, weren't you girl? But she's Howie's wife and welcome here."

Moon licked Vernie's face in apology. Out of the trees, Howie appeared and ran to Vernie, whining. She hugged her dog close, "it's okay, Howie. Just a little misunderstanding."

"Well! We've had our excitement for the day, I'd say. How about feeding your man now?"

LaVerne laughed and led the way into the cabin.

Forty-six

Spring came with a vengeance. Huge ice flows, some as big as houses, crammed the Yukon. Making their way down river, pushing against the banks of the river, the village came close to flooding.

LaVerne had been on the homestead alone for three days. Men from Joe's family, Stan and Milo had gone on a moose hunt for the celebratory potlach that would be a part of the burial ritual for Elk-tail and their uncle. The women in the village had spent the winter sewing special furs, trimmed with shells and beads, for the body shrouds.

She welcomed the time alone and after the chores were finished each day she sat in her rocker, with her guitar, and thought about writing some new music. Time had slipped by what with the hard life creating a homestead, running a trap line, the daily work that never ceased and married life. She hadn't written a line of music in all that time. She scribbled on a scrap of paper.

We met in a snow storm,
waiting for winter to go to spring-warm
We kissed under a hunter's moon
Our future became our past far too soon

The years fled past, far too fast
We knew it would never last
True love lives on
If only in a song,
If only in a song, If only in a song

She admitted to herself that she wasn't really certain whether the lyrics were about Milo or Charlie. In privacy she still mourned the loss of her good friend but was very careful that Milo never saw her sadness. She looked out over her yard. It was quiet with the sled team gone. The goats stared at her, munching their cud. The chickens pecked and clucked with self-importance. Moon and Howie slept at her feet.

She sighed in total contentment with how her life had turned out. Now the only thing missing was a family of their own. But time would take care of that missing piece. She looked down at what she'd written so far and strummed chords on her guitar, trying to find just the right feel to go with the words.

The dogs' heads jerked up and their ears pointed toward the trail-head. Howie growled deep in his throat then changed to a happy bark. Moon rose silently and watched the other side of the clearing. From the edge of the forest Milo's sled team burst into the yard and Howie and Moon rushed off the porch to greet them.

Milo dressed in trail fur and hat, with only his eyes showing, raised his hand in greeting. Guiding the team near to where their dog houses were, he stopped them and threw the anchor down. He pulled off his hat and grinned at his wife. Vernie was off the porch and running across to her husband. She ran into his arms.

"I missed you!" she cried.

"Missed you too, wife. Everything good here at home?"

"Yes. All's quiet. How was the hunt?"

"Good. We got two bulls and two big cows. Plenty of meat for the ceremony. I brought my portion home." He walked to the sled and uncovered a hind quarter of moose meat, "Let me string it up. Would you start settling the dogs while I do that?"

"Of course." Vernie began to unhitch dogs and walking them to their chains. Milo tied a rope securely around the leg of the meat and threw the other end of the rope over the pole of the storage cache. He pulled the hind quarter up until it was six feet off the ground and safe from predators who might be looking for an easy meal.

He began a fire in the pit and soon was cooking up a pot of hot food for his dogs. They'd worked hard on the trail for three days, living on cold food. Vernie had all the dogs secured and was cleaning water bowls. While they waited for the pot of stewed caribou and salmon to boil they sat on the steps of their cabin.

"Tell me about your hunt."

"Joe got the first bull. The cow was right beside him so I shot her. A couple of the elders bagged the other two. Stan got another cow. The elders were very pleased. The burial will be as it should be for two respected hunters. They thought it would be warm enough in a couple of weeks to dig the graves."

"They will let us know."

"Of course. I brought the heart home for dinner tonight, if you like."

"Yum. Fried up in the skillet--my favorite."

They sat in silence thinking of Elk-tail and the terrible loss. Milo sighed and getting up, walked to the fire. "Pot's boiled."

He lifted it from the fire and added some cold water to bring the temperature down. With a large ladle, which he kept for that purpose, he began to walk from dog to dog filling each of their bowls with the tasty stew. The pups soon forgot that they'd been left behind and clambered for food with the rest of the dogs.

"I'll get Howie's and Moon's bowls, shall I?" Vernie called to him.

"Yes, there's plenty for all."

LaVerne walked up onto the porch and over to her rocker. She stuffed the paper that the new lyrics were written on into her pocket and picked up her guitar.

"Been writing again?" Milo asked as he walked toward her. "That's good."

"Yes, just noodling around with a new song."

"It's been a while. I'll look forward to hearing it."

"It's not close to being finished, Milo. I don't even have the music written yet."

"Well, when the time comes I'd like to hear it."

Vernie walked into the cabin and set her guitar in a corner. She returned outside with the two food bowls and set them on the porch. Howie and Moon sat, tails thunking on the wood floor and gazed expectantly at Milo. Milo ladled food into the bowls and the two dogs began to wolf it down.

Milo looked at his wife and grinned, "Greedy little mutts."

"Come inside by the fire. I'm sure you're cold."

"Let me just wash out this pot and I'll be right in."

Forty-seven

Two and a half weeks later LaVerne and Milo took one sled, a team of four dogs, Moon and Howie and headed into the village to join the funeral pot-latch for Joe's brother and uncle. They planned to return each night to the homestead, for chores, but would participate in the three days of celebration and burial.

The purpose of the potlatch was to help the relatives of the decedent grieve. It was believed that the celebration would assist the deceased to transition from the living to the spiritual world.

When LaVerne and Milo arrived at the communal lodge they found that hitch lines had been set up for the various teams of dogs that would be arriving. The lines were spaced far enough apart to assure that the dogs, unfamiliar with each other, did not fight. A huge fire pit was burning brightly and a large grate sat over the flames.

Several very large pots bubbled and spit. These pots contained moose-head soup which would be the culinary centerpiece thanks to the hunting party that brought back a successful kill. Every part of the head was used; meat from the head, the brain, the nose and tongue. The feast would include every kind of wild meat. Duck, geese, white fish, salmon, moose, caribou, beaver, muskrat and bear.

The preparing and cooking of the meat was done, mostly outdoors, and only by the men of the tribe. It was considered bad luck for women, particularly young women, to handle fresh meat.

Following a prescribed pattern, the decedent's family designated the hunting party, hosted the potlatch, and gathered additional food, gifts and money for their guests.

It hadn't been appropriate for the guests to bring food. On this occasion all food had to come from the grieving family. So LaVerne had written a poem in the hopes that Edna, Elk-tail's mother, would include it in the ceremony or take it as a keepsake and token of hers and Milo's friendship. LaVerne would find a quiet moment to slip the piece of paper into Elk-tail's mother's hand and tell her how much she enjoyed knowing her son. Milo had read it and found it fitting and a gesture of love.

I travel the road in this life,
people gathered around me
only to find that they are mere shadows,
a wisp of spirit in a fleeting moment of time

Looking up after what seems but a few miles,
the crowd has thinned
until as the last valley approaches,
I find I am walking the road alone

the one I leaned on, loved, cherished was a
shadow, never to be touched again
impossible, I say
not to be endured, I scream to the heavens
my voice rolls out over the valley and mountain
and dies in the trees

I travel the road and reaching the final
destination, I end the journey as I began, alone

After greeting the family and other friends from the village, Milo and LaVerne set out their furs and blankets on the ground near their dogs.

"Have they already buried Elk-tail and his uncle?" LaVerne whispered.

"No. The potlatch will begin with the procession to the cemetery. The blood relatives are forbidden to handle the corpse and that is left to the in-laws. They were responsible for taking care of all the funeral arrangements including building the coffins, digging the graves, and carrying the coffins to the cemetery. The family and guests will follow the procession.

"I'm not looking forward to that," LaVerne murmured.

"I know, but it is expected of everyone. Once the burial is complete we return here and the feasting begins. The moose-head soup will be served first to the elders of the tribe, then to the family and then to the rest of the guests. Storytelling, singing, dancing and the distribution of gifts will go on for three days.

"Elk-tail would like that."

"Yes, Elk-tail was a fine storyteller and loved to sing even though he couldn't carry a tune in a basket." Milo stared out at the gathering, and remembered the years he had hunted with his friend and Joe. Sitting in camp out on the trail around a campfire while Elk-tail told his stories.

"Milo?" She had felt him go far away.

"Yes, my love. Anyway, the gifts that the deceased's family will give to the in-laws include blankets and rifles. The blankets traditionally symbolize warmth and affection while the rifles symbolize the ability to hunt and feed oneself.

"It all sounds lovely. I wish my funeral could be like that."

Milo smiled tenderly at his wife, "Plenty of years ahead to make those plans, my love."

On the third day LaVerne found herself sitting with Joe and Elk-tail's mother, Edna, and some of the elder women of the tribe. There had been singing, dancing, many stories, and feasting, from dawn until dusk, just as Milo had predicted. Now, the women drank coffee and gossiped about the potlatch. They shared stories of the women of Edna's family going back three generations. One of the oldest women, Little Doe, stared at LaVerne so long that she began to squirm. As the woman was very old, she chalked it up to senility and tried to ignore the elderly lady. She couldn't have been more mistaken. Finally she stared back and smiled.

"Daughter, you are quickening," the old one said in the Athabaskan language.

LaVerne didn't not understand and turned to her friend, Edna, with a quizzical look on her face.

Little Doe says you are quickening," Edna told her.

"Quickening? I don't understand." Vernie said.

The other women tittered and nodded.

"You are pregnant, Miss Vernie. Little Doe is never wrong." Edna replied.

"No, that's not possible." LaVerne looked around the fire at the native women. They beamed smiles back at her.

"Daughter, it will be a boy," Little Doe went on.

"What?" LaVerne turned to Edna once again.

"She says it will be a boy. She is famous, for a hundred miles up and down the river, for her knowledge. Expecting mothers come to receive her visions of a healthy child and an easy birth. She is never wrong."

"But, but," LaVerne sputtered. "I'm taking steps--we aren't trying--it's the wrong time."

"New life," another elder woman huffed, "there is never a wrong time. Always the right time."

"The circle of life," Edna, Elk-tail's mother spoke, "We lose two strong hunters and gain another."

"A baby?" LaVerne's eyes filled with tears. Maybe that explained why she was extra tired lately and wanted nothing more than to sleep. She tried to think back to her last flow. She'd always been irregular and just dealt with it when it came. She couldn't remember but she thought perhaps it was over two months ago. How could she have not noticed?

The old women gathered around her, petting her head and holding her hands. Tittering and laughing they began to chant and sing a song of welcome to the baby that secretly nestled within Vernie.

※※※

At dusk, on the last day of the festivities, Milo and LaVerne drove into their yard. It had been a wonderful three days of feasting and celebrating the two men that had been lost beneath the ice. But it had been exhausting too. LaVerne contemplated their routine as they arrived to the barks, naaa's and clucks of the animals that had been left behind. It was always the same, first take care of the dog team and see to their comfort.

Milo hurried into the cabin just long enough to get fires going while Vernie began unhitching dogs and leading them to their spots in the yard. They hurried through the evening chores and then walked arm in arm to the cabin.

"What was the big hullabaloo with you and the old ladies? They seemed very happy about something. Some of the men gave me funny looks and slapped me on the back. Strangest durn thing."

"I'll tell you over dinner." Avoiding looking at him, LaVerne hurried onto the porch and into the cabin.

At the end of their simple supper LaVerne was almost nodding off into her plate. Milo gently patted her hand and she jerked awake. Why don't you go on to bed? I'll do up the dishes and close up the house.

"Really? Oh, I would love that. I am exhausted. Can I go to bed right now?"

Milo chuckled, "Yes, my love. Right now. I'll be in in a little bit."

News forgotten and without another word Vernie rose and hurried across the room to their bedroom. Milo collected the dirty dishes from the table and placed them in the sink. He ladled hot water from the stove's reservoir into a dishpan. After washing and racking the dishes and pots, he cleaned the table top just like Vernie liked it done. He then poured himself a mug of coffee and settled in front of the fireplace. He stared into the flames remembering all the good times he'd shared with his friend, Elk-tail.

Forty-eight

The next morning LaVerne slipped from their bed and left Milo snoring. She would get the coffee on and begin a nice breakfast for her husband. What with all the food at the potlatch, the last thing they had wanted to do over the past three days was eat when they got home each night. Vernie cut thick slabs of bacon and set them next to the skillet. She got a bowl of eggs from the cool box. She began to cut thick slices of the bread that the family had sent home with them.

Suddenly the smell of the bacon overwhelmed her and she dashed for the door. She ran down to the end of the porch and, leaning over the railing, retched into the yard. When she was finished, she wiped her mouth on her shirt sleeve.

Ugh. I guess that confirms the elders' prediction.

She returned to the cabin hoping that Milo hadn't heard her. Her stomach rolled when she breathed in the aromas of breakfast. She had little experience but she was told stories by her sister, Lillas, of how rough the first few months could be when carrying a child. *What had her sister called it? Oh, yes, morning sickness.*

Vernie brushed her teeth at the kitchen sink and was just going to wake Milo up when he walked into the main room, fully dressed.

"Good morning! You're up early."

"Good morning, my love. Thanks to you I got a wonderful night's sleep," Vernie kissed him on the cheek.

"I need coffee, woman, not your pecks on the cheek," he teased.

"Sit. I'll get you a cup. Are you hungry?"

"Starved."

LaVerne placed a steaming cup of coffee in front of Milo and turned back to the cook stove. She filled the tea pot and put it to boil. A mug of tea suddenly appealed far more than coffee. The bacon hit the skillet and began to sizzle and snap.

"Could I have scrambled eggs this morning?"

"Certainly." LaVerne turned back and began to crack eggs into a bowl.

Milo watched in amazement as she suddenly bolted for the door again and rushed outside without a coat. He could then hear her vomiting off the end of the porch. There was silence for a bit and then his wife walked back in the cabin.

"Do you think you got some bad food at the potlatch? Or do you have influenza?"

LaVerne pulled the skillet off the stove and then joined Milo at the table.

"The elder women of the tribe gave me some news yesterday. You'll be glad you're sitting down."

"I saw them tittering and flitting around you. It was a curious sight. What did they have to tell you?"

"I'm expecting…"

"Expecting what?"

Milo looked so innocent and perplexed that LaVerne almost laughed in his face. She raised her eyebrows and grinned at him.

Milo's face got beet red, "Expecting--as in a baby? You--*we* are having a baby? That's why your breasts are--" He was uncomfortable speaking about such personal things in broad daylight. "And you haven't turned me away at that time of the month for--what's it been? Seven? Eight weeks? And now you're puking off the porch. My God, woman! You're carrying my child!"

He jumped up, pulling her up with him. Lifting her up with an arm around her shoulders and one under her knees, he twirled her around and around.

"My gracious, Milo! Put me down before I puke all over *you*!"

He set her down immediately and hugged her gently. He whispered into her hair, "A baby." He sighed. "I'm going to be a father. God, Vernie, I love you. Thank you."

LaVerne took his face in his hands and looked at him, "No thank you, husband for a wonderful life and for being so kind and gentle and loving. Our baby is going to be so happy with you as his Daddy."

"He?"

"Yes, Little Doe assures me it's a boy and she's never wrong, you know."

"Have you thought about names?" Milo asked as he guided her to the comfy chair in front of the fireplace. He sat on the floor at her knees.

"Milo! I just found out," Vernie laughed.

"Well, have you?"

"You know me so well. Yes, I'd like to call him Milo Robert Levi Robbins."

"Whew! That's quite a handle. I understand the Levi for your Pa but who's Robert?"

Vernie stared at him as realization dawned on him. "Oh. Robert Service, your hero."

"*One* of my heroes."

Milo blushed. "Well I like the name fine but I don't want to saddle a son of mine with my name. Kids make fun of kids with names like Milo. Let's switch it around--Robert Milo Levi Robbins. What do you think?"

"I love it. He can be Robbie when he's younger, Rob, Robert or Bob when he's a man."

Milo turned and pressed his face against LaVerne's stomach. "Hello, in there. Robbie? Can you hear your ole' Dad out here? I love you already and I can't wait to meet'cha."

Tears of joy coursed down Vernie's face.

Forty-nine

Two months later

Milo decided on his way back from Tanana that he would ride over to Charlie's old homestead and check on things. He had no responsibility to it or to her but it bothered him that such a fine place was sitting empty and alone. He was shocked when he saw smoke rising from the chimney through the trees and several dogs set up a howl at his approach.

As he came out of the trees into the yard three dogs came running, tails wagging. The yard was neat and clean, there were chickens in the enclosure once again. Charlie's corral had had some repairs done to it.

He called out just as the cabin's front door opened. "Hallo the..." In a normal voice he called out, "Welcome. I'm Milo your closest neighbor."

A huge man came out from the shadowy porch and stood on the top step. He was over six feet tall and all muscle. His hair was so blonde it looked white in the sun. His eye lashes and brows matched the hair. His eyes, now fixed on Milo, were an icy blue. Then he smiled and his whole demeanor changed.

"Welcome to our home. Step down and have something hot to drink at our table, ya? I'm Finn." The snowy mountains of Scandinavia flavored his speech.

"Don't mind if I do." Milo dismounted and walked his horse to the hitching post at the bottom of the stairs, where he tied one rein. The two men shook hands reintroducing themselves.

"Milo Robbins, nice to meet'cha."

"Finn Swenson, Milo, it's a pleasure to meet a neighbor. Come inside and meet my wife and children."

They walked up the steps and into the house. A pretty little woman, hardly five foot tall, was at the sink washing dishes. She was as blonde as her husband but her hair was darker, honey colored. On the hearth rug two small children were playing some kind of board game. They resembled their father and one might mistake them for albinos, they were so fair.

"Lillian, this is our neighbor, Milo Robbins."

The woman wiped her hands and came to shake Milo's hand. "It's lovely to meet you, Mr. Robbins. Can you stay for coffee or mulled cider and a visit?"

"Only if you call me Milo, Lillian." He grinned at her. "I'd love some coffee."

"And you must call me Lily." She bustled back to the stove, scooped coffee grounds into the boiling coffee pot and pulled it to the side to steep.

"Barn, come and meet our Nya vän…" Finn called his children to him.

"English please, Finn, we have a guest." Lily chided softly.

"Excuse me Milo. Children, meet our new friend, Mr. Robbins."

The kids rose and crossed to their father. The boy looked to be about seven and the pretty little girl, about five. Her thumb popped into her mouth as she leaned against her father's knee and stared at Milo.

"Say hello, barn."

"Hello, Mr. Robin." The small boy gave Milo a shy smile.

The girl's thumb made a popping noise as she removed it. "Hhh-whoa." The thumb returned to its place.

"Hello, children. What're your names?"

"I'm Liam and this is Astrid," he indicated his sister with a dismissive finger. "She's a baby."

The thumb popped out again, "Am not."

"Am too."

"Kinder, watch your manners, please." Lily walked to the table, placing mugs of coffee in front of the men. She went back to the kitchen and then returned with a plate of freshly baked strudel.

"Do you have children, Milo?" she asked.

"We are expecting our first."

Lily beamed at him, "Congratulations. Children will enrichen your life like nothing else." She turned to hers, "Go back to your game, kinder, while we adults talk." She turned back to Milo. "And your wife? How is she feeling?"

"Vernie! She's strong as a horse and won't listen to me when I tell her to rest." Milo laughed.

"Vernie? That's an unusual name for a kvinna--woman--ya?" Finn asked.

"Oh, sorry, that's her nickname. Her name is LaVerne."

"That too is…" Finn replied.

"Is very pretty is what Finn is trying to say," Lily finished for her husband.

"Ya, ya, very pretty and unusual."

All three laughed at Finn's gaffe and a friendship was forged.

"How long have you been here at the homestead, Finn?"

"We moved in--what has it been, Lily? Three weeks?"

"Yes, a little over three weeks. It's a lovely house and we are so happy to be in Alaska."

"Did you live in the lower forty-eight?" Milo asked.

"Yes, Wisconsin. I was born there and Finn, he migrated from Sweden with his parents when he was a child. And you, Milo? Have you been in Alaska long?"

"Yes, about twenty years."

"And your wife?" Finn asked.

"She's only been here for a couple of years. Came up from Washington and homesteaded her own place."

"Not by herself, surely?" Lily said.

"Yep, did it all by herself. Worked in Fairbanks until she could save up a stake. Then came here by flat boat and made a home for herself."

"A true Valkyrie, this wife of yours." Finn chuckled.

"Valkyrie? I don't know that word." Milo asked.

"It's a female warrior in Norse mythology, Milo. It fits your wife. How brave of her." Lily explained.

"That's what drew me to her, her tenacity, bravery, and kindness. She'll be so happy to meet you Lily. She hasn't had a woman friend close by since Charlie went back to Boston."

Lily looked at her husband, "The woman we bought the place from, Finn?"

"No, her name was Charlotte, hustru."

"Yes. That's her. She went by Charlie up here." Milo explained.

"Ah. We never met her. The sale was handled through her lawyers."

Milo turned to Finn, "What do you do, Finn, if you don't mind me askin'?"

"I'm a blacksmith by trade but I hope to run a trap line too. That's what I did in Wisconsin. I need to get a dog team together and build my sled before next winter. And you Milo?"

"I have a saw mill just north of Tanana, Finn, so if you ever need milled boards just let me know. We can also turn out some fine runners for your new sled if you want. I also trap fur. A blacksmith, huh? Your trade will be a much welcomed addition to our community."

"Ya? That is good news. I have my forge half completed in the barn now."

Milo reluctantly rose. "Well, I best get home. That was mighty fine pastry, Lily. Thank you."

Finn and Lily stood and the men shook hands.

"Please come to supper soon, Milo, so I can meet your wife. Would next week do? Wednesday?"

"We'd love to. I'll ask Vernie and if you don't hear different we'll be here. Thank you."

They walked Milo outside and watched him ride away into the trees.

"Oh, Finn, that makes me so happy to have another woman nearby."

"I know, Min kärlek, my love. Another woman to gossip with and drink gallons of tea with, ya?"

Fifty

Milo rode into his yard amidst a din of welcoming dogs. He shushed them as he rode over to the corral and dismounted. He swung the gate open and walked his gelding into the space. Removing Buster's tack he rubbed him down with the horse blanket and then checked his water and gave him a handful of oats. He carried the tack and saddle bags into the barn and neatly hung everything up. From the saddlebags he removed the few items that Vernie had asked him to buy at the village store and their mail.

Walking up onto the porch Milo toed off his boots. Spring meant rain so the yard was muddy. As he reached for the latch the door swung open and LaVerne leapt into his arms.

"Daddy, Robbie and I thought you'd never come home," she hugged him tight. "What took you so long?"

"We have new neighbors." Milo wasn't certain how his wife was going to receive the news that someone else now lived in Charlie's house. "They've moved into Charlie's place."

"How do you know? Is that what they are saying in the village?"

"No, I stopped by there, just to check on the place, you know? I met them."

"Oh! That's wonderful. I hated that her homestead was empty and neglected. What are they like? Is there a wife?"

Milo should have known Vernie wouldn't be hanging onto any false hopes that Charlie might return. After all, she'd promised that the past was the past.

"They seem very nice. And yes, there's a wife, maybe just a couple years older than you and there's two kids, seven and five."

LaVerne sighed, "Oh, Milo, that's such good news. How's does the house look? How long have they been there? What does the husband do for work? Are the kids girls? Boys? Tell me everything."

Milo laughed at his eager wife, "Steady, girl. One question at a time. The house looks cozy like always. They've been there a few weeks. Finn, the husband, is a blacksmith by trade. The kids are one of each."

"What made you go there?"

"I've been stopping by since Charlie left. I hated to see the place empty and forgotten. I don't know why but I check on it once in a while. They've asked us over for supper next Wednesday."

"But Milo I should be having them here for dinner. They're the new comers."

"Well, Lily—that's her name, Lillian--asked us first. You can always return the invitation, if you like her."

"Why wouldn't I like her...is there something wrong with her?"

"Will you calm down, wife? She's lovely, very nice to talk to and makes pastry to die for."

"I can't wait to meet them. What do you think I should take as a house warming present?"

"Your jams are always a big hit. Take them a couple of jars."

"Good idea. What time on Wednesday, did she say?"

"Supper time."

"Oh, you men! 'Supper time', indeed. You'll ride by there in the next day or so and accept their invitation and ask what time they'd like us to come. Please."

ᒫᒫᒫ

The following Wednesday Milo and Vernie walked their horses down the trail to the fork that led to Charlie's old place.

"It's going to be strange calling Charlie's homestead the Swenson place." LaVerne told her husband.

"You'll get used to it, especially when you get to know the Swenson family."

"I so hope Lily and I like each other!"

They rode on in silence, Vernie with her hopes of a new friend and Milo with his thoughts of how strange women could be.

Minutes later they rode into Charlie's old yard. Dogs barked excitedly and the cabin door opened almost immediately. Finn and Lily walked out onto the porch and waited but their son, Liam rushed down the steps and ran to Milo.

"Mr. Robin, Mr. Robin, we been waiting for you. I had to wash behind my ears and everything 'cause Ma said you was company comin'!"

Milo reached down, and grasping Liam's arm, hauled up into the saddle with him. As they reached the porch Lily beamed at LaVerne.

"Welcome, Vernie! I have so been looking forward to meeting you." She turned to her husband, "Finn, help Vernie down and then you and Milo can stable the horses. Come in, come in!"

Finn plucked Vernie out of the saddle like she was a thistle-down and set her on her feet. She walked up on the porch and took Lily's hand, "It's such a delight to meet you. I have been looking forward to this evening." Not taking her eyes from Lily's face she continued, "But Milo said you had two children, a little girl. But I don't see her anywhere."

Astrid was hiding behind her mother's skirts. Lily was well aware of what LaVerne was doing so she joined the game of trying to get her daughter to greet the strangers of her own volition. "She was here just a minute ago, Vernie. I can't imagine where she might be."

"Well, I guess I'll just have to meet her another time. I am disappointed."

"Oh, that's too bad." Lily smiled slyly at Vernie.

"Mama, I'm right here." Astrid stepped out from behind Lily and gazed up at Vernie.

"You're a very big lady." She announced.

"Astrid! What a thing to say."

"No, no that's all right, Lily." Vernie squatted beside the small girl. "I am very tall compared to your Mama, aren't I, Astrid. What a pretty name."

The young child looked at the floor and her thumb was headed for her mouth.

"Shall you and I go into the house with your Mama?" Vernie held out her hand and the little girl took it.

Vernie rose and the three went into the cabin. "I love what you've done with the house, Lily. Are you finding you like the area and Tanana?"

"Oh yes, very much. Sometimes I miss my parents and I hate it that the children don't see their grandparents. But they have promised to visit. Would you like some coffee or brännvin? Finn distills it from corn and potatoes and it is flavored with different spices. Please sit."

"Oh, it sounds much too strong for me, but I'm sure Milo will try it. Coffee is fine for me or tea, if you have it. Thank you Lily."

Milo and Finn came in, Milo carrying the saddle bags. He walked to LaVerne and took out the jam jars that she had brought. From the other bag, Milo removed a stuffed food sack.

"Finn and Lily, Milo and I would like to welcome you as neighbors. I've brought you some of my homemade jam. And Milo brought some caribou meat."

Lily came to the table to inspect the four jars. The tops were covered with colorful scraps of cloth and tied with twine.

"They're so pretty, Vernie. Thank you."

"Yes, tack, Vernie. That's Swedish for thank you." Finn said. "And meat. That's a welcomed gift. We look forward to the hunting season." Finn slapped Milo on the back, almost knocking him over.

I hope you like German food, I cooked Rouladen, a meat stewed with pork belly, chopped onions, and pickles and Kasespatzle, a noodle and cheese dish."

"It sounds wonderful, Lily." Vernie said.

Milo turned to Finn, "I thought I heard hogs."

"We only brought three with us, a boar and a pregnant sow but in a few months, with luck, we shall have a few more. I butchered the third so we would have meat until we can hunt." Finn replied.

"Children, come and wash your hands and then be seated please."

While they chatted, Lily placed steaming bowls and skillets on the table.

When everyone was seated the family joined hands with their guests and said a brief prayer.

"May I serve you, Vernie?" Lily held out her hand for a plate.

"Thank you, Lily. It all smells divine. Did your mother teach you to cook traditional German dishes?"

"My grandmother. She insisted that a good wife was a wife who could cook well."

"Daddy and I love Mama's Rouladen, Mrs. Robin," Liam announced.

The adults laughed and dedicated themselves, for the next several minutes, to the savory food before them.

"This is truly wonderful, Lily," Milo said. Finn's a lucky man."

"That is what I tell him frequently, Milo," Lily grinned at her husband.

"Milo, where do you suggest I look first for my trap line?" Finn asked.

"You must be careful, Finn. I don't know how it's done in Wisconsin but here in Alaska infringing on a man's line can get you killed. Most trap lines have been handed down from generation to generation. When we get some snow this fall, if you'd like, I'll take you to see some country that I know is free of established lines. We can check for sign so you pick an area that sees good fur moving through."

"You'd do that for me? You have my sincere thanks. I would not wish to accidently intrude on another's line and get shot," He laughed.

"Finn! It's not funny!" Lily scolded.

"Perhaps I can hammer out some horse shoes or meat hooks as a re-payment for your generosity?"

"That would be much appreciated, Finn. That's sure how we do things in Alaska. Trade our talents."

"Ya, back home too. Do you smoke? I usually take a pipe out on the porch after supper."

"No, but I'll join you while you do. Will you excuse us ladies?"

The men got up and went outside, leaving the women to get to know each other better.

"Vernie, Milo tells us you are expecting. Congratulations. When is the baby due?"

"I think around December." She laughed. "I didn't even know. An old woman in the village told me. Then I counted back to my last monthly flow and I thought it might be possible. No sooner had the elder informed me I was pregnant than I was puking off the end of the porch."

The two women laughed knowingly. "Astrid was also a surprise. Blessed, but a surprise."

"The elder also said it was a boy. Milo is over the moon about it."

"Will you go to Fairbanks to have your baby since it is the first? Do they have a midwife in the village?"

"No, I'll have it at home. If my mother could bring thirteen babies into the world by herself, sometimes with only the help of Pa if he was home, I think I can handle one."

"Whatever do you mean?"

"Well, for example, Mama was in her root cellar and her water broke. She couldn't make it back up the ladder and my brothers and sisters were too young to help, much less watch such an event. She gathered up some burlap sacks and tried to make a bed on the dirt floor and two hours later my sister, Ivah was born."

"Oh, Mein Gott! Finn called you a Valkyrie and I see now that you come from a family of women warriors."

"You should see Mama, Lily. She's so strong and sweet at the same time. She's the boss of five grown boys, Pa, and of course us girls. She's the true Valkyrie."

"And I must ask you if what Milo said is really true. That you came to this wild place alone and began your homestead? I can hardly believe it!"

"Yes, it's true and I must have been crazy but I did it with a lot of help from my neighbors and friends. You'll see, in the future, if neighbors hear you're in need of something they come running."

"What made you do it? How did your family allow it?"

"They didn't know. I ran away and hitchhiked to Seattle, then worked my way up to Fairbanks. I worked in the trading post for over a year to get my stake together."

"Oh my goodness! You're the bravest woman I've ever met!"

"Or the dumbest," Vernie chortled. "But it all worked out and I love my life here. I hope the same for you."

"I love it already. My children are flourishing. My husband is happy. And now I have a new friend just minutes away."

LaVerne pinked up at the compliments. "I'm so glad you and your family have moved in, Lily."

Her hostess rose and went to the door, opening it, "Come now if you would like dessert."

At the mention of dessert the two children, who had been playing quietly in front of the fire, came scrambling into their chairs, adorable looks of expectation on their faces.

"Did someone say dessert? LaVerne teased them.

The men came to the table and sat down. LaVerne could see that her husband liked Finn and she was happy that they had this lovely family so close by.

"Is it linzer torte, Mama?" Liam turned to LaVerne. "It's my favorite, you know."

"Yes, liebchen, it is. And we shall put a dollop of Vernie's berry jam preserves on top of it."

Lily set plates, forks and a pie dish on the table. She sliced it like a pie, even though it was a rich pastry. She opened one of the jars of jam and put a teaspoon of it on each serving. She returned to the stove to get the coffee pot.

Milo couldn't wait and eagerly forked a bite into his mouth. His eyes rolled back in his head, making the children giggle.

"Marry me, Lily, will you? You cook like an angel!"

"Sorry my friend, I saw her first. And besides she's already married." Finn chuckled.

The adults had a good laugh together while the children looked at them puzzled at someone wanting to marry their mama.

"We must do this again soon," LaVerne told them. "But I must warn you, Finn, I'm not nearly the chef that your wife is. Alaskan homesteader food is my specialty."

"Don't believe her, Finn. She makes a caribou stew that will have you weeping." Milo told them.

"Ya, I will look forward to that."

After a last cup of coffee, LaVerne and Milo rose and donned their coats. The women hugged and the men shook hands.

"I will walk you to the corral and help you with the horses."

The men left to bring the horses around to the house.

"Goodnight, Lily. And thank you for your hospitality."

"Goodnight Vernie. Oh! Wait one minute and I'll wrap a piece of the torte for you to take home. A treat for Milo."

She bustled over to the kitchen and found a clean cloth. Going to the table she sliced a large piece of the dessert and wrapped it in the cloth.

"Milo will be your slave in no time, Lily," she said.

"I shall see you soon, yes?" Lily asked.

"Yes, we'll look forward to another evening like this, only at our place."

Lily escorted LaVerne out onto the porch where the men were just walking up with the horses. Amidst cries of goodbyes, LaVerne and Milo disappeared into the forest.

Under the canopy of the primal forest it was pitch dark. Milo halted the horses and stepped down. Unpacking a lantern from his saddlebags, he lit it and walked his horse down the trail with LaVerne following. Their horses knew the way home, the lantern was for comfort and so Milo could watch the trail.

When they arrived home the dog team was nervous and barking a high pitched, alarm type noise. Milo walked the horses to the corral and he and LaVerne made quick work of getting them settled. The breeze shifted direction suddenly and Milo's big gelding began to snort and dance.

"What's wrong with him, Milo?"

"Buster usually acts that way when there's a wild critter around. Let's take a look around the yard. I don't like how the dogs are acting either."

As he exited the corral, he racked a cartridge into his rifle. In his other hand he carried the lantern. LaVerne closed the brush gate and followed on his heels. The light danced across a gaping hole in the wire fence that held the chickens and goats.

"Oh! Look! There's been something in the chicken coop. The light pierced the darkest corner where the goats slept. They were on their feet and bunched up in a corner. Their naaa'ing was pitiful.

"Where's Betty? Oh, Milo, something got Betty."

"Stay here, Vernie, and let me get a closer look."

Milo walked through the hole in the fence and studied the ground. There was a large patch of fresh blood on the ground and goat hair. Bear. Milo knew nothing else could have grabbed a full sized goat. Lynx were too shy to come this close to a house and nothing but a bear could tear through a wire fence like it was butter.

Milo walked back to Vernie. "Bear. I'm sorry, Vernie, but Betty is gone. It's comin' on spring and the bears are coming out of hibernation, half starved. Let me get some wire and brush to close up that hole."

"What if it comes back?"

The both knew once a bear found easy food it would be back again and again.

"I'm gonna build a big fire in the yard's fire pit and sleep on the porch tonight. Then tomorrow, first light, I'm goin' bear trackin'. I don't want to kill him if I can scare him enough to run him outta the area, but if I have to, I *will* kill him. Why don't you go on into the cabin and light some lanterns and a fire?"

"I'll get more lanterns so you can see what you're doing but I want to help with the work."

"Vernie, no, you don't need to be out here in the dark and the cold."

"Husband, we are a team. We share the work. No more to talk about. Anyway, I'll feel better about Betty if my hands are busy."

An hour later the fence had been temporarily repaired and a big fire blazed in the pit. Milo was positioned in the rocking chair wrapped in blankets, his rifle nearby.

"Do you really need to spend the rest of the night out here, Milo? It's so cold."

"I'm cozy as can be. Go in now and get a good night's sleep. Robbie must be exhausted what with the social evening and the work you did here." He put his hand on her slightly extended tummy and smiled lovingly at her.

"It was nice, wasn't it? The Swensons are such a lovely family. I think Lily and I will be close."

"Yes. And Finn is a good man. Now, off to bed with you."

Fifty-one

The next morning, at dawn, Milo was up and inspecting the dogs. He was relieved that the bear had not bothered them but who knew about the next time. If he didn't find the bear and dissuade him from returning he knew he wouldn't be so lucky when the bear did come back. He quickly did the morning chores, feeding dogs, livestock and the horses. He reinforced the repair he had done on the enclosure fence and then walked to the cabin.

"Good morning, husband. I've got a big breakfast cooked for you. All I have to do is cook the eggs when you're ready to sit down. I've made you a trail lunch of biscuit sandwiches and a slice of Lily's torte which she sent home with us."

"Really? That'll be a treat. Let me just get some fresh clothes on. A couple of heavy shirts and clean socks. I'll only be a minute." He walked into the bedroom.

Milo hurried through his morning meal and took the small lunch sack Vernie gave him. He would carry just his .338 Winchester rifle, a small knapsack with some emergency provisions and his .357 Magnum sidearm. Kissing his worried wife goodbye he promised to be home well before dark.

Outside Milo found the blood trail up behind the dog yard with scraps of goat hair stuck on bushes. The bear had carried his kill up the hill and west.

Two miles later, watching where he placed every foot, he heard the low grunting of a bear in the thick underbrush. He called out, "Hey, bear. Get outta here, bear!" Then he fired a round from his rifle into the air, immediately chambering another round.

Out of the brush a fifteen hundred-pound brown bear rose up on his hind feet. His muzzle was wet with blood. He had been feeding. Milo yelled again, "Go on, bear, get!" He fired another shot into the trees and racked another round into the chamber.

The huge boar, with a notable hump between his shoulders fell back to all four and charged directly at Milo. Without aiming, Milo raised his rifle at the bear and fired as the bear got within three feet of him. He kept coming and as he brushed by Milo hit him in the shoulder, knocking him off his feet and flat on his back, causing him to drop his rifle.

Milo jumped to his feet, yanking his handgun out of its holster and cocking it. He whirled around to find out where the bear was. Two feet from him, the bear lay in a heap. Milo backed away, watching the bear closely. He picked up his rifle and crossed around to approach him from the back and then poked him with the end of his rifle. Animals had been known to play possum and then jump up and attack. But his bear was dead and on examining him found that he'd made a killing shot to the heart. He secured his sidearm, dropped his knapsack and laid his rifle on the ground close by. He knelt by the brown bear and ruffled his fur with a touch of reverence.

"Bear, I didn't want to kill you. Why didn't you run off? We'd both a'been happier. Thank you for

the meat and fur you will be providing my family."
He'd learned as a younger man, from native
Alaskans, that a hunter should always respect and
thank an animal for giving up its life. And in this
instance, he truly regretted having to take this
majestic animal's life. It was so unnecessary.

Talking out his Bowie knife from its sheath, he
field-dressed the big boar. He threw the gut pile as
far away from the carcass as he could to try to
protect the meat from scavengers until he could get
back to pack it out.

An hour later Milo emerged down the hill and
into the homeplace yard. LaVerne was sitting on the
porch. She'd heard the shots and waited anxiously.
She turned ghost white when she saw all the blood
on Milo's shirt and sleeves.

"It's bear blood, Vernie," he yelled across the
yard. "Don't look so scared. I'm alright."

Vernie ran to him, weaving through the dogs who
jumped and barked excitedly. Moon and Howie
followed her and jumped up on Milo, fascinated by
the smell of the blood.

Milo opened his arms and Vernie crawled all over
him, inspecting every inch of him with her hands.
"Are you sure you're not hurt? So much blood. Are
you certain none of its your blood?"

"Positive. Cut it out, wife. You're getting blood
all over yourself."

She stepped back, "You had to kill it." It was not
a question.

"Yes. He wouldn't back down." Milo was
reluctant to tell his pregnant wife that the bear had
charged him. "I need to get back and harvest the

meat. I'm going to take one of the horses and pack the meat and fur out."

"I'm coming with you."

"No. That's not necessary."

"I want to help. I'm coming."

Milo knew that there was no arguing with her and there was little danger in her going with him. He just didn't want her upset by the sight of the dead bear. He saw that she was already dressed for the trail. Arm in arm they walked to the house so he could wash his hands and change his shirt. His horse would not be happy if he came near him with the smell of bear and blood all over him.

LaVerne walked to the sink and put out hand soap and a clean cloth. Milo walked to the bedroom.

"Bring your bloody shirt back with you, Milo, and I'll set it to soaking in some cold water."

Fifteen minutes later Milo's horse had a lead halter on and panniers strapped to his back. LaVerne carried clean meat sacks and her smaller gage rifle. Milo led his horse, carrying his .338. They started back up the hill and walked at a brisk pace to the kill site.

LaVerne took one look and started to gag. Milo put his free arm around her and turned her so she wasn't looking at the gutted bear.

"Easy, sweetheart. You don't have to watch. Here, sit on this stump and keep watch. Keep your rifle handy."

"Why?"

"Other bears can smell this kill for over two miles and as hungry as they are they'll head this way, looking for a meal. We have to be quick skinning it out and packing up the meat. Watch Buster's ears too. He'll hear and smell a bear long before we see one."

Milo carefully, but efficiently, skinned out the hide. It would make a beautiful blanket or rug once it was tanned. He cut up the meat into quarters. He bagged the back strap, heart and liver in one sack and each quarter into other sacks. He walked to his horse and let him smell the first sack. He spoke softly to the animal reassuring him that there was no danger. He then tied the sacks onto the panniers distributing the weight as evenly as possible.

"Milo, you're bleeding through your shirt. Your elbow. You're hurt."

Milo pulled his sleeve back and examined his elbow. There was a long bloody gash.

"Must'a snagged it on something when I fell on my ass," he murmured to himself without thinking.

LaVerne had come over to examine the wound. "Why would you have fallen on your butt? You're the most sure-footed woodsman I know."

"Uhh…" Milo stuttered.

"Tell me." Her tone brooked no prevarication from her husband.

"The bear didn't back down, I told ya."

Realization dawned. "And he charged you?"

"Well…ya…"

LaVerne's knees went weak and Milo had to help her to sit back down on the stump she'd just left.

"Why didn't you tell me? You could have been killed so easily," she began to cry.

"*That's* why. I didn't want you to get upset. It's not good for the baby, Vernie."

"But he charged you and knocked you on your ass. You said so," she cried harder.

"Vernie, stop. See? I'm here and alive except for a little scratch. If you'll stop cryin' I'll tell you the whole thing. But first we gotta get goin' before we have some unwanted company. I promise to tell you all the gory details when we get home. Just, please stop cryin'."

LaVerne sniffled and wiped her nose on her sleeve. "All right."

"Good girl. Grab your rifle and walk in front of me, back the way we came." As Milo spoke he shoved his rifle into a scabbard attached to one of the panniers and they began the trip home.

Fifty-two

The sun had set and a soft rain dripped off the edge of the roof line. Verne and Milo sat on their front porch, hands wrapped around steaming mugs of coffee. Lanterns burned at each end of the cabin's porch. When they had arrived home, Milo had unloaded the meat and hung it in the barn. With spring coming on the meat could not be frozen. It had to be preserved in some way. Tomorrow he would salt it down and then hang it in the smoker. He preferred a mixture of oak and hickory as wood for the smoker and had a special pile saved in the barn.

He had relieved his horse of the panniers and rubbed him down thoroughly. He made certain the horses had fresh water and food. He built a fire in the pit and put on the pot to boil up a bear meat stew for the dogs. LaVerne had watered the dogs and fed the livestock.

Chores done, they had enjoyed a dinner of fried bear heart and potatoes, with carrots on the side. Now they sat in perfect accord and listened to the forest come alive with night sounds and rain dripping from the trees. Their goats snuffled in their hay and the chickens clucked quietly on their roosts. Most of the dogs lay inside their houses with their heads hanging out, watching their humans. Howie lay at LaVerne's side and Moon lay across Milo's feet.

"So tell me," LaVerne said.

"I heard the bear first and started calling out to him hoping he'd run when he heard me. He spotted me and reared up on his hind feet. I started yelling louder and fired off a'couple rounds over his head. He didn't hesitate. He fell to all four paws and charged. I don't know if you know this, Vernie, but those things can travel at thirty miles an hour. I didn't even have time to aim. I just lifted my rifle and fired. It was a heart shot but his adrenalin carried him on after he was dead and he crashed into me. I thought for a minute I was a dead man, he hit me so hard. I lost my rifle." He scoffed. "Knocked me flat. I scrambled up and pulled my .357. But he had been dead on his feet and he lay where you saw him. End of story."

"I want you to promise me…you'll never put yourself in danger again. How would Robbie and I go on without you? You must promise."

"Yes, dear."

"That doesn't sound very sincere, Milo."

"My love, how can I make such a promise? How could you expect me to keep it? Things--animals will threaten our home, our family. You know it's true that bears come back when they discover an easy food source. It's my responsibility to protect our family, the dogs, and our livestock. What kind of husband would I be if I didn't?"

LaVerne sighed. "I understand. Then I want you to promise me you will be extra, extra careful and don't take any chances with your safety. Can you do that?"

"Yes, wife, I can do that. As long as *you* understand that I would give my life for you and our baby."

LaVerne got up and climbed into Milo's lap. "You are such a good man. I love you to the moon and beyond."

Epilogue

The spring and summer were a busy time every year, preparing for the long, dark, winter months. Stocking up on salmon, hunting deer, caribou and moose, cutting and stacking enough wood for the cold months. Harvesting a garden, filling the root cellar with vegetables, canning, and preserving food.

Now it was Christmas night and the Robbins had a house full of friends and family. LaVerne's Mama and Pa had come up for their first visit. Finn, Lily and their two children were there. Joe and his mother, Edna had joined them.

The men had hunted birds for the past two days and their Christmas dinner had consisted of wild goose, duck and a ham, from Finn's pigs. After the supper dishes were cleared away they all gathered in front of the fire and the adults told stories of Christmases past.

Suddenly LaVerne let out a squeak. She looked down in horror, as a wet stain spread across the front of her pants. "Oh!"

Pa, who was a father and grandfather several times over stood, "That's our cue to retire to the porch, gentlemen." He strode to the door followed quickly by the men. Milo hung back, not certain where his place was. He didn't want to leave his wife.

"Oooo," LaVerne doubled up in pain as her first contraction hit her.

Milo ran to her side. "I'm here, Vernie."

"Kiss your wife, Milo and then go out to the porch with the other men. We will call you as soon as your son is here." Edna told him, making shooing motions with her hands.

Vernie's mama sat next to her. "Breathe through it, daughter."

"Children, time for bed. Vernie, may I put them in the loft?" Lily asked as she led the kids to the ladder.

"Yes. There are pallets already made up." Vernie panted.

"Let's get you into the bedroom," Mama said.

"I'm fine. I can walk now." Vernie said as she rose and walked toward the other room.

Lily came into the bedroom a few moments later and the three women helped Vernie into a nightgown and got her settled into bed.

"Where are the baby's things for when he gets here?" Lily asked.

"Over on the…oooo," Vernie arched her body as another contraction came.

"Breathe, child."

"…dresser," Vernie finished saying as the contraction subsided.

♪♪♪

Twelve hours later the men were back on the porch. Joe, Finn and Pa had slept in the barn in their bedrolls. Milo had tried to get some sleep on the sofa by the fireplace but every time Vernie moaned from the next room, he sat up and listened for the next hour. When he rose at dawn, he crept around the kitchen making coffee and a cold breakfast for the men. Howie had never left the closed door to the bedroom. Moon had followed Milo's every step, whimpering once in a while.

Milo had just finished plunking down the coffee pot and handful of mugs, on the porch railing, when they all heard a loud squalling from inside.

"Boy's got a set of lungs on him," Pa beamed at the thought of his first grandson.

Milo rushed back inside and threw open the bedroom door just in time to see his mother-in-law laying his son on Vernie's chest.

"Come on in, Papa, and meet your new son," she said.

"Milo, you have a fine son, almost nine pounds is my guess. A great hunter," Edna pronounced.

As big a man as he was, Milo tiptoed to the head of the bed and knelt by Vernie's side. His son was already rooting around trying to locate his first meal. When he couldn't find it he let out a bellow that shocked Milo.

"Is he all right?" Milo sat back on his heels.

All the women laughed. "He's hungry and you know when a man wants his dinner he tends to holler," Mama told him. "Kiss your son and your wife and let us get back to making Vernie and Robbie comfortable."

When Milo returned to the living area all the men were there. Pa had stoked up the fire in the fireplace and Finn had filled the wood bin by the cook stove. Joe was frying up a pile of bacon.

"Did you get a son, my friend?" Joe asked.

"Yes. The women say he is close to nine pounds and he's got all his toes and fingers. That's all I care about."

"Congratulate me, boys, I'm grandpa to a grandson!" Pa chortled.

Joe left the stove and went to Milo. He shook his hand and beat him on the back. "A son, Milo!"

Tears suddenly coursed down the big man's face, so overwhelmed he had become, "Your mother said he would be a great hunter."

ACKNOWLEDGEMENTS

Musician, composer Gary Swindell who generously wrote the song, I Go Swiftly.

The people of the Athabaskan Nation.
http://www.ankn.uaf.edu/index.html

Other lyrics and poetry by Trisha Sugarek

'Stardust' by Hoagy Carmichael

Author's Notes

Credit is reluctantly given to Johnny Horton and Tillman Franks for the song '*North to Alaska*' written and released by singer/song writers. But family legend says that LaVerne actually wrote the song years before and someone allegedly plagiarized it. When this author was a teenager, she remembers seeing her aunt's name on a 45 vinyl record, under the title, *North to Alaska*.

This story is based upon true events.

About the author....

Trisha Sugarek has enjoyed a twenty year career writing stage plays, fiction, children's books and poetry. In addition to a half a dozen full length plays, she expanded her body of work to include four children's books, eight novels, of which five are a series of murder mysteries. She has written a collection of ten minute plays for the classroom. Most recently she created four journal/handbooks (instructional) for writers. Her active blog encourages and helps other writers.

Trisha lives in Savannah, Georgia with her golden retriever, Gusto and a ridgeback hound, Miss Molly and *their* cat, Fiona.

www.writeratplay.com

60790922R00209

Made in the USA
Charleston, SC
05 September 2016